ALPHA
UNLEASHED

AILEEN ERIN

INK MONSTER

INK MONSTER

First Published by Ink Monster LLC in 2015

Ink Monster LLC
100 Commons Road, Suite 7-303
Dripping Springs, TX 78620
www.aileenerin.com

ISBN 9781943858439

Covers by Ana Cruz Arts

For Jeremy.
Thank you for being my rock. I can't do it without you.
I love you the most.

CHAPTER ONE

ICE-COLD WATER RAINED DOWN on my head. Someone was screaming.

"Tessa! Wake up!" The command rolled through my mental bond to Dastien and I gasped.

Blinking the water out of my eyes, I tried to figure out how I'd gotten in the shower. It took a second for my sight to clear. Meredith's crystal blue gaze stared down at me.

I reached for the knob with a shaking hand and turned it all the way hot. "Jesus. That's the fifth night in a row." My voice wobbled.

Hands held me against a hard chest, and I knew from the feel of him Dastien was holding me under the spray. This had become a necessary part of our nighttime routine.

He kissed the top of my head. "You scared me this time. I almost had to get the doctor."

"No! Don't do that. Ever. She'll come at me with one of her shots." If there was anything that would turn this bad situation worse, it was Dr. Gonzales and her little messenger bag of horrors.

AILEEN ERIN

"Do you remember what you were dreaming?" Meredith asked. She sat next to the tub in our small shared bathroom.

I shook my head slowly. Every night had been like this since I escaped from *La Aquelarre*'s compound. I hoped it was some sort of PTSD, but the fear that still coursed through my veins made me think it was something more. Something worse.

I only remembered pieces of my dreams—hints of blood and terror—but nothing concrete enough to tell her. My visions had never been so vague, but they'd been changing ever since Dastien bit me, turning me into a werewolf. For a while, I hadn't seen anything. I thought they were gone for good. Then the visions came back, but only when I focused on trying to have one. And then—weirdest of all—I'd started seeing stuff that happened in the future.

The only thing I'd *seen* since Luciana stripped me of magic was about Peru. If I'd gone instead of Claudia, everyone at St. Ailbe's would've died.

I took a deep breath and immediately regretted it. "Do you smell that?"

Dastien ran his hand across my forehead, pushing the hair out of my eyes. "Smell what?"

"Sulfur."

Meredith and Dastien stilled for a moment.

Shit. If the smell was part of my "dream," then I was either dreaming of my last run-in with Luciana or whatever she was cooking up for next time. "You aren't smelling anything?"

"No, *chérie*. I don't smell anything but you right now." He turned the knob, shutting off the water, and then stood up, pulling me with him. "Let's get into some dry clothes. Then we'll talk, because pretending this isn't happening isn't working." Water dripped on the floor as he moved. His T-shirt clung to his body like a second skin, showing off each ripple in his

2

muscles. He stripped off his shirt and threw it in the tub with a wet plop before wrapping himself in a towel. Then he grabbed a second towel from the rack and turned to me, holding it open.

I closed the distance between us and let his warmth sink into me. He was right. Ignoring whatever was up with me wasn't working. Not even a little bit. But talking about this stuff made it real, and it was so much easier pretending that the last few weeks never happened.

That I'd never gone to stay with the coven. That my powers hadn't been stripped and stuck in two stupid jars. That Daniel was still alive, Raphael had never been attacked, and Claudia was still here.

Tears welled but I refused to let them fall, on principle. A pity party wouldn't solve any of my problems. I blinked them away as I thought about what could be causing my nightmares.

I followed Dastien into my room.

"Holler when you're dressed." Meredith left our adjoining bathroom for her room, closing the door behind her.

"Sure thing," I mumbled, still too caught up in my own thoughts to really focus on anything. The first time it happened, Dastien and I had torn up his cabin searching for a *gris-gris*. We hadn't found anything that looked remotely cursed, so I thought it was just a really bad dream.

But five nights in a row...

Dastien grabbed a pair of his sweatpants and quickly pulled them on. "Do you want me to help you get changed?"

My cheeks burned. "I've got it."

Even if he was my mate, we hadn't gone through the whole bonding ceremony yet. He was determined not to cross the line until we did, but we were true mates. Two halves of one soul. So, we already had somewhat of a bond. With it, we could talk silently to each other, feel each other's emotions, and I could see where he was when we were apart—but that last one wasn't a normal mate thing. That was an enhancement my witchyness provided.

I dug through my closet as Dastien turned his back, a gentleman to the end. After stripping off the wet stuff and tossing it in my hamper, I pulled on a pair of sleep shorts and a tank.

When I turned back, I blinked at the sight of the rainbow tie-dyed throw pillow in the center of my bed—the color was shocking compared to the painful whiteness of my room. Before I became a Were, I needed to be able to bleach my surroundings free of any vision-inducing elements, so white had always been more about practicality than an aesthetic choice. The pillow was the first decoration I'd gotten since I gained control of my visions. Now, I wanted to hurl it across the room.

I wasn't in control anymore.

Dastien reclined on my bed, and I crawled up next to him, hugging the rainbow pillow to my chest as I tried to hold it together. "We're dressed," I yelled.

Meredith peeked in and her hair fell forward. Her current dye job was black with streaks of hot pink. It looked fantastic against her pale, white skin. She was tall and thin, built like a runway model. On any other person, it might've been intimidating, but Meredith was my first friend here. My best friend, besides Dastien.

"So, what's the deal with the night terrors?" she asked.

"I don't know." I picked at the seams of the pillow as I tried to come up with an answer that had some substance. How could I forget something that affected me so much? Even now, all I could remember was the smell of sulfur. And the fear.

"What about your visions?"

"Still MIA." Although, I had a theory about what was

happening. Not a great theory, but one in general. Worry gnawed in my gut, but I had to voice my fears. "Maybe having my magic taken out and put back in changed things."

She sat on the foot of my bed. "But you don't think they're gone for good?"

"No. The magic is there. I felt it come back when the jars broke, but I wonder... No. It's stupid."

"It's not stupid," Dastien said. "Just tell us. We can't help if you won't talk to us."

"The thing is..." Crap. I wasn't even sure how to put this in words. "I feel it building in me sometimes. That little tingle that means a vision is coming the way it did before you bit me. But then the feeling goes away. Now, I'm wondering if I'm pushing it away. Maybe what I'm seeing is really bad, and I don't want to see it? Maybe my mind is protecting me? Only—"

"That makes sense," Dastien said. "You can't contain that kind of magic. It has to come out somehow. So, nightmares."

"Which does me no good." I tucked a strand of wet hair behind my ear as I processed my thoughts. "I mean, visions that I can't see are useless."

And I'd never needed to see the future more than I did now. There were too many alphas on campus to agree on a course of action, and half of them thought that sitting tight was the best plan. Which meant we were left sitting around like a bunch of morons, waiting for Luciana to make her next move.

Stupid. So freaking stupid. Not to mention frustrating. I hated doing nothing.

All the kids at school were on edge. Classes were canceled, and everyone was running the Cazadores' obstacle course and training like they knew what was coming. The Cazadores patrolled at night, but walked through campus like God's gift during the day. The alphas that had gathered—some of the ruling Seven Alphas were here with other key alphas from around the world—spent their days arguing in the conference room, accomplishing absolutely nothing. Fights broke out every few hours as the tension brought out the wolves in all of us.

In other words, the pack was a hot mess, and it didn't look like anything was going to change anytime soon. Not unless I changed it.

"If I could figure out what I was seeing, then maybe we could actually start doing something." I threw the pillow across the room in frustration. Maybe lack of sleep was making everything worse, but I couldn't shake the sense of danger. "Are the Cazadores still watching my parents and brother?"

Dastien grunted. "Of course. They're protected around the clock. Just like you wanted."

"And Tía Rosa—"

"Left yesterday for her family's estate in Mexico. Remember?"

"Right." My great-aunt had wanted to get far away from Luciana. At least that worry was gone. My family was safe. Whatever the vision was—it was about me.

"I know this isn't ideal, but the Seven say we wait, so we wait," Dastien said.

"Donovan doesn't agree with that, does he?" I asked Meredith. She was true mates with Donovan, one of the Council of Seven Alphas that ruled over all packs. I wished he were here, but tonight was his turn for the wee-hours patrol.

"No." She drew out the word. "But apparently he doesn't always agree with them. And since you and I are friends, they think Donovan isn't a fair judge of the situation."

"That's stupid."

"Right?" Meredith shouted the word. "That's exactly what I said."

"I have to figure out what I'm dreaming." If it was the past

6

tormenting me then I could deal with it. And if it was something that was going to happen, at least we could prepare.

"How?" Dastien asked.

That was the question. "I don't know."

"We could try yoga." Meredith led the afternoon yoga sessions. I'd gone to a few when I first got to St. Ailbe's, but hadn't had time in a while. "It's very centering."

She might be right. At this point, I'd juggle oranges while hopping on one foot and singing the ABCs if it'd fix me. "Okay."

"And if that doesn't work, maybe tiring your body out while you're awake will give your mind a chance to relax," Dastien said. "Either way, you need more sparring practice."

I rolled my eyes. This had become a thing with him. All the Weres had been training to fight their whole lives and Dastien was one of the best Cazadores—the Were fighters who hunted everything that went *bump* in the night. I'd say it pained him that I was so bad at fighting, but I knew the only reason it bothered him was because he wanted me to be able to defend myself. Which was probably a good thing, considering.

"Fine. A little gym time won't kill me. I've been spending too much time digging through old books anyhow." I drummed my fingers against my leg. The only productive thing I'd been able to do was cook up potions. I had a whole pile of vials on my desk, just waiting for the next attack. "And if that doesn't work?"

"We'll go for a run. Shift." Meredith sat on the edge of my bed. "We keep trying stuff until something works. You have to get out of your own way. Just break free from your thoughts and relax, and I'm sure your visions will come back."

Just relax. Easier said than done these days.

As soon as I thought I had a grip on my powers, they changed again. Even if they were working normally—whatever

7

that meant—Tía Rosa had made it clear that visions of the future couldn't be controlled. They'd come or they wouldn't.

She said I had to have faith.

Well, I had plenty of faith—but in myself?

Not so much. Not anymore.

CHAPTER TWO

I DID an hour of yoga with Meredith, but all I felt was exhausted. She wanted to do a long meditation after, but there was no way I wanted to fall asleep and go straight into another nightmare. So, Dastien got his way.

After two hours of martial arts training and zero visions, people started filtering into the gym. That was my cue to get the hell out. I was used to being watched—stared at—but ever since Luciana had stripped me, the attention made me anxious... Which in turn made me feel weak. It was dumb. There was no reason to feel this way, but I couldn't control it. Dastien said that I hadn't had time to deal with my emotions, but the problem was that I wouldn't have time anytime soon.

Eventually, I'd find a way to process all of it. I might even make some therapist rich with how much help I'd need. For now, I needed to focus on digging out whatever vision was taking up all the room in my subconscious.

After yet another shower—this one much warmer than the last—I decided food was very much a necessity. Dastien had stayed behind to train with the Cazadores, but I figured he'd end up at the cafeteria before too long. If I was hungry, he had to be, too.

In case no one else was eating, I grabbed a book on magic and headed across the well-manicured quad to the squat brick building that held the cafeteria. I passed two sophomore Weres. I wasn't paying attention to them until one shoved the other. They shredded their clothes as they shifted to their wolf forms—snarling and swiping claws at each other.

One of them let out a yelp of pain, and I froze.

I had two choices. Keep walking and let them work it out, or step in and stop the fight. Screw it. I'd had enough of the constant fighting.

"Knock it off!" I yelled the command at them, backed with a healthy dose of alpha power. The wolves froze. "Jesus. No more fighting. You're like a bunch of cranky toddlers." They rolled over, showing me their soft underbellies. I took that as agreement the fight would end there. "Have a nice day, boys," I said as I started moving across the quad.

But still, this was getting ridiculous. If the Alphas didn't come to some sort of agreement soon, I was worried what would happen to the pack. These little fights among the students were yet another glaring example of the division rippling through the pack bonds.

Someone had to step in and make some real decisions soon or there'd be no pack left to fight Luciana.

I braced myself as I opened the door to the cafeteria, hoping that Meredith or Donovan would be inside. Chris was definitely still in the gym. He'd come in as I was leaving. But I hadn't seen Meredith, and she wasn't in our suite. Adrian was probably out running the Cazadores' course yet again. That thing was a beast of obstacles, but he was determined to beat the challenge time. To become some ultimate fighter.

The scent of waffles, omelets, bacon, fruit, and some sort of sweet pastry filled the air. I'd definitely need to hunt one of those pastries down. They weren't an everyday thing, but man, when the chef made them, they were to die for.

As I moved through the room, conversations went silent. Of the thirty or so round tables, only one was completely full. Joseph's little clique. His dad was the Alpha of the Canadian pack, and he thought that made him God's gift to the world. Ever since Mr. Hoel died, they'd separated themselves. I hadn't noticed until I literally bumped into one of them and couldn't feel their connection to the pack. I'd brought it up to Mr. Dawson and the rest of the group, but no one was doing anything about it. No one seemed the least bit concerned.

But I knew in my bones that they were going to be trouble. If not now, then soon.

The group at the table had grown today. They had two girls sitting with them—a blonde and a redhead. My gaze stuck on the blonde. Something about the way she moved her hand...

If that's Imogene, then—

She turned, and I got a full look at her face.

Shit. That *was* Imogene Hoel. Just fantastic. Her father was part of the reason our pack was so fractured. If she was sitting with those guys, then this was definitely more of a problem than I'd thought.

And now I wanted to kick myself. I'd stuck up for her when they were going to boot her out of the pack. Which was one of the stupidest things I'd ever done. It'd seemed right at the time, but apparently it was coming back to bite me in the ass.

Imogene sneered at me and nudged the redhead beside her. The redhead turned.

Shannon. I fought to keep my face neutral as I returned her glare. Meredith was going to freak out when she found out that Shannon was hanging with that group.

Shannon shot me a nasty look and said something to the

AILEEN ERIN

boys, who started snickering. I guessed she wasn't over me yelling at her for going through my spell books. Or maybe she was still peeved that I had Dastien and she didn't. Whatever the reason behind that look, I didn't care. I didn't want anything to do with her anymore.

I made my way to the food. Shannon and Imogene would probably ignore me as long as I ignored them, but seeing them with those guys made me wonder about their connection to the pack.

As I heaped my tray with food, I focused on the pack bonds —the little strings of magic that tied all the Weres in the pack together. I'd never spoken to the guy who stood next to me, shoveling pancakes onto his plate, but I could sense my connection to him and to everyone else who obeyed Mr. Dawson as their alpha.

The strings of magic and alpha energy created a web through the cafeteria, connecting the werewolves to each other. Even some of the Cazadores, who weren't exactly part of this pack, had distant ties—barely visible, but there. Which made sense since nearly all Weres were tied to each other through the rule of the Seven.

Everyone except for Shannon, Imogene, and their round table of sucky people. I couldn't feel anything from them.

Dastien. I called to him through our bond.

As soon as I focused on him, I could feel his rapid breath as he backed away from whomever he was sparring. *Are you okay?*

Yeah. But that group is at the table again and I still can't feel their bond. And now Imogene and Shannon are with them...

We already told Michael. He said they're cleared.

Maybe they shouldn't be. It wasn't like Mr. Dawson was totally infallible.

I'll tell Michael about Imogene and Shannon, but there's

nothing we can do until they act out against the pack. Just keep an eye on them.

Will do. I didn't like it, but if the pack alphas wanted to hide in a room and argue all day, pretending the pack was fine, then it wasn't my place to question it.

Pushing my frustration aside, I ordered my usual bacon, cheddar, and avocado omelet. The more calories packed in there, the better. I had some serious studying to do and I needed to focus until lunch. I had a few witchcraft books I'd dug up at the back of the library, and I planned to keep working through them. The more I knew about magic, the better.

As I moved past their table, the hair rose on my arms. The group stayed quiet, and I purposely knocked my elbow into one of the guys.

"Watch it," he said.

"Sorry," I mumbled the word as I hurried past, but I'd already gotten what I needed.

There was no connection when we touched. It didn't make sense.

Unless they were working with another alpha who didn't answer to the Seven. But that was impossible. Mr. Hoel was dead. I knew it for a fact. I was the one who'd killed him. And the wolves loyal to him had left or been driven out.

So, maybe magic had made their bonds disappear. But they couldn't be working for Luciana... Could they?

No. And they weren't what I needed to be focusing on. Finding the magic to defeat Luciana and her demons was priority number one. I couldn't let whatever pranks they were pulling divide my attention. Especially when Mr. Dawson said not to worry about it.

I settled at a table by myself and flipped open my book— *Crystals: The Art of Harnessing Magic Through the Elements* —while I ate.

I was halfway through my second plate when Meredith finally showed. She saw me wave and headed my way.

"Hey." She looked flawless in her cut-off shorts and tank. Her hair was pulled back in a messy ponytail, showing off one big streak of hot pink down the side of her head. "I missed you in the dorms."

"I know. Where were you?"

A slow grin spread across her face. "On a run."

"Should've guessed." Now that she could shift, she was making up for lost time, going on forest runs with Donovan at every chance.

She pulled out a chair and settled down. "How was training after I left?"

I played with my half-eaten plate of hash browns. "It was fine. Ate more mat than I wanted to."

"That sounds awesome." Like every other Were, Meredith was an amazing fighter. Watching her and Shannon sparring during my first martial arts class had been insane. Not to mention intimidating.

"Yep. It was *super awesome.*" Sarcasm dripped from the words.

"Did you make any progress with your visions?"

I flipped the book shut and leaned back in my chair. "No. I don't know what's wrong with me, but I feel like there's something on the tip of my tongue. Something big that I'm forgetting. And it's driving me mad..." I trailed off when I noticed Meredith staring hard at something behind me. I quickly glanced over my shoulder. "What?"

"What's Shannon doing with that group?" Her lips pressed into a tight, thin line. "And is that *Imogene?*" Meredith and I might be split on how we felt about Shannon, but we totally agreed on Imogene.

I turned back to my now-cold omelet and took a bite. "I know," I said after a second. "Looks like they're BFFs now."

She scrunched up her nose as she thought. "Why is she with those guys? Shannon has nothing in common with them. She's from the Irish pack. And *Imogene? Really?*" Meredith stared at them like she could glean answers off them. "Maybe if we all try reaching out to her, she'll sit with us again."

I'd explained what happened between Shannon and me while Meredith was sick, but she didn't understand. For better or worse, they'd been friends since forever. Their parents were friends and they'd grown up taking vacations together. Meredith was loyal, almost to a fault, and that meant she refused to give up on Shannon.

"We tried that, remember? It didn't work."

"I should go over. Try talking to her again."

I nearly rolled my eyes. Meredith had tried talking to Shannon—and in her defense Shannon was still nice to *her*—but it was a losing battle. Shannon would obviously rather be with her new friends than with us.

Meredith started to stand up, but I grabbed her hand. "I wouldn't—"

"I have to try."

I let her go as I tried to think of a way to say what I needed to say without making it worse. "I don't know. I still can't feel *anyone* at that table through the pack bonds. Including Shannon."

Meredith crossed her arms as she stared down at me. "Whatever happened between you, she wouldn't do anything to harm the pack. Shannon's not capable of that."

I disagreed, but saying so would only hurt Meredith's feelings. "What if she thought it would help the pack?" *And what if they aren't part of our pack anymore?* I thought the words but didn't say them aloud.

For a second, Meredith's lower lip trembled, and I thought I'd gotten through to her, but then she shook her head. "No. I don't believe that. Not at all."

I kept my mouth firmly shut. If there was one person I didn't want to piss off, it was Meredith. She'd been my friend— no questions asked—from the beginning. She'd helped me when all I'd wanted to do was run away from St. Ailbe's. And when I'd sucked at running and kept jumping out of windows to get away, she hadn't made fun of me. Much.

"I just don't want you to be disappointed."

"I—" Meredith stopped in the middle of what she was saying and turned to the door.

It took me a second to figure out what was going on, but then Donovan came into the cafeteria and started our way. Maybe he'd be able to reach Meredith, because I sure as hell wasn't getting anywhere.

She laughed at something he must've said through their bond. "Donovan is going to keep you company while I talk to Shannon. I'll be back in a sec."

There wasn't any point in trying to stop her.

Donovan took Meredith's spot at the table. He wore sweat-pants and a T-shirt and his black hair was still messy from his run. His clothes gave off the scents of cedar and grass and dirt, and it almost made me jealous.

Maybe a run would clear my mind. Help me figure out a way around these visions.

"She's checking on Shannon, eh?" Donovan asked, bringing me back to myself.

"Yeah." I'd already said my piece to his mate. I didn't need to repeat myself.

He jerked his chin toward the table in question. "There's still something off about them."

My fork dropped to the plate with a clatter, and I glared into his crystal blue eyes. "Oh, come on. We're not doing this."

Donovan raised his eyebrows. "Not doing what?"

He had to be joking. "I just had this conversation with Meredith. I know how the whole mate thing works. There's not a chance she didn't tell you."

He gave me a wicked grin, and I knew trouble was coming. "Aye. But what you don't know is that I agree with you."

"You do?" Mr. Dawson had been all—everything's fine. Donovan hadn't said a word. Why now?

"Yes. I do."

"What do you know?" I leaned toward him, lowering my voice. Pesky Weres and their super awesome hearing. "Why are their bonds missing? I thought they couldn't leave the pack without putting in a formal bid to Mr. Dawson."

"That's true enough. I don't know what's going on, but I think you're going to find out. If this absence of pack bond is spreading, then we need to find the cause. Just... Don't say anything to Meredith until we're positive. All right?"

Whoa. I didn't keep much—if anything—from Dastien. "Do you think that's wise?"

"Keeping my opinions from my mate?" One side of his mouth quirked up. "Not usually. But she made her side clear enough with you, and I'd rather not start an argument that won't get us anywhere."

Who knew? Even the great Donovan—one of the all-powerful Seven—was afraid of pissing off his mate. The idea was a little preposterous, but then again—I didn't like upsetting Dastien either. I'd done it. But that didn't mean I liked it. That left me with one last question. "Why can't you keep an eye on them? You're probably way better at this pack bonds stuff than I am."

He raised an eyebrow. "In case you've forgotten, I'm not of

this pack. I'm an alpha, and can use that to overpower and override the pack bonds if necessary, but this needs more finesse. An insider's look."

"But your mate's in our pack." When Dastien bit me, I'd become part of the St. Ailbe's pack. I figured it would be the same for Donovan and Meredith and their mate bond, even if they hadn't gone through their bonding ceremony.

"Doesn't work that way. I'm already the alpha of another pack."

"So, what about Meredith? Is she still part of this pack?"

"Until she and Michael decide to let her move to mine. She'll keep it for as long as she's here, and I think that's best." He leaned forward. "I've heard through Michael and Meredith, but I want to know what it is you're feelin' from them. I've not experienced this before, and that's sayin' something to me." His Irish accent thickened, and I finally knew that someone else was as worried about this as I was.

"I don't know what to say except that I can't feel them. It's like they're there, but they're not." I sighed. "It makes no sense. Which is why Mr. Dawson blew me off when I brought it up. Shouldn't you be talking to him about this? He's the alpha."

"What makes you think I haven't already?"

The tension in my shoulders relaxed. It seemed like a good sign that two alphas were really talking about the problem. "And?"

"Nothing. If they've withdrawn from the pack, he's not feeling it." He leaned in closer, speaking so quietly that even I could barely hear. "But last night, he gave that group of boys from the Canada pack a direct command and they disobeyed. I backed the command and forced their obedience, but I shouldn't have had to. *He's* their alpha. It may be that Rupert Hoel's influence went deeper than those we've caught. There's still a major player out there, and I've a fine idea who it might be."

Holy shit. That was bad news. Only someone more alpha than Mr. Dawson could ignore his commands, and they weren't more alpha. At all.

"Who?"

"I think you might know. It's one who got away."

It hit me then. They'd kicked one of the Seven out of the Council. The one who hated me. Ferdinand. "Do you really think it could be?"

"Aye."

"But you didn't say anything when I brought it up before."

"It took me longer to feel what you were getting at. I like to suss things out before actin'. Get fully aware of the situation. If you feel anything else out of the ordinary, let me know. Just be aware that if that lot wants to leave, that's fine by me. They're welcome to go their own way, but they need to make formal bids to Michael and they'll have to tie to the Seven until they find their new packs. It must be done properly, or they'll be considered lone wolves. And if they align with Ferdinand... I'd like those youngsters to avoid that if possible."

My stomach churned, and suddenly I didn't feel much like finishing my omelet. If the pack was breaking up, then how were we ever going to defeat Luciana? We needed to be united if we wanted to stand the slightest chance of surviving.

Meredith came back with a tray of food. "What are you two talking about?"

As much as I didn't feel like eating, I reached for my fork and shoved a big bite in my mouth. I was crap at lying, and if I even tried, she'd smell it.

Man.

Visions of death. Hiding things from my best friend. Today was a real winner.

You okay? Dastien's voice came through our bond.

It used to weird me out when he did that, but ever since I came back from the compound, it felt natural. I found it comforting that no matter what, I could rely on him. He was there for me. *Yeah. I think so.*

If you're still stressing about your visions, don't. We're going to figure it out. I promise.

I hope we can. Because if we couldn't rely on the pack, we were going to need every bit of help we could get to stand against what was on the way.

CHAPTER THREE

AFTER I FINISHED EATING, I left Donovan and Meredith to their flirting and went to check on Raphael. Luciana's attack a couple of nights ago had left him looking the worse for wear. His bite from the reanimated zombie version of Daniel was horrifying for a lot of reasons.

That Luciana could do something like that to her own son…

Anger made my skin itch as the wolf rose, and I tried to remember that Dr. Gonzales was keeping a close watch on him in the infirmary. Still, there was a limit to what she could do. He'd looked pretty rough when I checked on him last night, but I was hoping she could cook up some good drugs to at least keep him stable until my cousin, Claudia, came back from Peru with a cure.

I made my way back through campus to the infirmary. It was never quiet in the mornings. People were always racing to get last-minute food before the melodic warning tone rang, telling us that classes were starting. But today, everyone seemed especially busy.

A group of Cazadores ran at full speed on a lap around the campus, but as they passed I noticed that they weren't in sync.

Usually, the footfalls matched and they looked like they were running as one—as a unified group—but one of these guys was completely off. His footfalls were exactly opposite the others. Another was just a fraction too slow.

The sight was unsettling to say the least. Even after being bitten, I'd been able to run in sync with my pack mates on my first jog around the gym. For the Cazadores, it should be like breathing.

Motion on the quad drew my attention away. Two Weres had shifted and were circling and growling in the middle of the grass. I wasn't positive, but going by the low rumbling sounds and flashing teeth, they weren't play fighting.

It seemed like everywhere I looked, the pack was falling apart. Maybe I was pushing my own suspicions on everyone, but I didn't think so. Not anymore. Especially not after what Donovan had just said.

Another Cazador's voice pulled me from my thoughts. He had a group of freshmen gathered around him.

"You have to be fast," he said as he paced back and forth in front of the group. His black hair was slicked back, but I couldn't see his face. I only knew he was a Cazador by his uniform—black jeans and a plain, black T-shirt. "If you see their fingers flick or their lips moving, they're cursing you. Act first. Slash your claws across their throat. If you can't get the right angle, biting off hands works well, too."

I rubbed my arms as goose bumps ran across my skin. It was probably good information for them to have, especially since we had a few bad witches under sedation in the feral cages—but still—the idea of killing witches willy-nilly was upsetting for obvious reasons. I shoved my hands into the pockets of my jeans and picked up my pace.

As soon as I reached the second floor of the building, the smell hit me.

Rotten eggs.

My stomach rolled, and I moved a little quicker. That scent brought back memories. None of them good.

The witches—Tiffany, Beth, Shane, Elsa, and Yvonne—were gathered around Raphael's bed. I briefly wondered where Cosette was hiding herself, but Raphael took all my attention as his breath came in loud rasping wheezes.

"He's worse than before." I'd thought we had more time for Claudia to find a cure and get back, but now... A shudder of fear ran up my spine.

"He's dying," Elsa said. She was shorter than me—which was a feat since I was barely over five feet tall—and rail thin. Her pixie cut made her appear even younger than she was. She usually liked to fade into the background, but every once in a while she said something that cut deep.

This time I hoped she was wrong. "Where's—"

Dr. Gonzales pushed past me, answering the question on my mind. "I've got an idea." She held one of her needles. "I don't know about the dose. He's human, but I think the demon's overpowering the human side. If I'm wrong, this could go very badly, though. I want—"

"Whatever it is, do it," Shane said. "He's suffering."

I'd never seen Dr. Gonzales so nervous. Her shirt was wrinkled and a strand of glossy black hair fell free of her usually immaculate ponytail. "No. I want to be absolutely clear. I've been monitoring him all night, but he's working through the drugs faster and faster. I'm taking a big risk here. I'm using enough sedative to put a full alpha down for a long nap. This could go badly."

"We won't hold it against you," Yvonne said a little too quickly.

The older woman stood at the head of Raphael's bed, gripping one of his hands. Her long gray hair was pulled into a low bun and her tea-length khaki skirt hung a little askew on her hips. I didn't think she meant Raphael harm, but she hadn't even considered the risks Dr. Gonzales mentioned. *Why?*

"What's happened?" I asked.

"He went into cardiac arrest early this morning," Dr. Gonzales said.

"About the time Claudia's plane took off," Elsa said.

I squeezed my eyes shut. Had I been wrong to encourage her to go?

"We finally got him more or less stabilized. His heart rate is still high, which means he'll be lucid and hurting again in a few minutes, unless I try something stronger. Whatever has a hold on him isn't giving up easily."

This shouldn't be happening. This wasn't supposed to happen. None of it.

A hand grasped my arm, and I opened my eyes. Tiffany stood there, staring at me. She was the one coven member I knew the least about. I'd never really talked to her, but if she was here instead of with Luciana, then it was a good indicator that she was a good witch.

"It's not your fault. We all told Claudia to go." She waited for that to sink in, and it did, but I still felt responsible for Raphael. For everything. "What Luciana does isn't in your control. She probably sensed Claudia slipping away, and this is retaliation."

"I didn't know that was possible."

"Many things are possible when you've taken a blood oath," Yvonne said.

Again, Yvonne hadn't said anything bad exactly, but her tone sent shivers down my spine. I pushed my concerns aside, and focused on Raphael. "What's in the needle?"

Dr. Gonzales sent me a look that said she was over my hatred of shots. "I had him hooked to an IV earlier, but his thrashing kept ripping it out. The syringe is filled with a seda-tive, painkiller, some antibiotics, and holy water."

She'd saved the best for last. "Holy water?"

She shrugged. "It's a guess, but it could weaken the demon so that the rest of the drugs can do their job."

Her logic seemed legit, but boy was it odd to think of a doctor shooting up a patient with holy water.

The witches made room for Dr. Gonzales around the bed.

The noise that Raphael made as the mixture went into him was nothing human. We stood frozen as he screamed. His back arched off the bed, and Dr. Gonzales pushed his shoulder down. "Hold him," she said as she pulled the needle out.

We all moved at once, each grabbing a bit of Raphael to hold him still as he thrashed. He jerked so hard that the bed nearly flipped.

I cringed as he convulsed. This wasn't right. "Does this happen every time you give him a shot?"

"No." She blinked twice. "It must be the holy water."

It took a few minutes for the convulsions to stop, but we kept holding him, unsure what was going to happen next.

The silence in the room was nearly deafening. And then it came.

At first, I thought it was just another rattle in Raphael's breath, but it wasn't. The sound built into a soft, slow laugh. Slimy energy ran against my skin. We all let go. I didn't want to touch anything he was touching.

"He's already mine." The rasping voice sounded like sand-paper on a chalkboard. It made my teeth hurt.

That wasn't Raphael. Not even a little bit. His skin was turning gray, and his eyes had gone from bloodshot to red.

Yvonne knocked into the chair behind her as she crossed herself and started praying.

"He's mine. Words can't protect you."

The demon had full control over my cousin. How was I going to tell Claudia about this? For the first time, I wasn't sure if her twin could be saved.

Dr. Gonzales stared down at Raphael. "I think if I—" She turned to me. "Watch him." Her voice was clipped, but held a hint of power as she gave the command. "I'll be back."

"Sure," I said, although I wasn't sure what else I could do but wait.

Raphael sat up, and we all moved as one to pin him down again. He snapped his teeth at Elsa, and she dodged out of the way. Her face paled as she glanced down at her arm.

"Did he bite you?" Shane asked.

"No. No." Her voice was wobbly. "He missed."

"Doctor!" I yelled. "Bring some rope when you come back."

She rushed back into the room. "Already on it." She moved around us, setting up the medical restraints and strapping Raphael down. He hissed and clawed. Yelled things that even made my ears bleed.

By the time she was done, we all stood a few feet from the bed watching Raphael. He strained against the bonds, but couldn't get free. If he got loose, he could probably infect others, and I didn't want to imagine what that would do to the pack at this point. It couldn't be allowed to happen.

"Are you going to try another dose?" I asked.

"No. Whatever was done to him, he's still human. I've already pushed his limits farther than I'm comfortable with."

"So what now?" I asked.

"We pray," Yvonne said as she pulled a rosary from her pocket.

"Pray?" That seemed like the least helpful thing to do right now.

"We have to wait for Claudia and have faith that she'll get back in time to save him."

"But that's going to take time." I tried to keep my cool, but I couldn't stop the urge to head down the feral cages and punch those witches in their faces for this. How could they do this to a member of their own coven? "His skin is gray, his lungs are rattling, and it looks like he's lost ten pounds since yesterday. He won't last days."

"Do you have a better idea?" Shane asked. He crossed his tattooed arms, and his biceps strained against his T-shirt.

"Not yet." But we had to do something. "What are our options?" I asked Dr. Gonzales.

She shook her head. "Like Yvonne said, pray. Have faith that Claudia gets back in time."

I chewed on my lip as I thought. "What if we move him closer to Claudia?"

"How? He can't fly like this. What if he starts convulsing? What if he gets loose? The plane would crash and then..." Dr. Gonzales' words trailed off. "No. We wait. In the meantime, I'll do everything I can."

That wasn't what I wanted to hear.

Maybe one of my books was hiding a spell that could help. It was a long shot, but worth a try.

I started to leave, and Elsa called out to me. "Where are you going?"

"To figure something out. I can't sit here and watch him die." I strode down the stairs and headed for the dorms.

Between the books I'd dug out of the library and the magic books Claudia had given me what seemed like ages ago, there had to be a few passages on demonic possession. I was ready to read every line if there was the smallest chance I could help Raphael.

THE SQUEAK of my highlighter against the page was the only noise in my room. Dastien had stopped by at lunchtime with sandwiches and snacks before heading back to the gym. He'd promised some people that he'd spar. He'd wanted me to go with him, but I was too busy to get my ass kicked again.

My eyes were burning as I switched books for the billionth time. All the ones I'd read so far had steered clear of any mention of demons or black magic. I needed more, and short of going back to the compound, I wasn't getting it.

I had no way to help Raphael. No way to defend us against the demons that Luciana would conjure.

Fear made my pulse race, but I pushed that thought away. I had to focus on one problem at a time. The most immediate one was Raphael.

My best idea so far was to somehow ship him down to Peru. At least then he'd be with Claudia when she found the cure, and she wouldn't lose a day of travel getting back to Texas.

But that was only saving her a day.

I was digging into a potion-making book when a ringing sound made me jump. It surprised me so much that it took a second to realize it was just my cell phone.

Yet another reminder how far I've come from normal.

Since I'd moved to St. Ailbe's, I seldom carried it on me. Who was going to call? Axel was busy being all collegiate. My parents stopped by sometimes, but we'd settled into a rhythm. They knew where I was, and that I'd call if something came up. In turn, family barbecues with Dastien and the gang were mandatory on Sunday afternoons. It must cost a small fortune to feed all of us once a week, but they did it without complaint.

I reached to my bedside table and picked up my phone, but the number showed as unavailable. I usually wouldn't answer, but with everything going on... It was better not to risk missing something important.

"Hello?" I said, more like a question than a statement.

"It's Claudia."

I sat up quickly. "Is everything okay?"

"Yeah. I'm fine. I think." She paused, and I let out a breath of relief. Even if the "I think" was a little vague for my liking. "That's not why I'm calling. You remember the guy I'm engaged to?"

I sure did. I clicked my highlighter shut as I grinned at the memory. When she first told me about him, she'd actually used a curse word. Very out of character for her. "The *douche bag* you told off the other night. Yeah, I remember. Why?"

"He's here." Her voice was soft as she said it, but the implications...

"He's what?" I wasn't smiling anymore. "Please, tell me that's a coincidence."

"I'm sorry. Luciana told him I was coming, and he managed to beat me here all the way from New York."

"More direct flights," I murmured. *And holy shit.* This was bad. If Luciana knew what we were up to, then... God, I didn't even want to think about what that could mean.

My mind went to Joseph, Imogene, and Shannon. They couldn't have, though...

No. They could. I just didn't want to believe they *would.* "Okay. So, what do you think? Is it a wash? Should you come home? We can figure out something else. Do some more digging in the library. I'm sure if we put our heads together we'll find something that can save Raphael. Maybe we should've tried harder before shipping you off, but it seemed like the easiest way to save him..." Although that was sounding more and more like wishful thinking.

"No. Muraco's right. I've never learned a thing about fighting demons and I grew up with *La Aquelarre.* It's been my

29

life forever. Maybe Luciana has something in her craft room, but—"

Chills ran down my spine. "No one is going in there. Never ever."

"I'd never ask that of you. But I could—"

Was she out of her mind? "No! We both know she's after your powers. She managed to strip me of mine, and now that you've left, she wants yours just as bad. You can't go anywhere near her." The problem was, we didn't have a ton of options. It wasn't just the fight with Luciana. Raphael's life was on the line. As crazy as it might be, this quest was still her best option. "I don't like the sound of this douche bag being in Peru with you."

"I know. But we all agreed. This is the best chance we have to save Raphael and stop Luciana."

"Right. Well, stay away from him."

"Thanks. I'll be okay. I've protected myself from Matt for years, but his being here isn't a good sign. I wanted to warn you. I'm not sure who is spying on us, but... Maybe look into Beth, Tiffany, and Yvonne."

"Yeah, I had the same thought. There's something about Yvonne." Maybe I wanted it to be her or any of the coven members, but my instincts said the pack could just as easily be the problem. "I don't know. And there are a few wolves who aren't acting right. They should be following Mr. Dawson's orders, but they're being shifty."

"They *are* shifters."

"Yeah. Yeah. Bad use of the word." I sighed. "I don't want you to worry, but Raphael—"

"He didn't... He's not..." She could barely say the words.

"No. He's still alive," I said quickly.

"Thank God." Relief was thick in her voice.

"He's hanging in, but he's in worse shape tonight than he was this morning. You just do your best, and then come home fast. I've got a feeling if you're not back soon, well..." I tried to pick my next words carefully, but the fact was Raphael wasn't doing well. "I'm not sure what you'll come back to."

"I know. I'm going to move as fast as I can."

"The thing is... He's fading faster than Dr. Gonzales expected. I'm wondering if it might make sense to get him to you. That way by the time you find his cure, he's there. She says we can't put him on a plane—he's not stable enough for that—" Dr. Gonzales was right. If he got loose in a confined space, he could kill everyone and crash the plane. "—but I can get a few wolves and maybe a couple of your *brujos* to drive him down to Peru. It'll take a few days, but could work out timewise. Then, once he's okay, you all fly back together." Raphael was running out of time, and if something happened on the road, they could pull over. Maybe it wasn't the best plan, but it was better than nothing.

"Who would drive him down?"

"Adrian and Shane for sure. And then I was thinking maybe Beth, and one or two more wolves. I have to see who else might be up for it. Who we can spare right now."

"Okay. I agree. Drive him down and I'll move as quickly as I can."

I hated to put more pressure on her, but if it were my brother, I'd want to know. "Just stay safe, Claudia. You can do this. I know you can. Call me if you need anything."

"Same to you. I'll be in touch as soon as I have more information. Call me if anything changes with Raphael."

"Of course."

"Bye."

I started to put the phone down, and then thought better of it. I shoved it into my pocket as I headed out. These books weren't getting me anywhere. Short of going back to Luciana's den of depravity, I wasn't going to find anything on the magic she was using. And that so wasn't happening. Not yet.

Hopefully not ever.

If I was going to get Raphael moved, I needed to start working on it now. My gut told me he didn't have a minute to spare, and I wasn't going to ignore it.

CHAPTER FOUR

ONE GLANCE out the window told me that the Cazadores were patrolling campus again. We were still on lockdown, but since I was known to fight against the witches, the Cazadores let me move around. They kind of had to. Their leader had tried commanding me to stay indoors a few nights ago, and it hadn't gone his way. Since then, they steered clear of me. I was pretty sure I made them uncomfortable, but that was definitely the least of my worries.

I stashed a few vials of my newest potion in my pockets— just in case something happened—before going in search of Dastien.

I went to the gym first, thinking our group would be there, but I didn't see Dastien or anyone else among the guys sparring. They didn't pay much attention to me as they fought, moving so quickly that their movements were hard to track.

Where was everyone? I thought about using the bond to find Dastien, but I hated to use that as a crutch. I wanted to be able to find him on my own.

The next logical place to look was the cafeteria. But again, only some Cazadores and alphas milling about, and no Dastien. No Meredith or Donovan or Adrian either.

So odd. If they were finished working out, why hadn't they come to get me?

I grabbed a drink and a cookie and finally gave in, opening the bond wide. *Where are you?*

The library.

As soon as he said the words, an image of him standing in front of the shelves as he scanned the spines of books came through the bond.

The library was on the first floor of the admin building. I started to head that way, but kept the connection open with Dastien. *You didn't come get me when you were finished?* My voice had a hint of whine. I hated that. I took a big bite of cookie. Chocolate chip with a hint of salt. God, the Were cooks were amazing.

I checked in. You were on the phone. I figured you'd find me when you were finished.

Which was what I'd done, so no point in getting annoyed. But why was I feeling needy all of a sudden?

I started up the three stairs to the entrance of the admin building.

Maybe because you were traumatized and you need to give yourself time to heal.

I nearly tripped. Sometimes it still surprised me that he could dig into my thoughts. *Right. Well, it stinks.*

I pushed through the door to the library. Everyone sat at study tables. Meredith and Donovan huddled over a book. When a chunk of pink hair fell into her eyes, Donovan tucked it back behind her ear. Chris was tapping a pencil against the table as he worked through his volume. His wavy blonde hair was getting long and poofing out. Chris was the most intro-verted of the group, even if he did like to flirt a little. I couldn't believe he'd actually kissed me once. That all seemed like forever ago.

Dastien stood off to the side waiting for me. He leaned casually against the bookcase, and grinned, showing his dimples. I rolled my eyes at how easily he got to me. Just one look and I was toast. "I sure hope you're right, because otherwise..." If I got any more addicted to him, I'd lose my mind.

"I'm always right."

I snorted. He liked to think so.

Adrian glanced up from his book. His short black curls were gelled just enough to be perfectly mussed and spiky. "What is he right about?"

I cleared my throat. "Nothing. But we have a situation."

That got everyone's attention. "What's going on?" Donovan asked.

"Have any of you been to see Raphael?" Only Chris had the decency to look sheepish. "He's not doing well. I've been trying to come up with a way to help, only I've got nothing."

"I thought Dr. Gonzales had him stabilized," Donovan said.

"Not even close." The eerie, cackling laugh of that thing inside Raphael echoed in my mind. "It's *The Exorcist* over there. She shot him up with enough sedatives to knock out an alpha, and it only pissed off whatever's possessing him. Best she could do was strap him down."

Adrian leaned back in his chair. "So, what now?"

"That's where you come in."

He pointed to himself. "Me? Specifically?"

"Yup." Adrian was pretty easygoing, and of all my friends he showed the most interest in getting closer with the *brujos*. He was also the only one in the pack that had *brujo* blood in him, even if it was a few generations removed. "I've been reading everything I can get my hands on, and so far there's nothing that would help Raphael. Claudia's his best shot, but she's more than a day of travel away. So, what do you think about going with Shane, Beth, and I dunno—someone else—to Peru."

"He can't get on a plane," Adrian said. "Not if he's that bad."

No kidding. "I figured that—"

"Yeah, if he's really bad off, I wouldn't chance putting him on a plane," Chris said. "It's too risky. What if something happens midflight?"

I rolled my eyes. "I know. That's what I'm trying to say. So, back to my original idea. You drive down."

"We'll get an RV. If they drive in shifts, they could be down there in a day or two," Dastien said.

"It'll take her at least that long to find a cure. That should be perfect." I tried to keep any hope off my face as I turned back to Adrian. "So, you game?"

Meredith snorted. "For some nearly alone time with Shane, I'd say he's in."

What? Why does he want alone time with Shane?

Probably because he has a crush on him.

Wait. Adrian's gay? How did I not know that? I tried to keep the surprise off my face, but Adrian narrowed his gaze, and I looked away.

Dastien shrugged. Why do you think we train together every morning at five? He's not pairing up with any girls. He thinks his only shot at making a difference is being a Cazador. And it gives him cover from his parents—who are a couple of complete assholes.

My world had just been rocked. I'd been so caught up in my own shit that I didn't really know the only friends I'd ever had.

Don't do that. His romantic life is between him and whoever he ends up with. Just like it's none of anyone else's business what you and I do or don't do.

That made sense, but I still felt like a moron. *But you all knew?*

That's because we've known each other a long time. This isn't about you.

Fine. I just feel selfish. Like a bad friend.

You're not a bad friend.

Meredith cleared her throat. "You about done?" She turned to Donovan. "We're not that annoying, are we?"

"Worse." Adrian groaned. "You're way worse. And being around the four of you is—"

"Nauseating," Chris chimed in. "It's nauseating. When I finally find my true mate, I'm not doing any of this shit."

Meredith threw a pen at him. "Big words, dork. You're going to be the worst of the bunch."

"So true," I said. "You're all into art and feelings. Which means you'll be even more romantic than the rest of us."

"Yeah, well, payback's gonna be a bitch." His voice had a hint of rasp to it as he laughed.

My smile faded as my mind wandered back to Raphael. "Okay. So, who else can we get to go on the trip? No offense, but I can only spare one of you. I figured Adrian was good to go since he'd get more time with the *brujos*."

"Good call," Adrian said. "I've been wanting to pick their brains. I feel like I could really get better at spells with their help, but there's been no time."

"Well, here's your chance."

"I'll find someone to go. Someone not too alpha, but a good fighter," Donovan said.

"Maybe Stephen? Or Kaden?" Meredith said.

I had no idea who they were. It was easy to forget that I'd only been at St. Ailbe's for a couple of months, but then things like this happened and I remembered that I really was just the new kid in school.

The door opened, and we all quieted as Mr. Dawson strode in. His gray-speckled hair was more messy than usual, which was a huge sign that he was stressed. He wore a pair of sweatpants and nothing else. Not even shoes. That meant one of two things: either he'd just been a wolf, or he was going to go wolf any second and didn't want to destroy his favorite pair of jeans.

"We've got a problem."

My breath quickened. I only had a few vials on me. If Luciana was here, they wouldn't be enough.

"The wolves we had issues with last night," he said to Donovan. "They're defecting."

I took a moment to calm down. That wasn't what I'd been expecting—which was good—but it still wasn't fantastic. What did this mean for the pack?

Dastien started toward the door. "Where are they?"

"The parking lot, but I'm worried they're part of a bigger problem. Some teenage Weres leaving the pack is one thing, but if Rupert did more damage..."

Even from beyond the grave, Rupert Hoel was being a pain in the ass. My patience was in the negatives and plummeting fast. There was no way I was letting those wolves get away. Not until Mr. Dawson made sure there was a clean break. We couldn't risk Luciana using them to gain power over the pack.

We booked it from the library, racing for the parking lot. Alpha energy pumped through my blood as I prepared for a fight. It made me tingle and feel alive as I ran. The sensation built with every step. Dastien kept pace beside me, but I was in the zone, focusing only on getting to the rogue Weres.

I spotted them piling into a white SUV and a little coupe. The same group from the table at breakfast.

"Stop," I yelled the command at them, throwing a healthy dose of alpha energy into it. Imogene paused for a second, but then jumped into the passenger side of the coupe. Engines roared to life as they gunned it.

What the hell? That much power behind an order, and it just rolled over them?

How was that possible?

Good thing I wasn't just an alpha. "Stop!" I put everything I had into that one word. The magic built within me—racing down my fingers—as I held my arms out, screaming the word, willing it to be possible.

Everything stopped.

Not just them. Everyone. Dastien had frozen in midstep. Chris and Adrian stood a few feet behind us, totally motionless. Even Mr. Dawson and Donovan had stopped. It was like someone had hit the Pause button on the world. None of them even blinked.

It took me a second, but I remembered Claudia had done this. When I first went up against Mr. Hoel, she'd frozen a whole mall full of people.

I grabbed Dastien and shook him, but he didn't unfreeze. "Wake up!"

He gasped, almost falling forward. "What the hell is going on?"

"No time. I don't know how long the spell will hold. Let's get them tied down."

"One second." He ran to the line of black SUVs parked in the front of the lot and popped the trunk of the closest one. After pulling out a bag of gear, he headed straight for the white SUV. "I'll do the grabbing. You zip tie their hands."

"Will that hold them?" Weres were strong enough to flip cars. There was no way a flimsy bit of plastic was going to stop them if they wanted to be free.

"There's some silver mixed in with the plastic, but even that won't hold a pissed off Were for long. But it should be enough."

"Enough for what?"

"To get them into the feral cages. Until we figure out what they're up to, that's where they'll have to stay."

We worked quickly, getting all eight Weres out of the cars and bound. Including Imogene and Shannon. I snuck a peek back at Meredith, still frozen. This was going to kill her.

"Okay, so how do you unfreeze everyone else?"

I chewed on my lip as I scanned their unmoving forms. I had no clue how to fix it. "I'm not even sure how I did it in the first place. I guess I'll go touch them and yell at them to wake up like I did to you." I stood up, brushing off my jeans.

"Do you think we should—?"

His question became moot as everyone started moving, almost tripping as their momentum caught up with them. I jumped back from Shannon as she struggled. The rest of my friends gathered behind me.

"What happened?" Mr. Dawson's voice was almost a growl. "What did you do?"

I wasn't quite sure how to answer in a way that wouldn't piss him off more, so instead I gave him a sheepish smile. "Caught them for you. What now?"

"Now, we release them." Waves of power rolled off Mr. Dawson so thick they were almost visible. "Anyone who wants to leave this pack, leave this land now." His voice was half-growl and laced with so much magic that my hair stood on end. I closed my eyes as his command tingled through my body, racing along the pack bonds.

"Those of you who have tampered with your bond are no longer welcome." His words vibrated through the magical web of the pack. Everyone in it—even if they weren't physically here —would hear him. "Any students who leave must go back to your native packs. You will be reported to your alphas and expected home. If any who leave interfere in our fight against

Luciana, you will be treated as an enemy of all packs. If you stay and harm the pack, there will be no tribunal. You will pay the ultimate price. You have five minutes to get off our land. Do not come back." He grabbed Joseph's zip-tied wrists. "Except you. You, I want answers from."

"You can't hold me here." His voice was full of whine. "My father's the alpha of the Canadian pack. I'm a student. I get to go home."

"I know who your father is. That's why I'm keeping you until he comes to pick you up." Joseph's face paled, and Mr. Dawson grinned. I never knew he could be scary, but I made a note to never do anything that would put me on the receiving end of one of those looks. "Yes. I'd be very afraid if I were you. Your father and I go way back. We're going to have a long talk about what you've done with the pack bonds."

"It was—"

A group of wolves approached the parking lot, and Mr. Dawson growled. "Keep your mouth shut until I say you can talk."

"Any Cazador who is not with us in this fight, leave now," Donovan added, and another wave of power rolled through the pack—even stronger than Mr. Dawson's. It was like a count-down, warning dissenters to get out now. While they still could.

I kept my eyes closed, focusing on the bonds. They looked like a big spider web. Mr. Dawson was in the center and the ties spiraled out from him. Farther out, a few strands were missing. And more of the distant, faint lines—the Cazadores who weren't part of our pack specifically but tied to us through the Seven— were evaporating by the second. Then more. Ten. Twenty. Thirty. More.

I opened my eyes. "They're all leaving." I tried to swallow down the panic, but it wasn't working. They couldn't leave.

"No, not all of them," Mr. Dawson said.

"But we need as many people as we can to fight Luciana."

"No." Donovan's tone was clear and firm, leaving no room for question. "Better to have fewer people fighting honestly than more fighting half-heartedly. Or worse, working against us. Best be done with it now."

Dastien took the zip ties off Joseph and the others one by one. I wasn't sure letting Imogene go was smart, but I wasn't about to argue with Mr. Dawson. But Shannon...

Meredith came to stand beside me. "You were right."

I leaned against her shoulder. "I'm sorry. I know you were close."

"If she's leaving the pack, then we weren't really all that close."

By the end of it, almost forty people left.

Some Cazadores. Some students. It didn't take more than a few minutes, but it felt much longer.

When the last of them were gone, Mr. Dawson raised his hands in the air. "The pack is now solid and closed. You will abide by my law or face the consequences. I am the alpha." The command in his words knocked me back.

Donovan raised his hands in the air. "By the power of the Seven, the ranks of the Cazadores are now sealed. Any who left are to be treated as dead." His command was stronger, and I nearly fell to the pavement as it slammed into me.

I focused in on the pack bonds. The lines that linked us were thicker and clearer than they'd been before. "Are you going to follow them? The ones who aren't going back to their home packs?" I asked Donovan.

"Yes and no," Donovan said. "They'll have to join another pack or stay lone wolves, but they're subject to Were laws regardless. If they're joining up with Ferdinand—"

"We'll have a mess on our hands."

"Aye. But it should keep for a while. I'll send someone I

trust to keep an eye on them. I'm not liking the fact that Rupert's daughter is in this bunch."

"Agreed," Mr. Dawson said. "Who will you send?"

"Mal."

Who's Mal? I asked Dastien.

One of the best wolves I've ever known.

Coming from Dastien, that was high praise.

"Good choice."

"Aye. He's been working on a problem for me in the area. Just going to have to expand his job a bit now. Pack is feeling better from my end. On yours?" He asked Mr. Dawson.

"Much better, but I wasn't feeling much before."

"And you?" Donovan asked me.

"Me?"

"Aye. What are you feeling?"

"It's good. As soon as you closed the pack, it was like every-thing solidified. It felt calm again."

"Good. We've had enough of that then. When this bit with Luciana is over with, I'll meet up with Mal. See what's what. Until then..." He turned back toward campus. A group of students and Cazadores were watching the flood of Weres leaving campus. "Show's over. Everyone who's not patrolling get to bed."

Mr. Dawson and Donovan headed for the admin building, hauling a very unhappy-looking Joseph between them.

I shook my head at the sight. I wouldn't want to be in his shoes. Not in a million years.

Finally, everyone dispersed, with Adrian giving orders on getting their road trip to Peru underway. Dastien and I started walking toward his cabin, but he was even more quiet than usual.

"Are you okay?"

"Sure."

"Why don't I believe you?"

He tucked a strand of curls behind his ear. "Some of the Cazadores that left—they were my friends. I trusted them. Fought with them. But they left? When we're in the middle of a war with the witches?"

"I'm sorry." I said the words even though I knew they probably wouldn't help.

He was hurting now, but Donovan had a point. We were better off cutting loose the Weres who weren't behind our cause. If we were going to beat Luciana, we had to be united.

If this was part of one of her schemes—to weaken the pack—it had definitely been a good one. Luckily, we'd caught it sooner rather than later.

I had a feeling it wasn't the last we'd see of those wolves. Maybe they'd stay gone until Luciana was out of the way, but we hadn't gotten rid of them for good. I just hoped this Mal guy —whoever he was—was as badass as Dastien thought.

For now, I was pushing away any thoughts of rogue Weres. That was one thing off my already-full plate.

Now, all I had to worry about were psychotic witches and night terrors that might be visions of the future.

CHAPTER FIVE

AN ECHO BOOMED through the empty gym as my back slammed against the mat. Air was wrenched from my lungs. "Fuck." I moaned the word as soon as I could catch my breath. It was the third time in less than five minutes that I'd ended up on the floor. The pain receded almost as quickly as it came.

At least being a werewolf was good for some things.

"You okay?" Dastien's voice had only a hint of concern.

Jerk. "No." I squeezed my eyes shut. If I pretended really hard, I could nearly imagine I was snug in my bed. Then I caught the scent of the highly polished wood mixed with the rubber in the floor mats and even I couldn't pretend I was anywhere but the gym.

After a few hours of fitful sleep, we'd seen Adrian, Shane, Beth, and Kaden off on their way to move Raphael, and Dastien had dragged me here.

It was half-past five in the morning, and he was convinced that getting me totally exhausted would loosen my mind enough that I'd finally *see* what I needed to see. "I'm dead. You killed me this time."

"You're breathing fine." My mate's voice lifted up at the

end, and I knew he was smiling at me. He was closer now. Standing right above me even though I hadn't heard him move. The scent of forest overpowered the plastic as he moved even closer.

"I wasn't a second ago. Can we be done?"

He nudged my leg with his foot. "I told you I wasn't going easy on you."

I finally opened my eyes. I was right. He was smiling.

No. Not smiling. *Smirking.*

"I think we passed the 'not going easy' on me and went straight for 'kicking my ass.' Really. This is getting a bit ridiculous."

"I have to go hard on you right now. You want to stop having nightmares, right?" I didn't like the stress in his voice. I wasn't the only one being affected by my dreams.

"Right." I wiped the sweat off my face with my T-shirt, but it didn't help much. My shirt was already soaked through.

"Come on. I know you're tired, but I think this is loosening you up. Just relax. Let your mind wander, and it'll come." Dastien reached down to me, muscles flexing under his gray T-shirt. His sweatpants hung low on his hips, and he was barefoot. The sight of him made me melt.

From the second I first saw him I'd wanted him more than I'd ever wanted anything. I'd fought our bond when I first became a Were—because the whole biting thing hadn't gone over well—but I was done with that. Long done.

He leaned forward, patiently waiting for me to take his hand. "Come on," he said again. When he smiled, his dimples made deep dents in his cheeks.

Damn it. He knew exactly what he was doing to me, but I couldn't deny that face. Maybe one day I'd get used to him and I'd be able to get my own way once in a while.

I put my hand in his and instantly our bond strengthened. "I'm glad you're enjoying this."

His grin got even bigger. "You can't lie to me. I know you're having fun, too."

"I'd rather do a different kind of wrestling on the mat." I raised an eyebrow.

"Don't try to tempt me with your wiles."

I shook my head. "Wiles? Seriously?" Sometimes he sounded way older than twenty.

"Let's try it again. This time you try and take me to the mat."

"But I don't know what I'm doing." A piece of my long brown hair fell in my eyes, and I pulled my hair out of its rubber band.

"Just do whatever feels right. This is good for you, beyond helping with the visions. We're going to be fighting for our lives. Maybe tonight. You have to be ready. I don't—"

"Want to lose you," I finished for him.

I'd heard this speech a lot the past few days. When Luciana stripped me of my powers, it had affected Dastien in a big way. He kept worrying about losing me or losing our bond. Honestly, I wasn't sure which of us it had hurt more. But it didn't matter. We were dealing with the fallout together.

This was Dastien's way. Preparing me for next time. Making sure there wasn't a next time.

I met his amber gaze. "You're not going to lose me."

He pressed his lips together. "Of course I'm not. Because we're going to be ready. I know you're frustrated—"

"I'm not frustrated." I tried to stay calm. Morning wasn't my most rational part of the day.

"Don't try to deny it, *chérie*. I can feel your frustration—at your visions, at your lack of ability when sparring, and most of all

47

at what Luciana did. That's okay. I understand what you're going through, but you don't get how scared I am. How hard it was being away from you, not knowing if you were okay. Then you came back, and you *weren't* okay. I feel like I failed you. I should've stopped you from going. I knew it was a bad idea. I knew nothing good would come of you going to the coven, but I agreed for the sake of the pack. Now, you have to let me protect you. Please."

My lip started to tremble and I bit it, trying to get it to stop the embarrassing fluttering. Those jars... It had been hard, but I'd gotten through it. I was getting through it. "I'm not broken."

"You're not broken, but you're fragile right now."

I wasn't sure how I felt about that statement. If I was honest with myself, I might agree, but that didn't make hearing it from him any easier. It made it more real. And that kind of sucked.

He moved toward me. "I know it was awful. I can't imagine... But I feel your fear when you sleep. I hear you cry out during your nightmares and there's nothing I can do. Nothing but this." He spread his hands out wide, motioning around the gym.

I couldn't look at him. Not if I didn't want to cry.

I'd done that enough. It was stupid. I had my powers back. I was okay magically—sort of. Physically. But being in that evil circle—where Luciana called the demon to take away everything that made me *me*... It had changed me. Knocked me off balance.

Maybe this whole exhausting-me-until-the-vision-came plan wasn't going to work. Maybe my visions would always be different from here on out, and I'd just see glimpses in my dreams.

"It's not your fault. It was my choice to go to the coven. Please, don't..." I didn't know what else to say. I'd told him before, but he wasn't hearing me.

He closed the distance, wrapping his arms around me. "I never should've let you go."

"Stop it." I pressed my cheek into his chest. "I had to." I laughed and the sound was muffled against him. "We're quite the pair. Each making ourselves sick over something that we can't change."

He ran his fingers through my hair. "The best pair ever."

"I'm going to be okay. It's really only been a few days."

He sighed, and then his bond opened wider. All his worry and fear—terror—flooded me. The pain of being apart.

I nearly gasped. I hadn't realized how closed off he'd been. I squeezed him tighter, fisting the back of his shirt.

God. I'd been messed up because of what Luciana did, but he'd been a wreck. I'd ignored that. Ignored my own mate's pain.

"I'm—" My voice wobbled and I stopped. "I'm so sorry. I didn't mean for any of this to happen." I couldn't help it now. A tear ran down my cheek.

He pulled back. "Hey. What's this?"

"You messed with our bond so I wouldn't know how bad you're hurting." His bond started to close again, and I shoved him. "Don't you dare shut me out again."

His mouth dropped. "I didn't know I opened it."

Why would he close it off in the first place?

"Because you were dealing with enough. You didn't need me adding to it."

"Well, stop it. I never asked you to protect me."

"It's my job."

Now he was pissing me off. The caveman needed to put down his club before he hurt himself. "Screw a bunch of that noise."

He gently cupped my face, wiping my tears away with a brush of his thumbs. "Hey now. I take my job very seriously."

Two could play at this game. "Same here." If being my mate was his *job*, then the reverse was true.

"All right. Let's give it one more shot."

I crossed my arms. "Seriously? Can't we just go get break-fast now?"

"One more round and then we eat. I feel like we're finally getting somewhere. I can feel it. You're more open. I know you're getting there. One more time."

"Fine. But after breakfast, I'm grabbing a nap." Between my nightmares and his patrols, we weren't getting much sleep. "And we're going to my dorm. It's closer."

"Deal."

Fine. He wanted me to go on the offensive, then I'd give it my best. I'd be back on the mat in five seconds. And then we could go back to sleep.

Or not.

I lunged at him, and he moved faster than I could follow. I felt him through the bond and twisted before he could snag his arms around me.

I lasted all of ten seconds—double what I'd guessed—before wind brushed against my face.

The world turned as I flipped through the air.

Then it started. The tingling. Dastien was right. A vision was coming, and I had a choice. A split second to decide whether I relaxed into it or shut it out.

Whatever the powers that be wanted to show me had to be big.

I took solace in what Dastien said.

"Let go!"

I almost didn't understand his words, but then I did. As my shoulder hit the mat, I let go.

A flash of white filled my eyes and the gym disappeared.

CHAPTER SIX

I STOOD IN THE CAFETERIA. *The smell of food told me it was lunch—pizza day. Baked ziti. Warm garlic bread.*

What the hell?

It was like I'd been sucked into a different place. It wasn't at all like the last time I saw into the future, mostly because I was aware that this was a vision. Maybe Luciana's magic really had changed my abilities for good?

I couldn't worry about it now. The vision was happening, and I surrendered to it.

I walked with Dastien, weaving through the tables to our friends. He balanced his tray piled with more food than I could eat—which was a lot—on one hand and held a bottle of Orangina in the other. He seemed to drink more of them when he was stressed. It must be a comfort thing.

This wasn't so bad. Not bad at all. Definitely not what was giving me nightmares.

Dastien looked back at me over his shoulder. "Don't worry so much, chérie. We will stop this, okay?"

While he was focusing on me, someone bumped him. The bottle slipped from his fingers.

Usually, if someone dropped something, it was caught before ever hitting the ground. Were reflexes were good. And Dastien's were extremely good.

Instead, we both stood there, watching the bottle as it fell to the floor and shattered in a mess of soda and glass. His eyes met mine and his panic washed over me.

The vision shifted. I was sitting between Dastien and Mr. Dawson in the conference room of St. Ailbe's main building. Twelve chairs surrounded the long oval table. Each one was taken. People stood behind the chairs, filling the room past capacity.

Everyone was arguing. Voices rose until they were impossible to differentiate.

Mr. Dawson's voice cut above the rest. "Yes, Tessa. Do you have something to add?"

The room went quiet as everyone turned to me.

I didn't have anything to add. What was everyone even arguing about? My heart rate picked up as I searched for what to say, but the vision shifted again.

I held hands with Dastien as we gazed over the lake. The sun hit the water in just the right way, making it shimmer in the sunset. I glanced behind us at the surrounding forest. We were on the land that Dastien had given to me. Someday we'd build a home here.

"Are you ready for this?"

I wasn't sure what he meant, but whatever it was, I was willing. He was wearing a white button down, rolled up to the elbows, and a pair of khaki pants. Definitely not what he usually wore. He was more a T-shirt and jeans kind of guy.

Something fluttered against my legs, and I looked down. I was wearing a white dress.

Dastien leaned in and pressed his mouth to mine. I closed my eyes.

The feel of his lips disappeared before it even registered.

The sound of shouting—human, wolf, and something I didn't have a name for—filled my ears. I was almost too scared to open my eyes.

The smell was my second tip-off. Sulfur so strong my nostrils burned.

Demons. The other sound was demons. The scuttling of nails. Hissing. And a deep, guttural roar.

My mouth went dry as gunshots rang out, nearly deafening me... But not quite. I could still hear the shouts as people cried out in pain. Something made an awful gurgling sound next to me and I gagged as the scent of blood filled the air.

This. This was what I didn't want to see. This was what had me waking up in sweats. Crying my eyes out.

I said a little prayer and opened my eyes. Instantly, I wished I were anywhere else.

I stood in a crumbling old church. It had cream-colored adobe walls with exposed beams. Pews were torn apart and thrown everywhere. Moonlight shone through shattered stained glass windows. Flares were lit randomly along the floor. They gave off a smoky red light, casting a hue of evil over the room.

But what caught my attention were the humans fighting alongside the wolves. They were dressed in riot gear—police.

God. They didn't belong here. They weren't strong enough to fight this.

Silver flashed at the corner of my eye. I spun and spotted Cosette fighting back to back with a guy I'd never seen before. His long white hair was clipped back in a low ponytail. Both of them glowed like moonlight, and every time they swung their swords, demons cried out.

I'd thought the Weres were graceful. But no. The fey. They were the definition of grace as they moved as one.

An explosion rocked the floor. Luciana stood at the front of the church. The ragged, yawning hole at her feet took up the space where the altar used to be.

Demons crawled out of it.

Big ones. Little ones. Some looked human, but their eyes glowed red. Definitely not human. The rest were the stuff of nightmares. Their gray faces, pointed teeth, and noseless faces would haunt me from this moment on.

I stood there, horrified by the scuttling bodies that kept climbing up from the hole.

Something was wrong. More wrong than just this.

And then it hit me.

Where was Dastien?

My skin chilled.

I turned in a full circle—scanning the people pressing against the horde of demons. Searching for Dastien in wolf or human form. But I couldn't find him.

Meredith and Donovan fought as wolves. A demon tore through Donovan's leg, and they both howled. Three more demons lunged at them, and I saw them both fall before I lost them in the pile.

No. This couldn't be happening. This wasn't happening.

Dastien! I screamed through our bond, but I wasn't really here.

Where was Dastien? Why wasn't he by my side?

Finally, I spotted him. Not far away. Just out of sight. I sprang over the few remaining pews and found him in the chaos. He stood alone, fighting three demons at once and holding his own.

But he couldn't see what I saw.

There was another. A fourth demon. It was crawling from the hole, nails scratching along the stone floor. Heading for him.

A jolt of adrenaline hit me, and I started running.

"Dastien!" I screamed so violently my throated ached. I was

going to be too late. There wasn't enough time. Nothing was going to stop the demon. Not my Were powers. Not my magic.

My heart tore as panic gripped me. I pushed myself to move faster, but the demon scuttled closer to my mate.

Dastien killed one, and turned—finally hearing the larger demon behind him—but it was too late.

I was too late. I was going to fail him. Fail myself. This was it. The end.

The demon ripped its long nails across Dastien's neck, and his body jolted.

I screamed as Dastien's head rolled into the hole, falling into hell. His body stayed in place, slowly crumpling to the ground.

No. No. This can't happen. I can't—I won't survive it.

Luciana's laugh cut across the numbness in my head. She stood glowing with power at the edge of the ragged hole and hate filled every inch of me.

All of this came back to her. I was moving before I could think.

I threw myself at Luciana. We hit the ground hard. She sat on me, her hands around my throat. I was strong enough to get her off, but there were too many demons surrounding her. I couldn't fight them all.

I had to stop this.

The portal she'd opened was just to the right. My life was over.

Dastien was dead.

The only thing left for me to do was end this fight.

I grabbed hold of her and rolled us into the hell mouth. It closed above me and fire licked along my skin as I fell.

And fell.

The heat burned as I plummeted to my death.

CHAPTER SEVEN

I SAT UP, roaring with terror. My throat burned, but I couldn't stop. Someone shook my shoulders, but I couldn't register anything but fear. Heartbreak. The burning fire. Dastien being dead.

Everything being over before it had a chance to begin.

Then ice-cold water crashed over my head. I coughed as it lodged in my airways.

"Tessa. Answer me. Are you okay?"

Dastien. My sight cleared and I saw him crouching in front of me. I leaped at him, tackling him to the ground, and started sobbing. I couldn't help it. My vision hadn't happened yet, but it would. I was going to watch him die, and then I was going to die.

I just...

No. My heart ached. I knew he wasn't dead. He was here. But I couldn't help feeling the loss.

He wrapped his arms around me as he cradled me in his lap, running one hand up and down my back. "Shh. You're here. You're safe. Everything is okay."

I shook my head, but didn't pull back from him. "It's not

okay. Everything is not okay. I can't—" I started crying again. Harder this time. The fear was too much. I couldn't lose him. It was too soon. We were too young. I was supposed to have a lifetime with him. A Were lifetime. And now I was going to get what? Weeks at best?

I didn't know how long we had, but Luciana was coming.

"You have to calm down. You're going to make yourself sick." He tried to pull away, but I clung to him. "*Chérie*, please. I can feel your fear and anger, but I don't know what any of it means. You're scaring me. Tell me what you saw. Whatever it is, we can fix it. We can change it. I know we can. But you have to talk to me."

"How do you know we can change it?"

"I don't know, but I can try. With everything that I am, I will try to stop whatever has made you so upset. But I can't do that until you talk to me. So calm down. Talk to me."

It was horrible. I said through our bond.

Chérie. *Tell me.*

I slowly described everything I'd seen—from the Orangina breaking to how I ended the fight with Luciana.

He stayed quiet for a long moment when I was finished, and then sucked in a big breath. "Okay."

I pulled back from him. "Okay? What about that was *okay*?"

"Nothing. Nothing about that was okay. But okay—now we can work to change it. If you hadn't seen that, then it probably would've happened, but now—we prepare. That gives us something to watch for. And there are markers along the way. So, as long as I never touch that Orangina, then none of this will happen."

I took a deep breath. "Okay. So, no more Oranginas for you."

"Hate the stuff. Never touching it again. Especially on pizza day."

I huffed a small laugh. It was pitiful, but something. "I can't do it. Watching you die... It was the worst thing ever."

He pressed his forehead to mine. "It's not going to happen."

"It can't."

I thought for a second. I needed someone who knew more about magic and visions to tell me that this could be changed. Going to the *brujos* that were still here seemed the most obvious choice, but Claudia was in Peru and I didn't know the rest well enough to tell if they'd blow smoke up my ass or tell me the truth.

Cosette would. Even if she might be a little more harsh than I could handle, her brand of truth would be preferable. I had to know how to prepare. Or if we should just give up now.

"Do you think Cosette might know anything about visions? She's mentioned a few things here and there—and I know she said that she didn't really know much—but I get the sense that she's not telling us everything."

"She's fey. Of course she knows more than she's saying."

"Who do you think the guy is?" If the fey were fighting with us against Luciana, it would definitely make a difference. I'd only seen Cosette and the one dude, but they'd been the only ones who weren't getting their asses kicked in my horror show of a vision. We needed more of them. We needed every advantage we could gather.

"I don't know, but the fey have strings. I don't want to say they're not welcome, but they'd add another layer of complication."

I chewed on my lip. I couldn't believe I was actually going to suggest this. "We should talk to Cosette. Ask her point-blank. See if we can get some fey backing, too."

"We can try. She's not a bad person. Just very fey."

I wasn't sure what that meant, but I'd do anything —*anything*—to stop that vision from happening.

I started to get up and then realized that I was soaked. "You threw a bucket of water on me?"

Dastien brushed the hair back from my face. "What was I supposed to do? You were screaming. It was tearing me apart. The water's there in case someone loses it during sparring... I figured it would shock you out of the vision."

"It was a good try. But now I have to shower again." And I wasn't going back to sleep anytime soon. Not after that vision. Until Luciana was dead and Dastien was safe and sound, that image was going to haunt me.

I couldn't—wouldn't—let it come true.

AFTER I HAD a long hot shower, we went in search of Cosette. It was still early, but I'd wake her up if I needed to. We walked from my dorm back across the quad to the admin building. Light broke through the trees, sending God rays down on us. If I could've felt peaceful, I would've, but I couldn't. The image of Dastien's head rolling into the mouth of hell was burned into my brain.

I blinked, trying to focus on the trees. On the ground underneath my feet. On Dastien's hand warm in mine... He'd barely let me out of his sight to shower and change, and I didn't mind that one bit. I was feeling more than a little clingy.

Stop thinking about it, his voice came through the bond.

I'm trying, but I can't help it. I'm really scared. I swallowed the lump in my throat. I don't want to die. And I definitely don't want you to die.

Your fear is drowning everything else out. You have to let go of it. It's not going to do us any good.

His determination that things would go well burned

through our bond, but he hadn't seen what I had. *Easier said than done.*

I know. Just try.

I was trying, but man—I was shaken to the core by this. How could I not be? Everything I had was on the line. Dastien. My friends' lives. Even my life.

There'd always been risk, but it had never felt more real. Even when I was scared for myself, it'd never occurred to me to be scared for Dastien. He was such a good fighter, and he'd always been so strong. I really thought he was invincible...

But he could die. We could all die. Tonight. Tomorrow.

This could be it for us. It wasn't a huge leap to understand why I was so scared. The terror gripped me until it was like I was moving through a fog.

Now wasn't the time to be foggy.

Because giving up seemed like a totally valid option at this point.

Running sounded pretty good, too.

But if I could stop it entirely—stop Luciana before we ended up in some crumbling church with an open portal to hell —then that would be fantastic.

I tasted blood, and let go of my lip. I hadn't even realized I was biting it.

Chérie. Dastien's rumble came through the bond. A note of warning lit his voice.

I know. I was freaking out, and I needed to stop.

We headed straight up the stairs in the main building, which held the admin rooms and offices on the bottom floors. Above that was the infirmary. The guest suites were on the top floor. They usually housed the parents of students, visiting teachers, or Cazadores. Even though plenty of alphas and Cazadores were staying on campus, they were all in the dorms.

The few witches who'd broken from *La Aquelarre* had the floor to themselves.

Mr. Dawson had thought giving them their own space would be best. They mostly stuck around there or the library. The only one who didn't care about the Weres and went where she pleased was Cosette. She'd been spending afternoons sunning in the quad, but she wasn't an early riser. I'd be shocked to see her anywhere before noon.

As we climbed to the third floor, I couldn't help but smirk at the idea of waking her up. If I had to be awake at this hour, it was only fair that she should feel my pain.

I wasn't sure which room was hers, but I used my senses to sniff her out. Her scent wasn't like anything else I'd come across. The best way I could describe it was sugar water in the moonlight.

Which was ridiculous, because moonlight didn't smell. But if it helped me find her, I wasn't going to question it.

My nose led me to the third room on the right. Of course. That room had one of the tinier windows, but the best view over the quad.

I knocked three times.

No answer.

I knocked two more times.

No answer.

As I was about to knock a third time, she spoke up. "You want to keep that hand?"

Oh no. She was not going to take that tone with me. "I need to talk to you."

"Come back in four hours."

"I can't wait that long." I jiggled the door handle, but it was locked. Not that it would hold against my Were strength. "I'm coming in. You can either let me in or I'll let myself in."

"You're going to regret it." The faint rustle of sheets carried through the door along with a lot of what I assumed were fey curses.

"I already regret the need for it." I leaned against the wall as I waited. "Do you think I'd be here this early if it wasn't important?"

The door swung open. Cosette stood in a sheer white robe that didn't quite hit her at mid-thigh. Her tiny, pale blue nightgown peeked from underneath and I shot Dastien a look. *Don't even go there.*

I wouldn't dare, he said through the bond as he stared at the ceiling.

I elbowed him and then pushed past Cosette.

The rooms up here were all the same. Small single beds in simple frames made with crisp white sheets and comforters. Each one had a small wooden table with a lamp and a full bathroom. With so little inside, the rooms were usually pretty tidy.

Not Cosette's. Clothes were strewn all over the floor. I wasn't sure if they were all dirty or if some were clean. I tried to watch where I was putting my feet, but it was no easy task. "Glad to see you've made yourself at home."

Cosette crossed her arms. God. She'd just rolled out of bed, but her hair fell around her face in perfect dark-blonde ringlets. That had to be something to do with being fey, because it definitely wasn't human. "If you woke me up to criticize my housekeeping, we're going to have a problem."

"No. Sorry. I..." I swallowed as the fear came back two-fold. "I wanted to talk to you about visions."

Cosette shook her head, making her curls bounce. "Hardly anything I know applies to your type of magic. You'd be better off talking to Yvonne or Elsa."

I sat down on the edge of her bed. Dastien leaned against the doorframe, hands shoved into the pockets of his faded and battered jeans. He gave me the slightest nod.

I met Cosette's brown gaze with my own. "I don't know them well enough to know if they'd lie to me." I hoped they wouldn't, but they might try to soften the reality. I needed brutal honesty. Cosette was the girl for that. "I know you'll tell me the truth, even if it's seriously sucky."

"That's true." She straightened. "What did you see that's got you so worked up?"

I told her the basics—leaving out the part about the fey dude for now—and then asked my million-dollar question. "Can I change what I saw? Or is it set in stone? I need to know if there's hope." I tried to keep the desperation out of my voice, but failed miserably. Holding my breath, I waited.

Cosette tilted her head from side to side as she thought about it. "I don't know."

Not exactly what I wanted to hear. "But it could change?"

"Maybe. Maybe not." She twirled the belt of her robe around a finger, her eyes out of focus and distant. "But is that the best question to be asking?"

Was she kidding? "What other question is there?" If I couldn't change the future...

I didn't even want to think about that.

"Don't worry about possible. Worry what to do with the information you have." Cosette leaned forward, peering at me so intently I almost leaned back. "Knowing what you know, will you still fight Luciana? Even if it costs your life?" She gestured toward Dastien. "His life? That's what I'd be asking."

Dastien seemed calm enough, leaning against the doorframe, but a trace of fear mixed in with his confidence and determination. Losing him would be awful. If I had to die to defeat Luciana, I at least wanted him to survive and I'd do pretty much anything to make that happen, even if it was selfish.

I knew someone else would stand against her eventually, but

could they win? Even if I tried to run, I had a feeling that I'd still end up in that church eventually.

Just with a lot more blood on my hands.

"I don't know how your visions work," Cosette said. "The fey teach that the future is changeable, but it's possible that all paths lead to that church for you. We might all die fighting." She shrugged, almost oddly unconcerned, but that *we* had to mean she was including herself. That was something, at least. "We all have some choices to make. I believe those choices will determine whether what you saw comes to pass."

Choices? I groaned in frustration. I needed something clearer. More definite. What good were these stupid visions if they didn't help?

"They are helping you, Tess." Dastien squatted down beside me. "You know what to look for. When we reach that moment, you'll either change it or you won't."

I wanted to wring his neck. "And you're okay with dying? Getting your head sliced off?"

"No! I don't want that at all. I have plans. Dreams. For us." He reached up to cradle my cheek and I leaned into his touch, trying to breathe in some of his calm. "I can only move forward, armed with this knowledge. We're going to do everything we can to make sure the worst doesn't happen. And if it does..."

I let out a slow breath. "If it does?"

"We'll be together. In this life and the next." He pulled me down until our foreheads touched. "You're stuck with me. No matter what."

"Can you guys move the snuggling elsewhere?" Cosette gave a wide yawn. "If we're done, I'm going back to sleep."

"You okay?" he asked as he leaned away from me.

"No. I'm terrified."

"You probably should be," Cosette's dark tone turned my head, but I couldn't snap back when I saw the soft concern in her eyes. "Fear's a great motivator. It might be exactly what you need to keep that vision from happening."

She sounded sincere enough, but I could never tell if she actually liked me or she was just twisting us all around for her own amusement.

"One more thing before I go. Any chance the fey will join the fight against Luciana? If we don't beat her, she's going to be a problem for everyone." I still couldn't decide whether telling her about the guy in the vision would help or hurt my case.

"I'd love to say yes, but it's been made *extremely* clear to me that it's not my call." Cosette gripped her wrist so hard her knuckles cracked. "For now I'll report what you've seen and we'll both have to hope it's enough to get the fey off the sidelines."

The knowledge that the fey existed was so new to me that I couldn't even try to comprehend what kind of pressure was on Cosette. But I appreciated that she was trying to help in her way. Whatever that was. "Thank—"

"Don't. If you thank me, you owe me, and I don't want that temptation any more than you want to be bound to me."

I pressed my lips together for a second. Cosette was saying I couldn't trust her? But she still warned me about it?

The more I learned about her, the more confused I was. "Got it," I said, even though I didn't really get it. Or her.

"Now get out of my room." She sat on the bed so hard the mattress shook. "And don't come knocking again before lunch."

"Sorry about that." I stood and tugged Dastien toward the door.

Cosette mumbled something that wasn't in English as she slipped on an eye mask. She was already under her covers when I shut the door. Apparently the fey took their beauty sleep seriously.

I'd wanted her to have some better news for us. As it was...

"Whatever happens, we'll get through it. One way or another."

That was what bothered me—the other way. I didn't like it. Not one bit.

It lit a fire in me. I had to figure out a way to stop Luciana. I had to be able to fight her. I had to be stronger. Much stronger. "Let's go back to the gym."

"You don't have to go back, *chérie*. You're exhausted already."

Cosette was right. Fear was a great motivator. "I do. I can do this. But I need your help."

"I'd do anything for you."

I knew he would. Just like I'd do anything for him. If that meant eating mat every day until I was ready for the fight with Luciana, then game on.

CHAPTER EIGHT

FOUR DAYS LATER, I was hanging by a thread. There hadn't been any more attacks on the school since Raphael had been bitten by zombie Daniel. That should've been a good thing, but I knew it wasn't. Luciana was building up power. Maybe saving up for the church but I had a feeling we'd see her before then.

Waiting for something to happen was killing me. It was like slow torture.

Adrian had only gotten to Costa Rica before he had to stop. Raphael was too unstable to go farther. All I could do was hope that Claudia would find a way to save her brother while I spent my days training with Dastien and my nights trying to antici-pate Luciana's next move. Sleep was at a premium. I knew I should be resting while I could—it was somewhere past midnight—but I just couldn't. Maybe when Dastien got back, I could relax a little. Even convince him to not set the alarm. We'd been sleeping maybe three or four hours a night, and I could barely manage that much.

The shitty thing was that I couldn't do anything else. Fixing the pack bonds had stopped most of the arguing among the alphas in residence, but they all agreed we should stay put.

Dastien said the Cazadores were watching the compound from a safe distance, just in case Luciana made her move, but that left me and most everyone else sitting around, waiting for whatever Luciana threw at us next.

So in the meantime, I was doing the best I could to prepare.

The more I dug into the pile of books surrounding my bed, the more I realized there was no way in hell I was going to be ready. There was too much to know. Too much that these books didn't talk about. Anxiety had my shoulders in one giant knot. I tilted my head to the side, and my neck gave a satisfying snap. If something didn't change soon, I was going to take action and it would probably be insane. The ideas I'd come up with tonight were scaring even me. And I could almost swear I felt magic in the air... But maybe I was just being paranoid.

A knock at my door pulled me from my books. I bit my lip as I waited to see if whoever it was would go away. I was in no shape to entertain. And if it was another Were coming by to ask me what I'd come up with, I'd lose it.

The knock came again.

Screw it. "Come in."

"Hey," Meredith said. "How are you doing?"

Why wasn't she just coming in? We were suite-mates. We'd passed the whole knock-before-entering thing weeks ago. "I'm... I have no idea how I am. How are you?" Ever since Shannon left, she'd been distant. I'd planned on giving her until tomorrow to deal, and then I was going to talk to her about it. But she'd just beat me to it.

She wrung her hands together and looked anywhere in the room except at me. "I feel like I should apologize again."

"Why?" She had nothing to be sorry for. Not in the slightest. "You already apologized, and you didn't need to in the first place. It's totally fine."

"No. It's not fine. I..." She licked her lips and let out a sigh.

"I was wrong. About Shannon. You kept telling me that something was up with her, and I kept thinking it was just because she was jealous of you and Dastien. I—I didn't think she was capable of defecting from our pack. But I was rude to you when you tried to bring it up and I should've listened to you."

I scooted to the end of my bed and stood slowly. "Seriously. There's nothing to apologize for. I thought it was all about Dastien at first, too, but after what happened with you... It wasn't right. The way she was acting. She was straight up nasty."

"I know. I saw it, but I kept making excuses. Seeing her leaving with the others was a rude awakening."

"Are you okay?"

She shrugged. "Doesn't it feel like these past few weeks have been nuts?"

"Past few weeks? Try past few months. My life has taken a serious turn for the crazy ever since I got to Texas."

"No kidding, right?" She scrunched up her nose for a second.

With that, I knew that everything was going to be okay. At least with us. "For sure."

"So, what now?"

I turned back to my bed, surveying the mess all over it. The white sheets were barely visible under the books and notes. I'd surrounded myself with every resource I had, determined to find some sort of magic spell to make all this go away. So far, I'd come up with nil.

I pulled my hair into a messy knot at the nape of my neck. "I have no idea. I'm trying to figure out how to counter Luciana, but without knowing what she's up to...." I'd been thinking of doing something totally batshit the past couple of days. Maybe it was because Claudia had brought up the idea, but now I couldn't get it out of my head.

Or maybe it was all the waiting around. But whatever it was, I couldn't do *this* anymore. I had to do *something*. "I have an idea. Something Claudia said on the phone the other day... But it's super dangerous—I mean it's *stupid* dangerous—and Dastien is going to freak out... But I mean—I'm not getting anywhere here."

"Oh boy." She crossed her arms. "What kind of crazy idea is in your head now?"

I braced myself for her to flip, and then spit out the words. "Believe me. This is the last place that I want to go. Really. But Claudia said that there could be something in Luciana's craft room and if we go—"

"What!" Meredith screeched.

And there it was.

"Have you completely lost your mind? No! Under no circumstances will you ever be going back there. Not only is it incredibly dangerous and stupid, but you're right—Dastien would freak out." Her eyes flared from glass blue to electric. "You weren't here when he lost it last time. You weren't holding him down to be sedated. You didn't help drag him off to the feral cages. And you certainly didn't watch him throwing himself against the door over and over and over, trying to escape and get you back. And you didn't see yourself when you came back here. Broken." She poked my breastbone hard enough to knock me back. "So, no. That's not fucking happening. Not on my watch."

All of a sudden, my room got much more crowded, as Chris, Donovan, and Dastien burst through the door.

Shit. She must've told Donovan on me.

Dastien came to stand between us, facing Meredith, so that he could protect me. Little did he know that he was about to be on Meredith's side. "What's going on?"

"Your mate over there thinks it's a good idea to go back to

the compound and dig around Luciana's stuff. For what? Some kind of clue as to what she's up to?"

Dastien's pain, anger, and fear ran through our bond before he turned. "*Non.*" He started yelling and gesturing wildly in French. I didn't understand what he was saying—I knew only three phrases and a handful of words in French—but the meaning and intention were clear enough even without the emotions pouring through our bond.

I took a breath, praying for patience. "I know. I don't want to go back there—please know that I don't want to. The thought *terrifies* me. But I've been at this for days, and if we don't start going on the offensive, we're always going to be one step behind. We will *lose this fight.* It's a war, and we're always reacting. Never acting. And we can't do that. Not anymore. When she did that to Daniel—her own son—she crossed a line. She has to be stopped. And after what I've seen—"

"Wait," Chris cut in. "You had a vision? Of the future? What did you see? And why haven't you said anything to us?"

Tears pooled at the corners of my eyes, but I quickly swiped them away. I'd been trying to live on the assumption that the vision wouldn't come true. Dastien hadn't gone near an Orangina in days. So, that first part hadn't happened, and maybe it never would. "It's bad. Really bad." The words were so strained, they barely came out. "Please. I'm not saying that I want to go alone. I'm not that stupid. But if we come up with a plan, then I'm just saying that it's an option."

"I agree," Donovan said.

"What?" Meredith whirled around. "You can't be serious! I don't care what she saw. It's not worth the risk."

"Love. Please. I'm not saying going back to the compound is wise, but maybe it's time we wake up the witches we've got. We were so worried about Luciana using them that we sedated them before doing any real questioning. It's been days. Maybe the danger has passed." He turned to me. "Let's wake them up."

With that last sentence, it was like I was weightless. The stress lifted. I didn't have to go to the compound and risk going into that room again. I could do something and not leave the safety of St. Ailbe's.

This—*this* was a good idea. Finally. A real way to make some progress. "I agree. Let's do it."

"Me, too," Chris said. "I'm all in for waking up the witches."

"Okay. Let's go."

We all kept quiet as we crossed campus. Dastien hadn't said a word to me. It killed me. *I wasn't going to go anywhere without you.*

You should've told me first, not Meredith. I'm your mate.

I know. I know. But I wasn't sure you'd hear me out. I thought Meredith might, but turns out—not so much.

It was a stupid idea, chérie.

That stung. Did he really just call me stupid?

He pulled me to a stop. I'm sorry. I didn't mean it that way. It's just—I can't see you get hurt like that again. I won't let you do something that could put you in that kind of situation.

Okay. It's okay.

That's usually my line. He bent down, running his nose along the side of my neck. *Je t'aime, chérie.*

The second we started down the hallway to the feral cages, I smelled it.

Something foul. Rotted.

Dead.

I strode down the hallway and unbolted the first door. The smell was even worse.

One of the *brujas* lay inside on a bed with rails. The covers were tucked up to her armpits and a clear tube ran from her withered arm to the IV stand hanging beside her head.

She's not breathing. Her skin was gray and wrinkly. It looked like she'd aged a century.

I stumbled back. "Are they all...?"

Dastien pushed past me to test the girl's pulse. After a few long moments, he gently set down her wrist. "Yes. Chris, get Dr. Gonzalez."

"I'm on it."

I grabbed the clipboard that hung from the door. "The papers say that Dr. Gonzales checked on them an hour ago. Their vitals were fine. Her handwriting is a little messy—" Typical doctor scratches. "But they were stable and still sedated."

What could've done this? It couldn't be the drugs. They could've died from a wrong dose, but that wouldn't make them look like bones covered in shriveled skin.

Not all of them. Not in the space of an hour.

Dastien lifted the girl's eyelid. The socket held what looked like a raisin.

I gagged and backed into the hallway before I threw up. "Luciana did this."

"How?" Meredith peeked into the room. "She hasn't been on campus. We would've known."

It hit me then. Yvonne had said that Luciana could do a lot through the blood oath they'd all taken. That oath tied the witches together, almost like the pack bonds tied us Weres.

I shivered as cold dread ran up my spine.

I needed to talk to the other witches on campus before I said anything. If Luciana had—

The sound of Dr. Gonzales' high heels clacking against the floor dragged me from my thoughts. Without a word, she went into the rooms and checked each witch.

The rest of us waited for her evaluation.

She zipped her messenger bag closed, settling it on her hip

before starting. "My first fear was that something was wrong with the drugs I administered, but I was here an hour ago, and they didn't look like this. There's nothing I could give them that would do this." A little wrinkle formed between her eyes as she thought. "My best guess is that witchcraft was used to drain their life forces..."

She kept going on about her findings, but I tuned her out.

They'd been drained, but maybe not of life-force...

What if Luciana had drained them of their magic? She'd drained my magic, but stopped before I died. I hadn't had time to wonder why, but it wasn't because she liked me. It was quite clear the opposite was true. She hated me.

So, I'd been kept alive because she still wanted something from me. With Luciana, it always went back to power.

Maybe with time, my abilities would've come back on their own? Then Luciana could've drained me again and again.

But what if she wanted as much power as she could get in one shot? She could drain someone—or lots of someones—to the point that they died.

Little dots speckled my vision as I followed that train of thought.

What was stopping her from doing the same to everyone in the coven? Not the witches who were still loyal to her, but the ones who'd left...

No. She couldn't do that. Could she?

I started down the hall. I needed to talk to the rest of the *brujas* now.

"Tessa!" Dastien yelled after me. "Where are you going?"

I didn't take the time to answer. I just started running. Fear coursed through my veins, making me run faster than I ever had before. The others ran behind me, but I didn't stop. I didn't slow. I had to see.

Because if Luciana had done what I feared, then—

I couldn't even go there. I had to find out.

As soon as I hit the quad, I took a breath.

"What's wrong?" Dastien asked. He touched my shoulder, but I wasn't ready to explain.

Cosette's scent hit me strongest, leading me across the quad to the cafeteria. Maybe they'd gotten hungry.

"Do you think she killed all the witches that left the coven? Could she do that?" Chris asked.

"Yes."

I knew something was wrong. With certainty. A pit formed in my gut.

Still, I hoped I was wrong. I plowed through the cafeteria doors. They crashed into the wall with a boom. The few Cazadores froze mid-meal to stare at me in surprise or curiosity.

But no witches.

I spotted Cosette sitting alone and flipping through a magazine as she picked at a bowl of strawberries. She stood as soon as she saw me, pushing her magazine aside. "What's wrong?"

"Where are the witches?"

"I left them in the library a few hours ago. What's...?" Her eyes slipped out of focus and she paled. "What am I sensing?"

The library. Shit. Why hadn't I checked the library first? "Something really bad."

She moved past me. "Let's go."

Dastien and the rest followed behind us. I moved faster, jumping the three steps to enter the admin building. I burst through the doors and ran down the hallway to the right.

When I reached the library, I finally stopped. If they were in there, I didn't want to scare them.

But one breath was all it took. I knew what I feared was true. I could smell death. And I didn't want to open those doors. Because then it'd be real.

I backed away slowly.

Dastien squeeze my shoulder. "Why don't you wait here, Tess?"

"Yeah. Please. Just tell me I'm wrong."

"I wish you were."

"We didn't protect them." Tears welled, and I blinked them away. "I said they'd be safe here. I *promised*."

"We don't know what Luciana's done. Just..." He leaned down until he was eye level with me. "Don't go in yet." He turned to Dr. Gonzales and waved her forward, but Cosette moved in front of her.

I should've moved down the hallway, but my body didn't want to move at all. As soon as Dastien opened the door, I saw two of them. Yvonne lay collapsed forward onto the table. She faced away from me, but there was only one reason she'd stay that still.

Elsa's tiny body lay on the floor, her arms at odd angles. Her skin was gray and wrinkled...

I'd seen enough. I couldn't... I didn't...

I turned to press my forehead against the cool wall.

They were dead. All of them.

All of them.

Fear rolled through me so fiercely that I could hardly breathe.

Oh shit. *Claudia*. Oh shit.

I needed my cell phone. She had to be okay.

Please, God. Let her be okay.

CHAPTER NINE

I RACED back to my room and snatched my cell off the nightstand. My hands shook as I searched my contacts for Adrian's number. I hit it and started pacing the room.

The phone rang. And rang. With each ring, my lungs grew tighter.

Until it stopped ringing. "Tessa?"

"The witches—"

"Raphael's fine."

Relief made my legs weak. I reached back, finding the edge of the bed, and collapsed as I tried to get control of my breathing.

"Your cousin is a total badass. She came in with a bag of tricks—I have no idea how she got from Peru to Costa Rica in basically five minutes flat—but, dude, she's awesome."

I swallowed. "And Shane and Beth... Their oaths—"

"Broken. The three with me are all sworn to Claudia now, although I'm not sure she wanted any part of that."

A broken laugh slipped free. "Thank God."

I finally looked up at Dastien, who'd followed me the whole

way here. He sat next to me, wrapping me in his arms. "It's going to be okay," he murmured.

I nodded as a tear slipped free. They were okay. It was going to be okay.

"What's going on?" Adrian said. "I hear Dastien. What happened?"

I told him in as few words as I could.

He cursed when I was finished. "How am I supposed to tell them...?"

"Don't. Just don't. They're going to come back to one big nightmare and a whole lot of heartbreak. Let them relax for a little bit and enjoy this victory. They deserve it." I let out a breath. "Get back here on the first flight you can get tomorrow. I'll take care of breaking the news."

"So, what do I tell them in the meantime?"

"Just say Luciana's up to something, which is sort of true and expected."

He agreed, promising to send me flight details when he had them, and then hung up. Some of my anxiety melted, but one giant question nagged at the back of my mind. I didn't want to think about it. I wanted to put an end to the night's craziness, but I knew I wouldn't be able to sleep if I didn't follow the thought.

"What's going on in that head of yours?" Dastien asked, breaking the silence.

"I'm..." God, I was tired. I just wanted to curl up in my bed. I rubbed my fingers along my temples dreading where this would go once it was out of my mouth. "I'm just wondering how far she went with this spell."

I stood and started to pace. The problem was that I kept coming to the same conclusion. Unless I went to the coven's compound, there was no way to know what Luciana had done, or how far she'd gone with the power drain.

I stopped pacing as a horrifying thought crossed my mind. "Do you think...?" No. She couldn't possibly be that awful.

She wouldn't kill her entire coven? Would she?

But she could've. That was something she was totally capable of doing. Especially if it got her more power.

The answer had to be yes. To open her gateway to hell, Luciana was going to need a royal fuckload of power that she didn't have. Since she'd lost access to both Claudia and me, she'd have to get that power somewhere else. Her coven was an easy target. They were there—linked to her by blood—practically begging to be drained.

I had to go check it out. "Don't freak, but I don't think there's a way around it. We have to go to the compound."

"What? Why?" Dastien half-shouted the words.

"Because we need to know how far she went. If she drained her entire coven of magic, we're going to have a bigger fight on our hands than we thought." Just thinking that scared the crap out of me. We hadn't been prepared before, and if she'd really just done what I feared, then we were screwed.

"Even if she did drain the coven, why risk going there? We're not ready to fight her."

"So we sneak onto their land. If she didn't drain anyone, then we get out fast. If she did..." I had a feeling Luciana wouldn't stick around with the bodies. "I just need to know. *We* need to know." I grabbed my messenger bag, jammed in all my potion vials, and headed for the door.

"Fine." He stepped in front of me, his eyes glowing orbs of amber. "But the second we're in danger, we run."

"Of course." We were definitely on the same page. "Let's get the others."

We'd barely made it to the middle of campus before Mr. Dawson, Donovan, Meredith, Chris, and Dr. Gonzales strode toward us.

"We need to check out the compound," Mr. Dawson said. "See if anyone's still alive out there."

"Totally agree." And I couldn't be happier everyone was actually agreeing for once. "I've got some potions in case Luciana's still there, but we need a full plan."

"I summoned a few quads of Cazadores for backup," Mr. Dawson said.

"What about campus? Shouldn't they stay in case she tries to attack?"

"We've enough wolves to protect the campus," Donovan said. "If Luciana is still on the compound, she has power to burn. Nothing wrong with bringing backup."

"Okay. Probably a good idea." I thought for a second. "The main problem is the warding on the compound. We can deal with the repulsion part, but the spell also alerts the coven of intruders. If Luciana or any of the coven is still there we're going to have to run fast."

"I can help with that." Cosette raised her hand and I almost did a double take.

I would've sworn she wasn't standing there ten seconds ago, but if she was going to appear out of nowhere, she'd picked a good time to do it. "You can?"

"Yes. I'm sure I can still cross the wards without setting off the alarm." Her lips pressed into a thin line. "Or I can get you across them easily enough. Either way, I'm going along for the ride."

I managed not to gape at her, but it was close. Cosette volunteering to help? Whatever her reasons were now, I wasn't going to question them. "Okay. Cosette and I will deal with the wards. What next?"

"Once Tess and Cosette give the all clear, we'll send in a small group," Dastien said. "We check the closest houses for signs of life. Everyone else stays out of sight unless there's a call for help. If that happens, we get everyone out and run. We'll keep our drivers ready for a fast getaway."

"Agreed. We're just checking on the coven. None of us are ready to go against Luciana tonight." We weren't even *close* to ready.

I strode to the closest SUV and got in the passenger side. Dastien walked around to the driver's side and motioned for one of the Cazadores to get in back. Chris hopped in next to him. In minutes, everyone was packed in cars and heading out.

I tapped my fingers on the armrest as Dastien drove through the gates. It was a thirty-minute drive and there was no chance we were going to have a relaxing ride.

Because if Luciana was there, we were screwed. And if she wasn't, and the worst was true...

Then we were already one step closer to the mouth of hell in my vision.

CHAPTER TEN

I STARED out the car's window, resting my head against the cool glass as the darkness blurred past. My mind wandered to dark places. If Mom had moved us back to Texas when she realized I had abilities, would I have ended up like them? Sucked dry of magic and life?

That could've been me.

I guessed that was why this was hitting me so hard. I saw myself in them. In the sliding doors of my life, if just one thing had changed, it could have all turned out very differently.

"Don't go there," Dastien murmured. The other wolves heard, but couldn't know what he meant. Still, I wished he hadn't said the words aloud this time.

I can't help it. There's so much wrong right now. So much that's messed up.

I know. And it's easy to focus on the bad, especially when there's so much of it, but you can't do that. If we're going to get through this, you have to focus on the good.

Yeah, right. How could I be positive right now? After that vision, thinking of the future is the last thing I want to do.

We don't know that it's going to happen. What if it was just a warning? What if—

She has the power she needs now.

Dastien was quiet for a second as the truth sank in. Then we work hard and change how it happens. We're going to stop her before it gets that far. Okay?

"Okay. Yeah. We'll stop it before it gets that far." It sounded weak, even to my ears, but I was trying to believe it. I had to believe that I could change the outcome, otherwise...

"What gets that far?" Chris leaned forward between the front seats.

Shit. I hadn't meant to say that aloud. "Nothing." When he didn't sit back, I rolled my eyes at him. "Don't you know it's rude to listen to other people's conversations?"

"Don't you know it's rude to have private conversations when other people are around?"

He had a point. "I'm not talking about it. Not yet."

"Telling them doesn't mean it's going to happen," Dastien said.

"I know." I thought for a second. "If the things I saw in the first part of the vision happen, then I'll spill. If not, well then, it's moot. Because that future isn't happening."

We rounded a sharp turn, and I knew we were almost on coven land. "Stop the cars. Cosette and I will check the wards alone. If we're lucky, no one else has to come." I was praying we'd see people walking down the dirt road that divided the compound, going about life as usual. Then we could turn straight around before anyone got hurt.

"I don't like that at all," Dastien said.

To be honest, neither did I. "I'll stay within sight."

The leather steering wheel squeaked under the pressure as Dastien tightened his grip. "If you go out of sight, I'm coming after you."

"Okay," I said as the car came to a stop. "Keep the car running, just in case." I slung my messenger bag of vials over my shoulder and slid down from my seat. I reached inside, grabbing two vials, just in case, and then turned to Cosette, who was getting out of the car behind us.

"You ready?"

"Of course." She tucked a golden ringlet behind her ear. "Just let me test them first and we'll decide who goes through."

"Whatever you need."

We snuck toward to the cattle guards that started just before the compound's gate. I usually felt the urge to run right about now—the slimy feeling of the wards rushing over me—but nothing was happening. "Do you feel the wards?"

"No." Cosette reached out, moving her fingers like she was strumming a harp. "There's nothing."

Before I could stop her, she stepped over the threshold onto coven lands.

"Are you crazy?" I whisper-yelled at her as I glanced around frantically, expecting an army of witches to come at us. I held the vials up as my heartbeat thudded in my ears.

Only... The compound was quiet. The dirt road was empty. Cars were haphazardly parked on both sides of the road, the same as always. Houses loomed down the dirt road, with the schoolhouse at the end. A few houses still had lights on. Odd for this time of night—we were pushing past one in the morning—but not totally out of the realm of the possible.

I stood frozen, waiting for some sign of movement, but there was nothing.

The wards were down.

"Tell the others they can cross." Cosette whirled and started walking. "I'll make sure Luciana's gone."

"Wait." I caught up to her before she got more than a few steps. "Not alone"

"Alone." Cosette waved me off. "This might all be a trap."

My pulse raced. "Then go. Hurry."

As soon as she slipped away, I called for Dastien. *Can you hear me?*

How is that possible? The wards always blocked our bond before. Every time you were on coven land, I couldn't feel you, let alone talk to you like this.

They're gone.

What does that mean?

Nothing good. I turned back to the compound. *"Get everyone. Let's go."*

I made my way to the first lit house, knowing that Dastien wouldn't be far behind.

Two steps led up to the front porch. The first one squeaked under my weight, and I froze, expecting someone to come out and yell at me for trespassing.

No one came. I gingerly took the next step, and then tiptoed to the window beside the door. It gave a good view of the living room and kitchen. A movie played on the TV. *Fifth Element.* Good choice. The back of the couch faced the window, but I could see someone's head facing the screen.

Thank God. I closed my eyes as I let go of the worry. Luciana had spared them.

As soon as I let out a breath, another fear grabbed hold of me. If they were alive, the wards shouldn't be down and we'd just walked into a trap.

Shit. We needed to leave. Now.

I started to tell Dastien as much when something caught my eye.

In the little break in the cabinets that connected the kitchen to the living room, someone was lying on the floor. The shards of a broken mixing bowl were scattered all around them.

The momentary relief I'd felt was gone. Replaced with terror.

If I was seeing what I thought, then Luciana had stolen everyone's magic. Killed every single person in the coven.

And winning the fight against her was about to become infinitely more impossible.

I needed to be sure, only I didn't want to go inside. Not one little bit.

Shit. There was no getting around it.

As soon as I opened the front door, the smell wafted out. It was exactly the same as the others, but I had to go in. I had to be sure.

Chérie. *What do you see?* Dastien waited at the bottom of the porch steps.

I'm not sure yet. I need to check... I entered the house. The person on the couch was a teenage boy. I'd never spoken to him, but I remembered him from the one class I'd taken during my stay at the compound.

He stared at TV. His skin was gray and wrinkled, like the others. And the eyes that had died watching TV were twin black raisins.

"Shit." I made an effort to breathe through my mouth as I moved past him to the kitchen.

His mother had died baking a cake. Two candles lay on the counter. A one and a four.

How could she do it? To kids? To families?

Dastien and Mr. Dawson came through the door as I left the kitchen. I wiped my hands down my face. "How could she do this? It was his birthday. He was only fourteen." They started to say something, but I waved them off. There was nothing to say. Nothing for us to do. It was too late. We were too late. "We can search the compound, but I think everyone here is going to be like this." I waved my hand around the gruesome scene. I didn't even know them, but they didn't deserve this. No one deserved this.

"Luciana's car is gone," Cosette said as she came through the door. "Her house is empty, but I'm sensing power inside. No other traps." She crouched on the floor and gently touched the woman's cheek. "What a waste. And what a selfish use of magic." Only she moved in the silent room, tucking a lock of hair behind the woman's ear and then closing her eyes. "Maureen was a kind woman. And Elijah was a sweet boy. All they did was listen to the one who was supposed to be leading them."

I swallowed the ache building at the back of my throat. It would be the same scene in every house. Forty people dead? Fifty? And all her own coven. I didn't have the words.

"Any idea where she might've gone?" Mr. Dawson said.

"None." When Cosette finally stood, she pressed her hands against her temples, not crying but showing pain in her way. "I have to report it, but as soon as I do, I'll get pulled home. There's too much danger. But I can't leave now." She started to push past me, heading for the door. "I'll check the other houses. I want to see their faces."

"Hey." I grabbed her sleeve before she got to the door. I'd forgotten that she lived with the coven for months before I got there. She knew them in a way I didn't. If this was weighing on me, it had to be even harder for her. "Don't blame yourself. No one could've guessed she'd go this far."

"I know exactly who to blame." Cosette patted my hand on her sleeve. Her fingers were gentle, but her eyes burned cold fire. "And take your own advice. You couldn't have stopped it either." She slipped away and I wanted to listen, but I couldn't help the guilt.

Even worse, my gut told me we were one step closer to meeting Luciana in that church.

When Dr. Gonzales came in to confirm the deaths, I went to stand in the road with Meredith and Donovan.

Wondering what Luciana might do with her new power would only freak me out. *First things first.* "What do we do now?" I asked Donovan.

"About?"

I motioned around me. "This place. All the bodies. And who do we tell? I'm sure some of these people have friends and family that should be told that their loved ones are dead." God. Someone had to call Tía Rosa. She was going to be devastated. I had to tell Mom. And my brother.

And Claudia and Raphael. What was I going to say to them? How could I tell them that everyone they knew was dead?

Mr. Dawson joined us on the roadside. "If it were my pack, I'd notify the families and then burn it all to the ground, but these are witches. I don't want another coven coming here and saying we killed them. It could start a war." He blew out a breath. "Some of the local cops know about the pack. I'll call them. But first, we should call your father. I want him here to make sure we handle this right."

I pointed to myself. "My dad?" He was a normal human. No witch or wolf or fey in him at all and I wanted him as far away from this as possible. "Why would we call him?"

"He's our PR guy and lawyer. If this gets out, we need to make sure we're covered. I want him here before we contact the authorities."

He had a point, but I still didn't like it. Not even a little bit. "I can call him." I pulled out my phone and was shocked to see it actually had service.

I snorted. That bitch. Luciana had put the kibosh on all forms of communication, but with her wards gone, I had full bars. Something I would've killed for when I was staying here.

Dad went into problem-solver mode as soon as I told him what was up. I could hear him getting dressed through the phone as I explained the situation. When he hung up, saying he'd get here as fast as he could, I settled down to wait. Cosette confirmed all buildings but Luciana's house were free of magic and then disappeared again, but I knew she wasn't gone for good. Not yet, at least.

After the magical all clear, the eight Cazadores divided the compound, searching the buildings one by one, just in case there were other enemies hiding. I understood it had to be done, but it still seemed wrong. Weren't they disturbing the scene of a crime? Or maybe I watched too many crime shows.

They agreed to save Luciana's house for me, but I didn't want to go in until I absolutely had to.

At least I wouldn't be going in alone this time. Dastien wouldn't let that happen.

It seemed like forever, but wasn't more than thirty minutes before my father pulled up. I stood, brushing the dirt off my jeans. Then a second car rumbled over the cattle guards. And a third. And as fast as that, three cop cars were pulling onto the compound.

I turned to Mr. Dawson. "I thought you didn't call them yet?"

He came to stand next to me. "I didn't." His voice had a bit of a growl in it.

This was so not good. "Then what are they doing here?" My voice sounded a little high, and I cleared my throat.

"I don't know." His growl deepened.

"What if they're not the cops on your payroll?"

"I don't have any cops on my payroll." He crossed his arms. "I just hope these are the ones I know."

I wiped my sweating hands on my jeans. "And if not?" I knew I was annoying him, but I wanted to know the answer.

We'd found a compound full of dead bodies and our first reaction hadn't been to call the cops.

Which made us look really bad. Basically suspects.

"Then it's a good thing your dad is here, because we're going to have a hard time explaining this."

I swallowed. Going to prison for murder might stop my vision from happening, but it wouldn't stop Luciana, and we'd be sitting ducks behind bars.

Except I doubted the Weres would take kindly to being shoved in the backs of cop cars. The Cazadores already formed a loose circle and their eyes glowed as their wolves neared the surface.

I swallowed again, praying this didn't turn into a fight.

CHAPTER ELEVEN

WE ALL GATHERED as we waited for the cops to leave their cars. The Cazadores stood behind us—me, Dastien, Mr. Dawson, Cosette, Chris, Meredith, and Donovan.

The first cop out was a woman. Her crisp uniform made her look more boxy than she probably was. Gray streaks ran through her hair, which was tied into a neat bun at the nape of her neck. "Michael," she said as she strode toward us. "I'm surprised to see you here."

Mr. Dawson met her halfway between the cars and us. "Honestly, I'm surprised to be here myself. How are you doing, Marlene?"

"Not good. I have four dead bodies in town. All of them listed this as their home address."

Shit. I hadn't even thought about the *brujos* who lived off the compound.

Mr. Dawson widened his stance—like he was bracing for a fight—as five more cops approached. "Where did they die?"

"Two at the movies. Two at a Whataburger. Witnesses said they just dropped and shriveled up. They all list this as their residence, and everyone in town with a decent-size brain between their ears knows that the people down here are off. And now you're here." She paused, pressing her lips together, and then tilted her head as if considering the situation. "So, what's really going on?"

Mr. Dawson huffed. "How many here know about us?"

Us meaning the pack. I crossed my fingers and hoped for best.

"All but Johnson." She motioned with her thumb to the young cop who stood back from the others. He looked a little pale and his skin glistened with sweat, but he was holding on. His night was about take a turn for the weird. "It's his first day on the job, but he's a good kid."

"Hell of a first day," Mr. Dawson said. "These bodies aren't for the squeamish."

Dad cleared his throat. "Marlene. Good to see you."

Marlene didn't even try to hide the disgust on her face. "What do you need with a lawyer?"

Yikes. Wonder what Dad did to piss her off?

Mr. Dawson shrugged. "Just covering my ass. There's a lot of death here."

Marlene cussed softly. "How many you think?"

"Over fifty before we stopped counting. We haven't found anyone alive."

"Jesus Christ Almighty." She put her hands on her hips "What is this place? I always thought it was some kind of cult, but with you here and the look of those bodies... Please don't tell me I've got some kind of satanic ritual suicide on my hands."

I held my breath as I waited. Telling the cop too much wouldn't fly, but if we didn't say enough there was no telling how she'd react.

"In a way," Mr. Dawson answered. Perfectly vague.

There was a long pause, and I chewed my lip. Cops made me nervous, and if this didn't go well there were two very possible and equally awful outcomes. The Weres—especially the Cazadores—could freak and kill humans. Which would be horrible. Or we could cooperate and then we'd rot away in prison while Luciana got to play tiddledywinks with all her new powers. Also horrible.

"We're going to search the place. I'm leaving these nice people with you, Johnson." She yelled the last over her shoulder at the young cop. "He's seen about all he can handle," she muttered under her breath, but all of us Weres could hear it. "If you wouldn't mind, stay here while I check things out," she said to Mr. Dawson. "I know I can trust you to keep yours calm and under control." There was a hint of threat in her words that set me on edge.

"Of course. We'll be right here," Mr. Dawson said. He seemed so much calmer than I was, but it had to be a show. I mean, what were we going to do? Cops plus dead bodies equaled arrests. Didn't it?

A trickle of sweat ran between my shoulder blades.

She strode past us with her four other colleagues and started going from house to house. They talked among themselves as they went. Giving theories. Debating what was going on.

Were hearing came in handy.

Some of the houses had more evidence of magic users— herbs and spell books—so they kept throwing the word "cult" around.

I should've been happy they thought it was a cult. That meant that they probably wouldn't arrest us. But as they deemed the artifacts evil and the coven satanists—it bothered me. It wasn't true. At least for the majority of the coven. Luciana was her own special case.

When I heard something break in my cousins' house, I ground my teeth. Only Dastien's firm grip on my arm kept me from going in.

"They're just doing their job," Dastien said.

"I know." I stared at my cousins' house, waiting for the cops to come out. Too bad I was one of the most impatient people I knew.

I sat down on the dirt road. Dastien stood behind me, and I leaned against his legs, reaching around to hold one of his ankles. He grounded me as I relaxed.

Eventually, my eyes grew heavy, and he sat down behind me and pulled me into his lap. He slid off my messenger bag and set it beside him. "Sleep, *chérie*," he whispered as he pressed a kiss to my forehead.

The command in his words rolled through me. Fighting it was an option, but I didn't really want to. It was already past two in the morning, and I was exhausted. I let my eyes drift closed as a deep and easy sleep took hold of me.

I didn't wake until Dastien's voice rumbled against me. "You don't want to go into that house."

"You don't want to be telling me how to do my job," Officer Marlene's tone was snippy. "I've worked in this town long enough to not be afraid of you and your kind. At least not while that one is around."

I opened my eyes and it took me a second to really comprehend what was about to happen. They were at Luciana's door. They didn't know her house from any other. They didn't know what they were about to walk into.

I jumped up. "No! Don't go in there."

The newbie cop—Johnson—pushed me as I started toward them. "You want to stay where you are."

"Get your hands off my mate." The words were more growl than anything, and the threat behind them was enough to set even me on edge.

But Johnson was a moron. He didn't see the fury bubbling

under the surface. And he certainly didn't know Dastien could turn into a wolf in a split second and rip out his throat.

Instead of calming down the situation, Officer Johnson did the worst thing possible and reached for his gun. "You need to sit your ass down while I deal with her."

Oh no he didn't.

Cold fury ran through our bond, and I knew Dastien was about to lose his shit.

Marlene stopped on the porch. For a second, I thought she was going to listen to me. "Johnson. You do your job. Keep them under control while I go in."

Terror gripped me, and suddenly I didn't care so much about being thrown into the back of a cop car. "You don't understand." Officer Johnson grabbed my arm as I tried to move toward the house, but I ignored him. She couldn't go in there. "The owner of that house was the leader of these people. It could be booby trapped. There could be dangerous things in there. Things you don't have the capacity to deal with."

"Young lady, you'll want to watch how you talk to me." She pointed her finger at me. "You sit your ass down. Understand that I'm an officer of the law, and if there is something dangerous in there, then *I* am the one who should deal with it."

Another growl added to Dastien's.

This was going south. Fast.

"They have nothing to hide and no part in this," Dad said as he moved to stand between the growling alphas and the cops. He turned to the one who was still grabbing me. The cop's fingers dug into my skin. If I were still human, I'd have bruises, but I wasn't that fragile anymore. "Let the girl go. She's going to cooperate fully."

The young cop listened to Dad, finally letting go. I caught Dastien, right as he was about to reach for the guy's throat, and pushed him toward Dad. I kept his gaze as I lowered my voice, talking fast. "They can't go in there. It's too dangerous."

The spot between Dad's eyebrows wrinkled as he leaned toward me. "Why?" he whispered.

"It could have wards or..." I didn't even know what to expect. It could be anything, but it wouldn't be anything good. "Who knows what black magic she left for us to find?"

He pressed his lips in a firm line as he stared at the house in question. "We can't stop them, kiddo. They're going to do their investigation, and then they're going to come question all of us. Then we go home. But right now, they're in charge."

"This is beyond stupid." I needed my messenger bag. It was still on the ground where we'd been sitting. I reached into it, touching the vials inside and dreading whatever chaos was about to be unleashed. Luciana wouldn't abandon her compound without leaving a nice surprise or two for us to find. "They're a bunch of fucking idiots. They don't know what they're messing with."

Dad smiled, and little wrinkles formed in the corners of his eyes. "I'm not going to argue that point. I raised a smart girl." He wrapped an arm around my shoulders and squeezed me into his side. "Even if she does curse like a sailor."

I shook my head. The vials in my hands grew slick with sweat as I grasped them. There was a small tingle of magic as they went through the door, and it was growing. It danced across my skin, making all the little hairs on my arms stand on end.

Dastien came to stand next to me. "You okay?"

"Yeah." I paused. "But I don't know that they're going to be okay. Magic is brewing in there and—"

The first scream turned my blood to ice. I thought about dashing into the house to help, but the gurgling noise told me I was already too late.

One cop was definitely dead.

For a second, everything went silent.

Then the smell of sulfur filled the air so strong I nearly choked. This was bad. This was so completely bad.

Four gunshots broke the night.

I stepped in front of Dad. "Get to the car. Now."

"I'm not leaving you here. I'm the Dad."

Another quick succession of gunshots rang out. I started dragging him away from the house. "And I can't be killed by a stray bullet." Unless it was a headshot, I was reasonably certain I could heal it. It'd hurt, but I'd live. "You can." I shoved him toward the car. "Go. Now."

He froze for a second before pointing to something behind me.

"Oh my God." Officer Johnson's voice spiked. "What is that?"

A creature slunk out of the house. Its skin was brown and wrinkly. Long nails hung from its clawlike hands, scraping wood as it stepped down from the porch.

And its beady red eyes bore into me like it was peering at my soul.

I recoiled from it, stumbling back a step before I could stop myself.

"That is a demon," Cosette said, chill as a cucumber.

"What the hell is this place?" Officer Johnson sprinted to the closest cop car and dove into the backseat. The locks clicked behind him.

He was smarter than I'd thought. Running was definitely the safest thing for him to do.

I pushed Dad. "Get to the car. Now!"

He started moving slowly backward. I trusted that he'd listen. Or—at the very least—stay out of the way.

Gunfire broke the night again. Officer Marlene stumbled

out the front door, one arm hanging limp at her side. She fired at the thing, and it spun toward her with a screech. Then it leaped and sank its teeth into her neck.

She tried to get her gun on it, but collapsed before she could fire another shot. Blood pooled on the ground as Officer Marlene bled out.

One second she was there, and the next she was dead.

The demon shook her like a dog with a toy. When it finally pulled away, it grinned at us. Now its dripping red fangs matched its red eyes.

A shiver ripped down my spine. How could we fight this?

The Weres reacted faster than I did. Already shifted, the Cazadores moved into a V-formation. Mr. Dawson, Chris, Dastien, Donovan, and Meredith all formed a half circle, ready to run the creature down no matter what direction it went.

I wasn't good in wolf-form. But I had potions.

Since I hadn't found mention of demons in my books, I'd modified the potions the *brujos* used against vampires, adding holy oil and pieces of a relic Tía Rosa had given me. Shaving the relic into bits was probably sacrilegious, but I'd been desperate.

I still had two vials in my hand from my bag. I had fifteen potions. My entire stash. Now I could only hope that they'd work.

"By the power of Christ, I banish you." I threw a vial.

It hit the demon and exploded in a blast of smoke and white light. The demon's high-pitched scream burned my eardrums.

Then it leaped for me.

Dastien swiped at it from the side as I dodged. His claws slashed it, sending a stream of black sludge to the ground. It splattered, fizzing like acid. Dastien yelped in pain, as some of it hit his back.

Shit. "Don't let its blood get on you," I yelled, adding a bit of a command to back up the warning.

The Weres circled the demon as it hissed. Scorches covered its skin where the potion vial had hit. That was something, but it wasn't going to be enough.

One of the Cazadores lunged at the demon, but the creature dodged, swiping its claws across the wolf's belly. Blood sprayed. The wolf crashed to the ground and convulsed for a few long seconds. Then the motion stopped.

Shock rooted me to the ground. Dead. In one hit.

What were we going to do? The wolves had no advantage against this kind of enemy and my potions were only pissing it off.

Instead of attacking, the wolves hung back, containing the demon in their circle, dodging and lunging to keep it corralled. But they couldn't hold that for long.

Cosette slipped around the wolves to get to me. "How many vials can you throw at once?"

I reached into my messenger bag and grabbed as many as I could. "Six. What are you thinking?"

"Blast it with everything you've got. If that's not enough, step aside and let it charge me."

"What? Are you trying to get yourself killed?"

"Why? You think my life is in danger?" She asked like we were at a freaking tea party.

"Are you insane? If we don't fight back, we're both dying here."

"That's what I thought." Now she grinned and her expression had more than a little bloodlust. She might be having a moment, but I didn't have time to play games.

The Weres were circling. The demon hissed and tried to dart between them, but the wolves closed ranks, slashing at it.

"Will that work?"

"I've never fought a demon before, but I'm perfectly able to defend my life." She shrugged. "Plus your potions might fry the thing. Either way, it'll come after the magic."

It was worth a try. Killing this bastard without getting blood on us was going to be hard. Especially for the wolves. They used their teeth and claws. Not exactly from-a-distance type weapons. Plus, I'd seen Cosette fight.

"On three," she said. "One. Two. Three."

I threw six vials and invoked them. As they activated, the blast knocked me back. Heat licked along my skin, but the demon kept on screeching. When the smoke cleared it was lunging for us.

"Move!" Cosette ordered the wolves, and they parted.

There was a cracking noise, like a falling snow globe, and then Cosette was holding a sword that came from nowhere.

The demon thrashed around, moving too fast for her to strike. She kept pace, dodging and lunging, but the effects of the potions were wearing off. The liquid boiled off its skin in a cloud of steam. Cosette either had to kill the thing or get away before she got hit.

It moved too fast. If we could just slow it down—

I sucked in a breath. Maybe I could do better than slowing it down.

I could freeze it.

I focused on my magic. I'd learned that believing the spell would work was half the battle, so I put all my will and faith into one word. "Stop!" The demon froze. Not for long, but a split second was all Cosette needed. She swung her sword in one smooth motion, and the demon's head separated from its body.

It unfroze as the head fell. Its mouth opened and let out an ear-burning cry. The thing was still yelling as a hole opened in the dirt. A ray of black and gold light exploded from the ground, wrapping the demon and sucking it down. Its scream didn't end until the earth snapped closed again.

It was so quiet I could hear my heart pounding in my ears.

"Holy shit. What was that?" It had happened so fast, I almost thought I was dreaming.

"That was hell." Cosette poked the scorched ground with her toe. "Somewhere I hope none of us visit." Her sword had disappeared, but a faint glow still lingered under her skin.

I staggered back from where the demon had fallen. Only the burned ground and persisting scent of sulfur said anything had happened.

A car horn honked, and we all jumped.

Fuck. Officer Johnson was still in the cop car. I could smell his panic and fear from here.

"What do we do now?" I said. "We've got a compound full of dead bodies, five of them cops." I had zero clue how to handle this situation.

I heard someone shift behind me and chose not to look. Unless it was Dastien, I didn't want to see any of that.

"I'm open to suggestions," said Mr. Dawson.

Dad cleared his throat as he walked toward us, carrying a few gallons of gasoline. "I turned off the cams on the cop cars. It took some doing, but thankfully Officer Johnson was thoroughly distracted by the end of that fight." He set the bright red canisters down and brushed off his hands. "I think it's time to cover our tracks."

My jaw dropped open. "Dad! We can't burn this place. All these houses... It's wrong."

He sighed. "This *is* wrong, kiddo, but there aren't a lot of options. Not unless you want to come out to the humans about Weres, witches, demons, vampires, and whatever else is out there."

Cosette met my gaze and subtly shook her head.

Yup, that's as bad of an idea as it sounds. "But what do we do about the other covens? Won't they blame us?"

"I'm on supernatural damage control." Cosette rubbed her hands together and I heard a faint crackling noise at the edge of my hearing. I hoped she was still powered up because I had no idea how to fix this without her help. "I'll contact my coven in Colorado and get them to spread the news of Luciana's draining. Then I have to report to the mother ship." She shuddered at the thought.

"What about Johnson over there?" I pointed to the cop car. "Do we get rid of him, too?" I said with a thick coating of sarcasm.

"I'll make a deal with him," Cosette said. "He won't remember a thing."

I knew she was fey, but I still had no idea what her powers were. After tonight, I realized how much she was hiding. There was more to Cosette than a flirty girl who liked her rag mags. "You can do that?"

She nodded, her blonde curls bouncing. How she appeared so sweet and innocent after decapitating a demon, I'd never know. "I can do a lot of things."

"Good to know." I had to wonder what else "a lot of things" included, but I wasn't going to ask as long as she was using her powers for us. "Fine." Not that anyone really cared what I thought. It seemed like everyone already knew what to do. Who was I to object?

"If you can handle Johnson, we'll take care of the compound," Mr. Dawson said. "I'll have my contacts at the coroner's office make the four bodies in custody disappear." Shit. I'd totally forgotten about the others. He sighed. "And Kelly. I'll have to notify his family."

I swallowed as I took in the lone wolf lying still, his fur

matted with dark blood. We'd already lost one fighter, and that was just one minor demon.

I hadn't even known the Were's name.

"I'm sorry for your loss. You take care of yours, and I'll get baby cop to take me to the station so I can tie up the rest of our loose ends." Cosette sighed.

I winced at the sound. She was really putting herself on the line for us. "How much trouble are you in?"

"I'll spin it somehow." Then she smirked. "Why are were-wolves so much trouble?"

I shrugged. "Don't ask me. I'm still new here."

She laughed. "For being so new to the supernatural world, you're handling it well."

That was high praise coming from her. "Th—" I caught myself before I thanked her. "I mean, that's nice to hear?" My manners were too ingrained. It felt wrong not to say thanks when she was putting herself out there for us.

"See? You're used to it already."

A wolf head-butted my hand, and I glanced down at Dastien's white and gray coat. "Did you get any of its blood on you?" He gave a small whimper and licked my palm. I couldn't sense much pain from him, but I could've sworn some of the blood got on his fur. "Gross."

I wiped my hand on my jeans and squatted down, pressing my forehead to his. His love came pouring through the bond, and I reveled in it for a moment. He was here. Safe. We were both alive. I could breathe easier for a second, before the tension built right back up. I hadn't thought a demon would be able to latch on just from a wound, but after what happened to Raphael...

"Let me see where the blood hit you. Was it your back?" I leaned over him and sniffed. The charred patch of fur smelled like sulfur. No way did I want him to end up like Raphael. I had to do something before any demonic energy took hold. I didn't have any holy water. Nothing that could cleanse it. Except...

I reached into my bag and grabbed one of the vials. The potion looked like dark gray sludge but it was brewed with holy oil and bits of the relic.

I slowly unscrewed the cap. "I'm going to put this on your back."

"Is that a good idea?" Meredith asked. "Don't those explode when they hit the demons?"

"Dastien isn't a demon." I was pretty sure it wouldn't damage him, but the potion should be strong enough to burn off the demon's blood. It would be worth a little sting to make sure there was no chance of him being possessed. "Guess we'll find out." *This might burn a little, okay?*

Dastien yipped, and I poured out the vial, quickly muttering the words to invoke it.

He snarled as the potion hit his skin. The vial slipped to the ground and I grabbed him, holding him still. "Give it a second. The burning should stop." I muttered my prayer activating the potion, hoping I wasn't lying.

There was a flash of white light, and then Dastien quit struggling.

Donovan squatted down next to us, back to human and sporting a pair of generic black sweatpants. "Shift back."

Dastien shifted, and suddenly I was staring at his naked back. A small burn—a little bigger than the size of a quarter—marred his otherwise smooth skin. It was raw and red, weeping a little bit of blood. "It isn't healing?"

"No." Donovan shook his head. "That's a supernatural hurt. Those heal slowly." He leaned in and sniffed Dastien's burn. "But it smells fine now. No infection."

I let out a breath of relief, but wondered—if I'd acted faster

—if I'd known what was going on with Raphael, could I have stopped it before the demon took hold?

Donovan patted Dastien's shoulder. "You should be okay. You've got quite the mate."

Dastien laughed. "I agree."

He looked back at me, and I couldn't help running my fingers through his hair. "You're okay."

He nodded.

I took him in, and my eyes widened. "You need some clothes. Like now."

"I guess I do. Be right back." Dastien headed for the SUV, and I tried not to steal a peek. Much. The rest of the wolves followed. I saw Mr. Dawson's brown wolf dart past, and knew the coast was clear of naked bits I didn't want to see.

I stared at Luciana's house. We had a small victory—one not without cost—but Luciana was out there. Somewhere. "I'm going to have to go in there, aren't I?"

"Probably. I'd help but I have to deal with our cop friend." Cosette tilted her head toward the car. "He looks like he's about to pee himself. If he hasn't already."

I grunted my agreement, but stayed there, staring up at Luciana's place. It was white, with forest green shutters, and a matching door. The white porch seemed almost homey. It might be, if not for the blood dripping down the steps. Not to mention Luciana's craft room...

Shuddering, I turned away.

How Daniel had lived there, I had no idea.

Thinking of him brought up a host of emotions I couldn't deal with yet. I shoved them down, but I couldn't ignore the question that keep coming back to me. "How could Luciana do this to her people? To her son?" I asked Dad.

He sat by me. "I don't know." He put his arm around me,

and I leaned into him. "I'd do anything to make sure you were okay."

I motioned to the red plastic containers. "Clearly."

He pressed a kiss to my forehead. "You're mine. No matter what's happened. I'll do everything I can to protect you."

I closed my eyes and breathed in his scent. He smelled like home. I could even smell Mom's lavender lotion. "I know. Love you, Dad."

"Love you, too, kiddo."

I patted Dad's leg and then stood, brushing myself off. There was no time to waste. Not when Luciana was out there, doing God only knew what. If I wanted to live through the next fight, I needed to be ready and the potions I had weren't going to cut it. If there were any books on demons hiding in the compound, they'd be inside.

As I started toward the house, my hands shook.

You can do this, Tessa. I told myself. You can do this. You're strong. You got out of there once. She's not even here. Keep your head on straight, and it'll be fine.

I snorted. No way was everything going to be fine, but I made myself move forward anyway.

At this point, I was the only one who could sort through whatever was left of Luciana's magic. It wasn't going to be fun and it wasn't going to be pretty, but I didn't have a choice in the matter. At every turn, Luciana did something more and more horrific. Someone had to stop her.

Maybe I wasn't the best person for the job, but I had to try.

Even if it meant coming face to face with my worst nightmares.

CHAPTER TWELVE

THERE WAS nothing worse than entering a quiet, dark house just before three in the morning. Especially one a demon just came out of. Yup. Not on my top ten list of things to do.

The door squeaked as I pushed it open. The metallic smell of blood hit me first. I swallowed my disgust, praying I wouldn't throw up. Then my toe bumped a severed leg and I nearly lost it.

Three dead cops sprawled in pieces around the living room.

This was so not my jam.

I tried to ignore the bodies as I headed down the hallway. The craft room's door hung open on one hinge. I pulled it the rest of the way open and took a steadying breath.

Memories of being trapped in the circle on the floor rushed over me. I lurched back before I could help myself. The urge to run away was almost unbearable, but if there was something in here that could help us, I had to force myself. If nothing else, we could clear out all the books.

"Wait," Dastien's voice stopped me. "Why are you going in without me?"

He stood behind me, wearing a pair of generic gray sweatpants from the SUVs. "You were getting dressed, and I thought..."

"No. We do this together."

I gripped the strap of my messenger bag. "Okay." Having Dastien there was a weight off my mind, but it still took me a few minutes to work up my courage. After a lot of deep breaths, I stepped into the room.

A layer of dried blood coated the floor, cracking as I walked over it. Hundreds of unlit black candles stood on pedestals of fallen wax. Whatever potion she'd last cooked up smelled like burnt plastic.

And the circle the demon had come from was still active.

Waves of magic thrummed against my skin like electricity. If I looked at it out of the corner of my eye, a yawning chasm opened in the center of floor. Pieces of the fourth cop lay sprinkled around the edges—he must've triggered it, releasing the demon.

This was a shitshow waiting to happen.

Thankfully, there was nothing crawling out now. At least not yet. "Wait at the door. The circle's still working."

"Be careful."

"Just give me a second." Thank God I'd been reading all those magic books. An active circle was dangerous, especially since I had no idea how to close the chasm. But I could bind the circle, making it impossible for anything to cross out of it.

All I needed was salt and a little bit of magic.

God. Why did she have to put everything in unlabeled black canisters? I didn't want to touch anything I didn't have to, so I opened one of the biggest canisters—hoping for salt—and gagged.

The smell was enough to do it, but the sight of eyeballs floating in some green gelatinous goo put me straight over the edge.

"That was so not fucking salt." I screwed the lid on and set it back as quickly as I could before wiping my hands on my jeans. "If I were salt, where would I be?"

"I could try the kitchen?"

Now that he was here, I didn't want him to leave. "She's got to have some in here. Every witch does. It has to be right in front of me." I moved farther into the room and grabbed the next likely canister. "Please, don't let it be eyeballs."

Nope. Hair. Thin chunks of it were tied with pieces of twine and labeled with people's names.

I closed the canister and slipped it into my bag. We'd have to take care of it later. Luciana could do all kinds of hexes with hair.

"Hey," Dastien said, suddenly behind me.

I jumped and let out a very uncool scream.

"Shit." I clutched my chest. "I told you to wait outside."

"I was bored."

"Just don't touch the circle." I pointed at the markings on the floor.

He took in the room. "It smells awful in here."

"I know."

"Is this where she…"

I nodded, trying not to think about the past, and focused on scanning the shelves. What if I needed some of her ingredients for a potion? If we burned the house, then all her supplies would be destroyed.

Nope.

If I needed something Luciana had, then I was doing the wrong kind of magic. "Let's just take the books." I gave him my bag. "Stuff in anything that looks handy. As much as you can fit. We'll sort it out when Claudia gets here tomorrow."

"You got it."

"Now I just need some salt."

Dastien faced the shelves and grabbed a medium-size canister. "There you go."

"What?" I unscrewed the lid and, sure enough—salt. "How did you know where it was?"

He tapped his nose.

"But it reeks in here."

"You have to learn to separate the smells. Search for the one you want. It takes a little practice, but most Weres can do it."

"I can't." Not with all the gross smells in here. I wouldn't even know where to start.

"You're new at this. When I was a kid, it was overwhelming. All the scents that humans use—especially girls." He gave me a wink. "All those soaps, lotions, perfumes..."

I shook my head. "Somehow I doubt that stopped you from flirting."

"I'd be happy to show you my smooth ways of... Scenting things."

I laughed. Here. In this room. I actually laughed. "Thanks for the distraction."

"You seemed tense. Let's get this sorted and get out of here, okay?"

"Deal."

He started clearing out the books while I took care of the circle. Sprinkling salt, I walked around its edge, not daring to step even one hair over the line. When I completed the lap, magic rose. I held out my hands to it. "Nothing leaves this circle." I forced my power through the words, willing them to be true. The magic snapped into place, trapping Luciana's evil mojo inside the larger circle of salt.

I wiped the sweat from my brow. I was already tired, but doing that one bit of magic made me even more exhausted.

Dastien froze. "What was that?"

"A seal." I grabbed a handful of salt and threw it at the

circle. It slammed against an invisible wall and sprinkled to the floor outside the ring. "Nothing's getting in or out of that thing." That was one less problem to worry about.

Dastien zipped the messenger bag and hefted the strap over his head. "Let's get out of here."

"Yes, please."

Outside, more Cazadores had gathered. The rest of our group had shifted back and everyone wore the same gray sweats. Mr. Dawson, Donovan, and Dad were huddled together, planning how to torch the compound. Only Cosette stood off to the side, leaning on Dad's car as she stared up at the moon.

It was weird to be handling all this without Claudia. She should be the one to decide what happened to the compound.

I joined the group, and Mr. Dawson paused, giving me a chance to say my piece. "Are you sure this is a good idea?"

"Do you have a better one?" Dad asked.

"No. Not really, but Claudia and the rest of what's left of this coven will be here tomorrow. I hate to do anything drastic like burning down her home when she's already on the way."

"And then what? This is a mess." Mr. Dawson gestured around the compound. "If humans don't stumble in here, animals will."

"Why don't we give them a proper funeral? Although I don't know what's right for witches." I turned to Dad. "I mean, at the very least we should call Mom and ask. Or Tía Rosa."

"I'd rather not drag your mother into this."

"She's going to find out about it."

"I know, I just... I want to protect her from making that decision."

Mom was going to flip when she found out that he didn't consult her, but if he wanted to suffer the consequences, I couldn't stop him.

"What if this is too big to hide?" Chris' hair was way poofier

AILEEN ERIN

than normal—a sure sign he'd been messing with it too much, something he tended to do when stressed. "We've talked about coming out to the humans. Why not now? Instead of covering everything up?"

"Not like this." Mr. Dawson shook his head. "If our first impression is death and violence, then humans will assume from the start that supernaturals are dangerous. That's exactly what we don't want."

"We should follow our usual protocol. We cover our tracks. Get rid of any sign of supernatural goings on. Dispose of bodies and the evidence of spellcraft. In a secluded area like this, burning the houses is a fine way to do it," Donovan said. "I know this is not ideal and, yes, it's a sizable cover-up, but it wouldn't be the grand first impression we'd hoped for. When we tell the humans we're here it has to be done extremely carefully, or we'll end up on the losin' end of things."

Donovan's words hit me hard. I didn't like covering this up. It made me feel like I'd done something wrong, when that was the farthest thing from the truth.

"Destroying Luciana's house is smart. Burning those floor-boards is the only way to make sure she can't do any more of her evil magic in there. But the rest of it..." Suddenly I was more than exhausted, and when Claudia got back tomorrow, it was only going to get worse. "Just do me a favor and tell Mom *before* you set everything on fire."

"Okay, kiddo," Dad said. "Probably a good idea."

"We'll leave it to you," Dastien said. "Unless you need us for anything else...?"

"I can handle it from here." Mr. Dawson nodded to Donovan. "You want to take the students back?"

"Aye." Donovan put his arm around Meredith's shoulders. "That'll be for the best. It's been a long night for all of us."

In that moment, I was glad to be considered a student. I

wanted no part of this. Going back and getting some sleep sounded like a much better option.

"I'm off, too," Cosette said. "We're running out of time to wipe memories."

"Chris," Mr. Dawson said. "Go with her. I'll tell my contact at the coroner's office you're heading that way. Cazadores to me. Let's get this cleanup done."

I gave Dad a quick hug and headed for the closest SUV. Meredith and Donovan piled in back while Dastien tossed the bag of books into the trunk.

"Well, that was a hell of a night," Meredith said as she buckled her seat belt.

I leaned into the soft leather. "For real." I closed my eyes. "Did we really fight a demon?"

"You're damned right we did," Meredith said, and Donovan laughed over her words.

I reached back and high-fived her "We're seriously badass." Laughing right then was probably asking for something worse to happen, but at this point I needed the laugh. So, I took it.

BACK AT DASTIEN'S CABIN, I showered and then threw on some sleep shorts and a tank. He set a plate with a heated-up burrito and some chips on my lap, but I put it on the nightstand.

"You have to eat."

"I'm way too tired." I flopped down on the bed, pulling the covers up around me.

He moved in front of me. One of his dark brown curls fell in front of his face as he bent over. "Please eat."

I took in the sight of him in his gym shorts. His chest still glistened from his shower. He was gorgeous. His body was perfection. Each ab muscle well defined. And his arms...

Thank you, God.

"*Chérie.*" He had a knowing smile on his face as he leaned down, trapping me between his arms. "You're somewhere else..."

I licked my lips. "You could say that."

He ran his nose along mine, before finally leaning in for a kiss. "Maybe you're hungry for something other than food?"

"If you're going to prance around in that outfit, then yeah. I'd say so."

His deep laugh ran through me, warming me from the inside. "Prance? Outfit? I'm feeling a little objectified."

I sighed, dreamily. "You should be. I'm definitely objectifying you right now." I ran my hands down his stomach, and he leaned forward, biting my lip.

His kisses were addictive. They drowned out all the bad. All the scary. And I had a lot of that going on in my head. But one touch, and I was gone.

I moaned as his tongue touched mine, and then I melted into the bed.

Yeah. I could get used to this. As he reached under my tank top, all coherent thought fled. All I wanted was more.

I let myself get lost in the sensation of his body against mine.

More. I needed more.

CHAPTER THIRTEEN

I NEVER DID GET AROUND to eating that burrito, but after our heavy make-out session, I slept like a baby. When I woke up, I reached over for him.

The sheets were cold.

Dastien.

"I'm here," he said.

The tone of his voice was off. Too quiet, with a hint of annoyance. Something was wrong. I sat up. He had the TV on silent, and the news was on. It played helicopter footage looking over a street of burned houses in the middle of the woods.

My heart stopped. "No." I slid from the bed and moved to his side. Dastien's hand found mine as he turned off Mute on the TV.

"...dashboard camera footage led the police to this compound. The suspects in question—"

I sank onto the couch and muted the TV again, unable to listen to more. "How did this happen?"

"The video auto-uploaded to the police servers. Someone leaked it to the media." Dastien rubbed a hand against his head.

"How much did they see?" And please don't say everything...

"From the moment the cars rolled onto the compound, until your dad turned off the cameras. It's all on there. Three cop cars. Three angles."

My heart pounded in my ears as the realization hit me. "The whole world knows about us."

"It gets worse."

I swallowed. "What do you mean it gets worse? How could it possibly get any fucking worse?"

He put his arm around me. "You have to calm down."

I wiggled free of him and stood. "Don't. Don't tell me to calm down. Just tell me what's worse."

He cleared his throat. "The demon didn't appear on film. At least, not how we saw it."

It took a second for that to sink in. If the demon didn't show up on film, then it was just werewolves, a fey, and a bunch of dead cops. "What do you mean?"

"It's better if you see." He rewound the news, stopping in the middle of the fight.

The video was a little grainy, but I could make out something moving in the middle of a ring of snarling wolves. I moved closer to the TV as the demon swiped at Kelly. The demon's motion turned it toward the camera and I stopped breathing for a second. The camera hadn't been close enough to pick up the red eyes, but I should've been able to see its skin color. Its nails. And its proportions that were anything but human.

Except the thing in the center of circle, surrounded by wolves, didn't look like a demon. If I didn't know—if I hadn't been there myself—I wouldn't have known it was a monster. From the video, it looked like a hunched over man. If you looked close enough, you could tell because it didn't *move* like a human, but I doubted anyone was looking that closely.

I closed my eyes and sank back down on the couch. "So what now?"

"Your dad and Michael are with the police. They're trying to get it sorted, but..."

I buried my face in my hands. "This is so messed up."

"It is."

"What's everyone saying online?"

"It's bad. You don't want to check."

He had to say that. Now all I wanted to do was look.

"Since you didn't shift there's a lot of speculation whether you're a Were, but because you grew up human, your records are out there. Maybe someone from your old school will talk or they'll match your photos, but it's only a matter of time before the media gets your name. And when they do..."

"I'm going to be hounded." Forget "Freaky Tessa." This was going to be a whole new level of crazy.

"Cosette, too, but she's MIA. We're not sure when—or if— she's coming back."

She'd be back. She had to be. We needed her, especially if she was that good against demons. I didn't know anyone else who could whip weapons out of thin air mid-battle.

"Lots of theories about the vials and the explosions. They know it wasn't us who killed the cops, and the footage shows the body getting sucked into the ground—but we've still got problems." He leaned back against the couch. "The local cops are freaking out because the FBI came down and now... It's like they just learned the *X-Files* are real."

This was too much. My mind was blown. I pulled my knees to my chest and held them as I watched the soundless TV. "So, what now?"

"Donovan, the Seven, and the rest of the alphas are in the conference room. They're talking to every pack alpha they can get on the phone, discussing options. So, it's going to be a while before anything gets decided. Until then, everyone's confined to campus." He sighed. "Which is probably a good thing. Your dad had a problem getting here. Apparently, there's a mob at the gates."

"I don't know how it's possible, but everything keeps getting worse."

Dastien tucked me against his side. He turned the volume on, and we sat there listening to their crazy commentary. Most of it was painfully wrong. I was half-convinced I should call in and correct them, but that was probably the worst idea in the history of bad ideas.

It kept bothering me that there were people at our gates. Would they go home at night? And if not, would Luciana still attack? How could we protect them when we could barely protect our own? And we couldn't have cops on campus if we were at war with the evil bitch.

A war that they weren't remotely equipped to fight.

Someone knocked on the door.

"Come in," I said without asking who it was.

"Teresa?"

Oh no. Claudia.

I raced to the door. She was wearing clothes that didn't really fit—not her usual skirt and peasant shirt. Her hair popped out of her braid and her eyes were rimmed with red.

She already knew.

"I'm so sorry," I said, even though sorry didn't even begin to cut it.

She started sobbing and wrapped her arms around my neck. "I don't understand how this happened. I saw the news, and I just—" She hiccupped, and I patted her back.

"Come inside. Sit down." I pulled her over the threshold.

It wasn't until then that I noticed the man behind her.

He was one of the most handsome men I'd ever seen—which was saying something. He radiated power, and I knew in an instant that he was an alpha. So much energy vibrated around him, he might even be more powerful than Donovan. His dark eyes met mine, and I couldn't look away. It was a dominance thing, not attraction. I wouldn't be the one to look away first.

He gave me a wink and started looking around the room.

Technically he'd looked away first, but with that wink, he was telling me he wasn't playing the game.

No fair.

Dastien hit Mute on the TV and stood as Beth, Shane, Adrian, and Raphael came in after him.

The *brujos* spotted the footage and were captivated.

Dastien crossed the room, reaching out a hand to the new guy. "Dastien Laurent."

The man wore simple track pants and the arms of his long-sleeved T-shirt bunched at his elbows. If I couldn't feel his power, I would've thought he was just a normal guy.

"I'm Claudia's mate," he said, and my jaw nearly hit the ground.

How in the hell did she get mated already? There hasn't been enough time, let alone a full moon, I yelled through our bond.

I don't know. But we can definitely ask.

"Lucas Reyes," he said as he took Dastien's hand.

For a split second, Dastien froze before shaking Lucas' hand. "It's good to meet you."

Who is he? It was the first time I'd ever seen Dastien react to someone like that.

Alpha of the pack in Peru. A very, very strong Alpha. But he hasn't left Peru in ages.

I had so many questions for Claudia, but first things first. "I'm sorry. I didn't want you to find out this way. I wanted to tell you in person when you got here—not over the phone—but I woke up a bit ago and the news..."

She nodded. "What happened?"

123

I stood in front of the now-dark TV and waited until everyone had found a place to sit in the small room before I started. I didn't stop when they started sobbing, but my throat got scratchy. I had to tell them. From beginning to end. Drawing it out wasn't going to make the truth any easier.

Still, as Beth leaned into Shane and Claudia sobbed on Lucas' chest, my throat grew tight and tears rolled down my face. Raphael stood behind the couch, taking the news like a good little soldier, but he was grinding his teeth so hard that his jaw was white.

When I finished, I sat on the coffee table. "I'm so sorry. I told you that you'd all be safe here with the pack. I promised to make sure you'd be okay, and I've broken my word. First with Raphael, and now this..." I swallowed. "I hope you know that I didn't mean for any of this to happen. And the compound... I'm sorry. It's burned, and I tried to stop it, but they were..."

"Covering up. Yes. It's procedure," Lucas finished for me.

Claudia covered her face as she started sobbing again, and Lucas moved to kneel in front of her. He whispered sweet nothings to her in Spanish. Affirmations that it would be okay, even when we all knew that it wouldn't be okay. There was no way that any of us could ever make this right.

With each sob of pain from my cousin, it felt like someone was stabbing my heart. I couldn't help her. I couldn't spare her from this, so I waited. She was going to have questions, and I needed to be here for her.

After a while, she wiped her eyes. "It's too much. This is too much. God. I just got my brother back. I thought we'd have some room to breathe, and now this. I can't—it's too much." She clutched her hand to her chest. "Everyone I knew my whole life, all gone. Even after Luciana is dealt with, what am I supposed to do? Where do I belong?"

Lucas ran his hand down her cheek. "You belong with me.

We'll make sure everyone here is safe, and then we go on with your plan. You don't have to worry about abandoning anyone anymore. Everything we talked about is still possible. Focus on that and we'll get through this."

I smiled through my tears. He was nice, this guy. He was good for her, and that at least was one thing that Claudia could count on.

When she finally calmed down, Claudia met my gaze, and I knew something was coming. Her eyes were rimmed with red, but something else flushed her cheeks. I recognized the spicy scent coming from her. Pure rage. I just hoped it wasn't directed at me.

"Where is *she*?" She nearly spat the last word.

Luciana. She wanted to kill Luciana. "We don't know. I don't even know where to start looking. All I know is that she's got more than enough power to do whatever she wants, and... She's made life complicated for us. It's not like we can just pop out and look for her. Not now."

"But we have to go after her," Raphael said. "She can't get away with what she's done. She's murdered everyone we know." He gripped the back of the couch. "I don't know what's happened to her, but if she can do that, then she's not the Luciana we knew. She's pure evil."

I nodded. "I agree. All I know is that we're stuck here. The alphas are trying to decide what to do next, and until then—I guess we wait."

Shane nodded, and I looked at Beth. A steady stream of tears ran down her face, but she wasn't looking at anything. More than any of them, she was the one who seemed utterly broken by this.

"Is she okay?"

Shane squeezed her. "We'll take care of her."

"I'm sorry. I—"

"Don't. This isn't your fault. There's nothing to apologize for. Luciana did this, and we'll make her pay." His words were so final that I couldn't do anything but nod.

"She will. I think we're all agreed on that."

Claudia wiped her face and cleared her throat. "What did you do with the bodies?"

I blinked as I tried find a way to answer Claudia's question that wouldn't upset her more. "I think they were burned at the compound."

"No. I mean Elsa. And Yvonne. Tiffany. They weren't at the compound."

"I—" I wasn't sure. We'd run off so quickly. "I don't know." I turned to Dastien, who was leaning against his kitchen counter.

"I think Dr. Gonzales has them. I don't think she's done anything yet."

"I want to see them."

Shane nodded. "Me, too."

"We should all go," Raphael said as he stepped toward the door.

"I should warn you. They don't... They look..."

"How bad?" Lucas said.

"I couldn't really look at them." I squeezed my eyes closed for a second as the image of Elsa on the floor of the library came to mind.

"Adrian?" Dastien said.

"Yeah." He stood up from where he was sitting—at the foot of Dastien's bed.

"Can you take them to see Dr. Gonzales?"

"Sure. Of course." Even he seemed a little pale. He moved slower than normal as he opened the door.

Claudia pulled me into a hug. "I'm sorry, too. This had to be so hard for you."

I huffed. "Me? No. I really am so sorry. If I knew—if there was something I could've done—I would've."

"I know. Me, too. I feel like this is my fault. I didn't do enough. If I'd moved against her sooner..." She stepped back. "But we can't know that. We could've done everything right and still gotten to this same place. So we have to keep moving forward. I'm going to see to my friends' bodies, and then we can look at what I brought back from Peru."

I nodded. "Whatever you need. I'm here."

"I'll call you," she said.

Lucas followed her out of the room, giving us a small nod, before closing the door behind them.

I melted down onto the couch. They'd only been here for a couple hours, but it felt like years. It was like I'd been hit by an emotional eighteen-wheeler. Even if Shane and Claudia said it wasn't my fault that this had happened, it felt like at least some of the blame fell to me. If I hadn't ended up with the pack, if I had been with the coven, maybe I could've prevented all this.

Dastien joined me and my head rested on his chest. I let his steady heartbeat soothe me. I knew he was probably listening in to my thoughts, but I didn't care.

What the hell were we going to do now? Everything was such a mess.

After a while, he pulled me off the couch. "Come on."

"Where are we going?"

"You can play 'what if' all day long, thinking up all kinds of scenarios to torture yourself, but it's not going to do any good. Do you trust me?"

"Always," I said as I looked into his amber eyes. It was the truth. I trusted him with everything that I was.

"Then come with me." He pulled me. "Let's shift. We're going for a run."

127

It'd been days since I'd had time to shift. My wolf was aching to get free. "Okay. Where are we going?"

"You'll see. Just shift and follow me."

In a blink of eye, his form changed. He stuck his wolfy tongue out at me, and I shook my head. I circled my finger in the air. "Turn around."

The sound he made might've been a laugh, but I couldn't be sure.

As I traded my skin for fur, all my worries melted away.

This was a fantastic idea.

CHAPTER FOURTEEN

WIND WHIPPED against my fur as I ran through the forest. There were so many scents to chase. So many things to see. Dastien herded me where he wanted to go, with a nip here and a chase there. Finally, the forest opened up and we were standing in the middle of a clearing.

Our land. He'd taken us to our land.

Wolf-Dastien ran off behind a tree and appeared a minute later dressed in a pair of sweats. "There are clothes for you back there."

I followed where he pointed. A plastic crate sat half hidden in the bushes behind a stand of trees. Supplies were stashed everywhere around campus—generic sweatpants, T-shirts, water, and granola bars—but I didn't know Dastien had stashed some here.

Ever since I'd stopped fighting my shift, it had quit hurting. Now it was a sweet release. My muscles rippled, bones moving so quickly that one moment I was wolf and the next human.

I flipped open the top of the crate. Inside were a bunch of clothes and some swimsuits. Although if Dastien thought I was ever swimming in that pond, he was going to be sorely disappointed. I found a pair of smaller sweatpants and a T-shirt and slipped them on.

Dastien waited by the pond. "I thought we weren't allowed to leave campus."

He shrugged. "Eh. Who needs rules anyhow?"

I shook my head. We were so getting our asses reamed for leaving, but he was right. I needed a break from it all. Ever since my birthday, it was like the hits just hadn't stopped coming. There hadn't been any room to relax.

If I didn't take a little time for myself, I might crack. I rubbed my temples as a headache pounded. It was only just after lunchtime, and I was already exhausted. I could've gone back to bed right then and slept for another million years. It wasn't just the physical exhaustion of the fight yesterday, but the emotional drain. Telling Claudia that her whole coven had been murdered by Luciana had been worse than I thought. The only good thing was that at least she had someone to lean on. Lucas seemed like a good guy. And if he was anything like Dastien and Donovan, he'd treat her like his queen.

I leaned into Dastien as he wrapped his arms around me. Being here—standing next to the pond with him—made me nervous. What I'd seen in my vision wasn't going to happen. We hadn't talked about it and I wasn't wearing a white dress... But still, nerves creeped in.

"Are you okay?"

It was probably stupid to mention it, but I couldn't help it. "In my vision, we—"

"No. Don't worry about the vision. I haven't had an Orangina in days, no matter how much I want one." He tickled my side, and I squirmed away, laughing. "That proves we can change what you saw."

He sat on the ground, pulling me down with him. The grass dampened the back of my sweatpants as we sat cross-legged, knees touching. The tension in his shoulders told me he wanted to talk about something serious. I was worried I couldn't take much more today, but he wouldn't have brought me all the way here if it wasn't important.

"I thought we both needed a moment. It's been one thing after another, and it's overwhelming, you know?"

"I was thinking the same." It was nice when we were in sync. It made me feel safe. "I just feel so terrible for my cousins. I can't imagine what they're going through."

"They'll get through it. And so will you."

I huffed a laugh. "You don't know that. Especially not now." My fear of what I'd *seen* clung so thick it was like I was wrapped in a blanket of it.

Dastien tilted his head to stare out over the pond. He searched the calm surface like the answers to all our problems were in the murky depths. I could feel his anxiety, like he was building up to something, but I didn't want to pry. He was always patient with me, so I'd do my best to be patient with him.

Finally, Dastien turned back to me. The sunlight shone around him, giving him a glow. A curl slipped free from behind his ear, and he shoved it back. "I think we should finish bonding before Luciana attacks again."

I licked my lips as I processed his words. I didn't want to upset him, but he had to be kidding.

"That was the last thing I saw before—" Why would he want to risk it? It was like taking one more step down the road that led straight to both of us dead. He had to be overstressed or he never—*ever*—would've suggested it.

I stood up, swiping my hands down my butt, but then gave up and started marching off—not even sure where I was going.

"Tessa, wait."

I spun to him. "No. You wait." My vision changed everything. *Everything.* For all we knew, going through with the ceremony now—before we defeated Luciana—was exactly what got us killed. "You talk about changing the future, and that's what we're trying to do. Staying away from Orangina is easy enough, but what if I find myself in the conference room? We have no proof that anything has changed. Bonding now could send us straight to our deaths in that church."

His eyebrows rose as he took in my anger. "I disagree. You're putting way too much stock in the vision. You can't let your fear of the future rule your life."

My breath came in sharp pants, and fur rippled along my arms. Shifting now wasn't a good idea. We had to talk this through. Which meant that I needed to calm down, but the fear of what might happen was so overwhelming, I could barely think straight. "You don't get it. I *saw you die* and it was the worst thing I've ever experienced. After what happened at the compound, that's saying something." My hands shook. I was so scared of what might happen. "If we end up there, I'm going to do my best to keep *you* and everyone else alive, but I won't do anything that could push us closer to that happening."

Dastien's face flashed from pensive to angry to sad. "*Non.*" He grabbed my shoulders and a burst of power followed his word. "You think that if we end up in the church *you'll* have to save *me*? If we end up there, it will be *our* responsibility. We can fight better as a team. That's why everyone is so jealous that we're true mates. We're far more powerful together than we are apart. Remember?"

I'd spent so much time alone that I was used to it. I knew we were a team, but *knowing* it and *being* it were two different things. Now doubt niggled at me. What if delaying our bonding was weakening us? "But what if it sets off a chain reaction that ends with you dead? It would be my fault for not stopping it now and then I'd be alone. Without you. I don't know that I can survive that."

He drew me against his chest, and his heart thumped steadily. I closed my eyes as I relaxed against him. "There's always a chance that something could happen to one of us. That's part of being alive. But none of that will ever be *your* fault. I didn't mean to bite you, and I take responsibility for that —but it happened. If I'd done it a different way, could that have changed Luciana's reaction and everything that happened since? I don't know, but if I thought that way, it would be easy to say this is all *my* fault."

I wanted to argue his logic, but I couldn't. If I tried to accept blame, then he had some, too, and I didn't like that. Not one bit.

"Something tells me that Luciana has been going down this road for a very long time, and nothing anyone could've done— not you or me—would've stopped it." He ran his fingers through my hair. "No matter what happens, you have to place blame where it belongs. On Luciana. She's the one who cast the spell on Meredith. Who attacked us? Who drained your powers and murdered her own coven? You didn't do any of those things. Accepting blame for any of it is crazy."

"That doesn't change my mind about bonding. I know you want it—and believe me, I do, too—but we have very compelling reasons why we shouldn't go through with it right now."

He cupped my cheek. "Fighting Luciana is going to be hard, especially now. We need everything we can get. Being a full unit, thinking like one, can only help us in a fight."

"But we'd bonded in the vision, and we still died."

"Did you see that part happen? You said in the vision that you couldn't find me for a second. If we were really bonded, you could never lose me."

Technically, I hadn't seen us go through with the ceremony.

I'd just assumed. We'd been here, on our land. I was wearing white, but maybe it wasn't what I thought. The only thing I'd really seen was us kissing. "I just assumed since I was in a white dress and you were in khakis and we were here, that it had to be because we were bonding."

"See. Anything could've happened. What if we'd only been here for a date? What if we started to bond, but something came up again?" He shook my shoulders. "You've got to stop thinking the worst is destined to happen."

I couldn't hold his gaze. "I'm scared. Like really, truly terrified."

"That's understandable. *I'm* scared of what might happen when we face Luciana again. But not living our lives because of what might or might not happen? That's not okay."

He was totally right. This was crazy, but he was right. Maybe what I saw in the vision was going to happen. Or maybe it wasn't.

If I cut myself off from him because I was scared, then I wasn't really living. I was getting by.

And if I really thought about it... If the worst happened, I'd regret not doing this and I'd forever wonder if completing our bond would've made a difference.

"Okay," I whispered the word.

"Yes?" His eyes flashed brighter, glowing amber.

"Okay. Yes." I said it a little louder this time.

He swept me up, and my feet hovered above the ground as he spun me in circles. I couldn't help but laugh as the world blurred around me.

When he set me down on my feet, I leaned into him. He cupped my face in his hands. "We're going to have a long, happy life here. In the house we're going to build. With the kids we're going to have. I know it. I can feel it in my bones. We're going to get through this, and then we're going to have the most amazing life."

I sighed as his conviction washed over me. I hoped he was right. I wanted it so badly I could taste it, but we had so much to get through before we got there. It seemed almost impossible.

But none of that changed how I felt about him. "I love you."

Dastien pressed his forehead against mine. "*Je t'aime, mon amour. Toujours.*"

Half of me couldn't believe I was agreeing to this. The other half was one hundred percent, totally all in. "Okay. Let's do this. What do we need to do?"

"Let's go back to campus to avoid any crossover with the vision. Then we'll figure out what Lucas and Claudia did, and we'll do it. Now."

"Right. Because Luciana could attack tonight."

"No."

"No?" Did he know something I didn't?

"No. If the past few weeks have taught me anything, it's that life is precious, and I can't stand wasting another minute. I want to be with you. I want to be your mate. Your husband. Your partner. I want it all. I don't want to wait. I don't want something else to come up. I want us to take the time we deserve and do this just for us and no other reason."

I wasn't sure how he managed to surprise me... But he had. He took my breath away. I couldn't even think. Instead of trying to find words that would never say enough, I opened my side of the bond as wide as I could, letting him see exactly how I felt about him.

One of us moved, and suddenly I was kissing him. My fingers in his soft curls. My legs wrapped around his waist. I couldn't get close enough. I growled as he tugged on my lip. Fire licked through my body and he pulled away, resting his forehead against mine. There were no more questions in my mind. As our breath mingled, I knew what I wanted.

"Not one second more." He panted the words.

I grinned so big my cheeks hurt. "Not one second more."

No matter what happened, we'd be together. We had some big obstacles in our way, but in that moment, I didn't care. All I wanted was to be with Dastien.

CHAPTER FIFTEEN

WE DECIDED to meet in the clearing where the pack meetings were held. That way, there'd be no overlap with my vision. Just because this was happening, didn't mean that anything else would.

Dastien talked to Lucas while I changed and caught my breath, but we decided it was going to be just us. I was too paranoid that someone would barge in again. The last Full Moon Ceremony hadn't gone as planned. Not even close.

Instead of the white dress—which I was sure I didn't own—I put on a pair of jeans and a blue Helio Sequence T-shirt. Dastien had been wearing a similar one the first time we saw each other. It seemed fitting for today. Although anything was better than the Weres' white ceremonial robes.

According to Lucas, all we had to do was make a promise—an oath laced with magic—and bind it with our blood. The bond would click into place. Just like that.

It seemed so easy—so different from the ceremony of last time—but I didn't need all that. I didn't want any of it. If there was one thing I hated, it was being center of attention. Especially these days.

Dastien wanted time to set up something at the pack site, but I was ready and antsy as I paced my room.

Are you ready yet? I asked through the bond. Waiting around was driving me slowly insane.

Go ahead and come. I should be finished by the time you get here.

What are you doing? He'd been at it for over an hour.

You'll see. And no peeking through the bond!

I laughed quietly to myself as I headed out of the dorm. I wanted to be annoyed, but I totally wasn't. It was really nice that he was going to all this trouble. Although as much as I appreciated the thought, he didn't have to worry. No matter how it happened, it was going to be special.

Butterflies filled my stomach as I walked across campus and made my way into the forest. I passed a few Cazadores and some classmates along the way, but I didn't really see them. If they said hello, I didn't hear them. I was focused on where I was going. This was it.

I smelled the fire first. The cedar gave a spice to the air that I loved. I breathed it in deep as I wove between the trees. The sun would be setting soon, but for now, the sunlight cut through the leaves.

When I got to the pack circle, Dastien stood in front of the fire. A thick blue blanket was spread under his bare feet. A picnic basket sat to the side of the blanket, and more blankets and pillows were piled on top. He wore his usual worn-in jeans —thankfully not the khakis from the vision—and the exact same T-shirt as me.

I laughed. "We're the biggest dorks ever."

He actually blushed a little as he grinned at me. I'd coordinate outfits all the time just to get that look on his face. "I guess we're already in sync."

That was true. So what would it be like when we were bonded? How much closer could we really get?

He reached out to me, and I took his hand, kicking off my shoes before moving onto the blanket. He sat, and I did the same.

How did we start? There was no dearly beloved here. No priest. No minister.

"What—"

"I—"

We laughed as we talked over each other. I could feel his nerves through the bond, and that made me relax a little more. It was a big deal. This was a big deal. But as I stared into his eyes, my nerves turned into excitement.

"Before we do this, I wanted to say that I love you." Dastien squeezed my hand. "I know we're young, and this probably seems crazy to you, but I feel like I've been waiting for this forever. I was nervous before, but now I'm just excited."

"Me, too."

"I don't want you to be afraid of this because of the vision. If I thought bonding would make that future happen, then we wouldn't be doing this. I promise. This will only help us."

"I hope so, but right now—" I let go of all my worries and focused on him. Only him. "I just want to be with you and forget everything else."

He grinned. "Me, too." He reached behind him and pulled something out of the basket. "Lucas told me the words he used to bond with Claudia, but first..." He held a knife out to me. "I know you didn't like the idea of biting me. Instead, we can cut ourselves and mix our blood."

This just kept getting weirder. Although I had to admit, making a little cut on my hand would be easier than biting him. The idea of hurting him—even for a good cause—turned my stomach a little. "So we'd be like blood brothers?"

Those stupid dimples dented his cheeks as he laughed. "Kind of. Which would you rather?"

"I'd rather not do either." For real. What was the deal with all of the biting and cutting? Couldn't we just make the promises already?

"Tessa." There was a hint of warning in his voice.

"But—if I must—I think I'll take the knife."

He held the handle out for me. "We have to move fast once we make the cuts. It's not a supernatural wound. It'll heal quickly."

"Right." I blew out a breath as I took the knife from him. "Does it matter where I make the cut?"

"Lucas didn't say it mattered, but they used their hands."

"Works for me." I held the knife above my left palm, and paused. "Oh man. This is a real pain in my ass."

Dastien gave me a fake growl. "I'll show you a pain in your ass."

I gave him a wicked look. "Promises, promises."

He laughed. "You're killing me. Just do it."

"I think I need a countdown."

"Like when you get a shot?" His eyes glittered in the fire-light. "Just make the cut, Tessa."

Okay. I can do this. Just slice this super sharp knife over my palm.

I squealed, a very uncool, high-pitched noise as I ran the blade over my palm. A drop of blood dripped onto the blanket. I dropped the knife, but Dastien caught it. "Shit. That fucking hurts." I closed my hand holding it against my heart. "Hurry up. I'm not doing that again."

Dastien slid the knife along his hand like it was nothing.

"Show off."

"Give me your hand."

I reached out, and we joined our hands together.

Dastien's power hit me and I felt like I was drowning.

I gasped. "Oh God."

It was overwhelming. For a while, I'd thought I was more powerful than him. More alpha because my *bruja* blood gave me an advantage. But I was wrong. So fucking wrong. Dastien was powerful. He had so much more in him than I'd thought. How did he keep it tamped down?

"What's mine is yours and yours is mine. From earth to air to fire to water. Moon and sun. I will be yours to the end of time." Dastien's words rolled through me, and our bond flew open—wider than it had ever been before. All I could see was white as a vision flashed before my eyes.

A man that looked like Dastien, only older, stood before me. His father? I'd seen a picture before. It had to be.

He sat in a field, playing blocks with a little boy, maybe two or three years old. Dastien. He giggled and I laughed, too.

He was so adorable. He must have his parents wrapped around his little finger.

A castle loomed behind them. Bright white stone and a dark black roof with spires reaching up into the sky. Little square windows dotted the outside, almost too many to count.

As they played, a woman ran to them; her long blonde hair flowed down her back like golden silk. She said something in French, and the boys laughed. When she started running back to the castle, the little boy jumped up with a squeal to chase her.

Another wave of Dastien's alpha power rolled through me, pulling me out of the vision. "Knowing what I have to offer, will you accept me and this bond?"

"Yes." I managed to say the word before another flash of white sucked me into a vision.

Dastien was a teenager. His hair was shorter, and his shoulders weren't as full.

He sat in the breakfast nook in Mr. Dawson's cabin. The kettle whistled and Mr. Dawson got up to fill two mugs.

"You have more power than any wolf that I know, but you're young. You have to learn to control it or you'll never be able to leave St. Ailbe's. I won't be able to allow it."

Dastien threw his mug across the room, but Mr. Dawson didn't flinch.

"I'm trying, but I... What am I going to do? Who can be with me? I'm dangerous."

His pain was so deep that it caused a stabbing ache in my heart.

"No." Mr. Dawson leaned across the table. "You're not dangerous."

"But Rupert said—"

"He's wrong, and he's jealous. There will be someone for you. A good match. But it won't be Imogene. She's trying to manipulate you." He crossed his arms, giving Dastien a fierce stare down. "She's a waste of your time. There will be someone for you. She'll be your perfect match. You just have to wait here."

"Wait here? But I'm graduating in two years and I have to decide if I'm bonding with Imogene—"

"No. You're not allowed. As your guardian, I don't approve the match."

With that, Dastien's pain vanished. A slow smile broke out across his face. "You don't?"

"No. I'll get you a cabin. You stay on here and—"

Another wave of alpha power hit me, pulling me back to the present. "With these words the bond is complete. I share all my power with my mate." Dastien's words held power. My soul ignited, and as the bond cemented, I saw so many things. Dastien's life passed before me. I knew him. Things he'd gone through. How he thought. Felt. All his hopes and dreams.

It was interesting and invasive and crazy. There was so

much there that I hadn't been seeing before—that I didn't know about Dastien—and as the visions slowed, I realized how right Dastien was.

We were infinitely more powerful together than we were apart.

Beyond our bond, I felt the pack. The web of ties that linked us all together was much clearer than before. I could draw power from the bonds so much easier with the two of us tied together. Before, it'd been a reach. Now, the pack was just there.

For the first time in a long time, I felt like we could actually do this. We could win.

I blinked as my vision cleared. "Holy shit. That was intense."

He pulled me into his lap. "What did you see?"

I ran my hand through his hair and the soft curls parted, turning into a fluffy mess. "I saw a lot of things. You and your parents at a castle?"

Through the bond, I could feel his heart warming as he thought of it. "Not a castle. That's my house in France."

House? Nope. "That's not a house. That's a fucking castle."

He gave me one of his Gallic shrugs, but I knew he was laughing on the inside. He loved that castle. "Same thing in this case."

That was nuts. People in Los Angeles had ridiculous estates, but that monstrosity of a "house" was bigger than anything I'd seen before. It was something out of a fairy tale. "Then you and Mr. Dawson were talking about you sticking around campus. Not bonding with Imogene. Yikes. I'd say you dodged a bullet with that one."

Another shrug, but this one was filled with regret. "She wanted it to be, but it wasn't right. She'd make me so angry— push my buttons—and back then, I wasn't in control of myself.

It was scary, for everyone else and for me, too. I didn't like who I was when I was with her."

I poked his ribs. "Of course she wasn't right." He laughed as I wanted, and the regret he was feeling melted away. "But I'm glad you're more in control. I mean, throwing that mug? Was that really necessary?"

"I told you it was hard for me before I met you. Before I had you to balance me out. I always had to keep such tight control on myself, and then you came and everything got mixed up again for a bit. And then it got better. So much better."

"Yeah." It was half-word, half-sigh. I didn't want anything to ruin this, but the vision of the church filled my thoughts.

"We're not going to let it happen, okay?"

I guessed he was in my head as much as I was in his. "Okay," I said, even though I knew he couldn't promise that. Neither of us could.

He squeezed my hand. "We're a team."

He'd said that before, but for the first time, it really was true. I was stronger with him. With this bond, I could feel his strength—all the alpha energy he was hiding from everyone pulsed against me—and that made me stronger. I had a partner in all this craziness, and I'd fight to keep him.

I pressed my lips against his and surrendered.

As his tongue brushed against mine, I could feel his attraction to me, and that made me feel the same for him. The feeling snowballed until I was going crazy—needing to feel him. I ripped at his shirt, and the material parted.

He leaned back for a second. "I need you."

"Now."

He nodded, and his nose rubbed against mine with the movement. "Now."

I didn't care that we were outside. That night had fallen. I needed him. Something told me that we were safe out here.

That he wouldn't have brought me here if he wasn't sure of our safety or privacy.

Dastien rolled until I was on my back. His hand brushed my hair aside as he leaned down. His lips brushed against my neck as he peppered kisses up to my lips. The second he deepened the kiss, I got swept away in the moment. In the movement of our bodies.

Waiting for my soul mate—for my mate—was worth it. He knew exactly where to touch and when it was too much. He made me feel like I was flying, and I never wanted it to end. As his hands ran over my body, I wanted more. I was addicted to his touch. With every movement, he owned me that much more, and I was totally fine with it.

We lay there after, sweating, catching our breath, and I knew I was cherished. Treasured. Even if the worst happened, this moment was worth it. It was worth everything.

Because love was worth it.

Always.

CHAPTER SIXTEEN

DASTIEN'S CELL RANG, waking me up from the best night of sleep I'd ever had. *Whoever that is, it better be important.*

"Yeah." Dastien's voice, still thick with sleep, held a bit of rasp to it.

"The alphas have come to a decision. We're meeting in the conference room in ten," I heard Mr. Dawson through the phone and swallowed the lump in my throat. "I need both of you there."

"Okay." Dastien hung up, and I rolled closer to him—laying half across his body. "We have to get dressed." He brushed his hand down my back, sending comfort in its wake. "I have a feeling it's going to be a long day."

I blew out a breath. I sure hoped he was right. Otherwise...

We quickly threw on some clothes and then grabbed a few power bars to eat as we walked to the admin building.

Before we stepped inside, Dastien grabbed my hand. "Whatever happens in there—even if it matches up with your vision—know that it's going to be okay. We might end up in that church, but we know what's coming now. We can fight it. So don't freak out."

I licked my lips as I stared at the door. "I know. Freaking out in a room full of Alphas is probably a bad idea, too."

"Exactly."

I stepped over the threshold, tugging him along with me. "Let's get this over with."

We heard the group inside the conference room arguing as soon as we entered the hall. I glanced at Dastien, and he shrugged.

The pack had been more stable since we'd gotten rid of the dissenters. More peaceful. No more fighting in the quad. The alphas had all agreed to stay put while we planned our next move. Seeing Weres on the news seemed to have ended that truce.

Dastien knocked twice. Before he could knock again, the door swung open.

Donovan stood in the doorway. "Good. You're here."

What is this about? I asked Dastien.

Your guess is as good as mine.

Judging by all the yelling, I should be running in the other direction. Not only was it intimidating, but in my vision, there'd been a lot of yelling.

I wiped my sweating palms on my jeans and stepped into the packed room. A long oval table took up most of the space. I quickly scanned the room. Mr. Dawson, Donovan, Lucas, and Sebastian were the big Alphas I knew at the table. Claudia sat next to Lucas, their hands twined together.

There were two other people that had a lot of power at the table that I didn't know. A blonde lady and a man with ebony skin. The leader of the Cazadores—Keeney—sat on the far left side of the table. He wore all black, his head shaved totally bald. Today he'd added a black blazer to his usual all-black attire. He gave me a little nod.

Meredith sat next to Donovan, but none of my other Were

friends had been invited to the war council. Cosette sat on Meredith's other side, and the relief that she hadn't disappeared for good was tangible. She was the only one leaning back in her chair, looking relaxed as she twirled her hair around a finger, but the dark circles under her eyes told a different story.

Three other alphas sat at the table, but they weren't as strong as the members of the Seven.

Dastien said something to one of them in French, and he answered in kind.

Who's that?

The French pack's Alpha.

Two seats were still open next to Mr. Dawson. Dastien rolled one chair back and waited for me to sit before settling down next to me.

My knee bounced under the table as my nerves took hold. This was looking eerily similar to my vision.

Donovan stood at the head of the table, commanding the room. "Thank you for coming, Tessa. You know most of us here. Though you've not met Lisabetta or Jackson." He motioned to the two unknowns. "They're two more of the Seven. We have Blaze and Muraco on the conference line as well."

"*Hola, chica,*" Muraco's voice came through the black speaker in the center of the table.

"Hi, Muraco," I said, hoping that I didn't sound too nervous, but that was a pipe dream at this point.

"The others here are the Alphas of the Canadian, French, and Eastern European packs."

"Nice to meet you," I said, wondering when the shoe was going to drop. The last time I'd been in front of this many alphas, I'd been on trial.

"We've got quite the situation on our hands." Donovan moved to the TV and my gaze shifted to the images behind him. Someone at the station had had way too much fun picking the worst possible images out of the police footage, and they scrolled past in a terrible montage.

The wolves looked terrifying on-screen. Teeth bared. Faces frozen mid-growl. Circling and slashing with their claws.

Then Cosette flashed on-screen. They'd slowed down the moment her sword materialized and the freeze frames showed her gracefully lunging through the air, glowing a pearly white shade that wasn't anything close to human.

Finally, my face appeared. My hands were full of glass vials and my skin looked pale. Afraid. Probably because I had been.

I'd seen the footage yesterday, but that didn't make it any easier to watch now.

"We can't undo what's been seen. For the last twenty-four hours we've been discussing what our next step should be, and Cosette advised us to bring in a human element before we come to a final decision. As someone who was once human, but is now of our world, we're hoping you can provide some insight."

Everyone began shouting at once. The room got so loud, I couldn't distinguish one voice from another. It was as if the air was suddenly thick and hot to breathe in. I reached up to tuck a piece of hair behind my ear, but noticed my hands were shaking and hid them under the table. *This was part of the vision. It's happening...* I said to Dastien.

Even if this part is happening, it doesn't mean the rest will. I haven't had an Orangina or broken any kind of bottle, right? So, the visions aren't necessarily connected.

That made me feel a little better, but not much. I'd rather have *nothing* from the visions happen.

"Some of those here want to go back." Donovan's commanding voice brought me back to the discussion. "They want to pretend this didn't happen. Cover it up."

Everyone looked at me like I had some magic answer. I pressed my hands against my thighs as I thought. "I don't think that will work. I mean, humans aren't stupid. The video speaks for itself."

"I still think we could play it off as a hoax," the Canadian pack leader—Joseph's dad—spoke up. "My son is a huge movie fan, and the effects they have these days are amazing."

"What do you think?" Donovan said. "Can we make this disappear? Will humans believe it's some sort of a stunt?"

I looked back at the news. The footage was a little grainy, but not *that* grainy. "This is just my opinion..." I wasn't sure why it mattered what I thought, but I guessed I was the only human—or former human—they had access to.

"Go ahead, *chica*," Muraco's voice came through the speaker. "They need to hear what you think. That is why you're here."

I cleared my throat. "I think it's too big. The cops had families. I guess Cosette could wipe their minds and whatnot, but it's too much. So many people saw it on TV, or knew people who were personally affected by it. It's already too late to get rid of the video. Once it's online, it lives forever. And you want to come out to the humans eventually, right?"

"Aye," Donovan said.

"So, say you somehow manage to cover it all up. You find every human that saw the witches drop dead at the movies and the Whataburger, and every person that was in contact with the cops. The rest of the humans buy the story that this was just a well-constructed hoax. It becomes a legend. And then, five years down the line? Ten years? You decide you want to go public. This will come back. They'll realize you lied to them. That you tricked them. Why should they trust you then?"

"But would you not say this already looks bad?" Lisabetta's accent gave her words a pleasant singsong cadence, even with the hard subject matter. "We burned many homes and disposed of bodies. It is bad, no?"

I couldn't deny that. "It's bad."

"See?" She threw her hands in the air. "You see? This is why we must cover it up. She agrees."

"She didn't say that," Jackson said.

"You think we should cover it up, no?" Lisabetta's command brushed against my skin, but I shook it off.

What do I do? I asked Dastien. She's doesn't want my real opinion. She wants me to agree with her.

Tell the truth. That's all you can do.

Yeah, but the truth was going to get one of the Seven pissed at me. "I don't know."

She growled.

Dastien reached over to hold my shaking hand. Lisabetta was making me nervous. More so than any other member of the Seven I'd met. "I know that's not what you want to hear, but you could make the case either way. The only fact I know is that this mess—" I waved to the TV. "Humans won't forget this. Maybe we can outlive them, but you'd need to wait at least another... I don't know fifty, seventy years, maybe more before coming out. And with today's technology, it'll only be a matter of time before another video crops up. What then? Another cover-up?" I paused. "I'm not sure what your plans were, but you'd have to wait a long time and make sure nothing else happens between now and then, or else this cover-up will come back to bite us. And it won't be pretty."

"She is biased." Lisabetta wrinkled her face with a look of disgust. "Her father has spoken with her."

What was she talking about?

"Tessa," Donovan said. "Have you spoken to your father in the last day?"

"No." I winced. I probably should've checked in with him. "Not since we left the compound."

"See. She doesn't smell like a lie," Mr. Dawson said. "And

before you say that she could be hiding her scent, she doesn't know how. She's too new."

At this, everyone started talking at once again. The voices rose until Donovan slammed his hand on the table. "Enough. We've delayed too long already. What we need is someone to talk to the press. It can't be me or Michael. We shifted on camera, makin' us one of the monsters. But we have to make a statement—one way or the other—and we have to decide on that right now. The crowd at the gates is growing restless, and I'm not sure how much longer we can peaceably hold them off before they break in." He paused. "So we vote. Those in favor of *not* covering up this incident, say aye."

A chorus of ayes answered. Only three of the alphas—the Canadian, French, and Eastern European ones—and Lisabetta —stayed silent.

"Right. That settles it. Thank you for your thoughts, Tessa. We'd been evenly divided until now."

Wow. I'd actually helped? "Of course." This hadn't been so bad.

"Now, we just need to decide which of us is going to speak to the press."

"I will do it," Lisabetta said.

"No," Muraco's voice fuzzed through the speaker. "You were against this. You'll paint us in a bad light."

She growled. "I would not. I am insulted that you would say such a thing, Muraco. After all this time?" She tilted her chin up in the air. "Not only am I one of the Seven, but since I do not agree with this plan, I'm the only one who would say what was necessary and no more."

Yikes. That seems like a bad idea.

Agreed. But I'm not going to be the one to tell her.

Me neither. You think if we keep quiet, they'll forget we're here. Or better yet—do you think we could sneak out?

I wish. We'd better stay until we're dismissed.

So, I settled back in my chair and waited. The voices rose, and once again it was too much. I couldn't pick out the voices when everyone was so loud. I tried to focus on what was going on, but after a few minutes I gave up.

And then someone kicked me.

I glanced around the table, and Cosette motioned to me, nodding her head to the side.

What, I mouthed the word.

She nodded her head to the side twice. More sharply this time.

I don't understand, I mouthed. What the hell was the side nod about?

The room stopped.

Mr. Dawson's voice cut above the din. "Yes, Tessa. Do you have something to add?"

My heart sped up. Nope. This was from my vision. And I definitely had nothing to add.

I shook my head, keeping my mouth firmly shut.

Cosette kicked me again. Harder this time. She nodded her head, and it was then that I realized she was motioning toward the TV.

I sat up.

You do it, she mouthed at me. She kicked me again, and pain radiated up my leg. If she kicked me one more time, she was going to get a taste of her own medicine.

She pointed at me again, and before I could think, words were rolling out of my mouth. "I could do it?"

I froze. Suddenly everyone was staring.

Motherfucker! I screamed through our bond. I didn't actually suggest that, did I?

His heart was racing. *You did. I can't believe you just offered that up.* There was more than a hint of growl to his voice, and I didn't need to be able to feel his emotions to know he was pissed off.

It was Cosette's fault! She kicked me and then her nodding. And then she pointed... And everyone was looking at me. I can get out of this, right?

"I think that's a fine idea," Donovan said with a big grin. The glint in his eye made me think I'd just been royally played. They'd set me up. He'd wanted me to volunteer all along.

A chorus of "I agree" and "Yes" and "Seconded" rang through the room.

All except Lisabetta's gang of four.

I sighed. What had I gotten myself into?

Donovan crossed his arms. "I know this isn't your cuppa, but you're the only one of ours who maintained a human shape in the video. People have been calling and asking about you. You've got a human record, and they might have no reason to trust you yet, but they'll hear you out."

Someone knocked on the door just before it opened. Dad stepped through, wearing one of his ubiquitous suits. His hair was still damp, but combed into place. "It got quiet in here. Have you made a decision?"

Donovan nodded. "I was just thanking Tessa for offering her help."

At first I was thrilled to see Dad. I knew he'd get me out of this. I just knew it.

Then he grinned. "That's my girl."

I couldn't help the wince of betrayal. He knew I didn't like being in the spotlight. "You want me to do it?" I said the words slowly, so as not to be misunderstood.

"I know it's not what you want, but I think this is the best way to go about it. Believe me, I want to protect you from this, but it's already happened and the media knows who you are.

The phone at the house has been ringing nonstop. Your mother finally unplugged it."

"Shit." The word slipped out before I could stop it. "No one's called my cell phone."

"It's unlisted, but that won't stop them for long." He took a breath. "The other option would be to hide, but this isn't some Hollywood scandal that will blow over in a week. This is a major upheaval in society and we don't want people to panic."

"Agreed," Donovan said.

"Agreed," Mr. Dawson echoed.

I bit down on my lip to keep from trying to argue my way out of this. *I just made our life so much harder.*

Dastien squeezed my hand. We're never going to have a quiet life. There's always going to be something. But remember what I said. You and me—together—forever. We can get through it. As long as we're a team. You might be the spokesperson, but I'll be there with you. Whatever you need, I'm here for you.

I nodded. I can't believe I'm agreeing to this.

I think you'll do great at it.

I shot a look at Dastien. The boy had lost his mind. Clearly. "So, Dad. You got a speech for me?" If I knew my father, he had this all planned out, and the notecards to prove it.

"Of course." He patted his suit coat pocket.

Good thing. I had no plans to go off the cuff announcing to the world that werewolves were real.

"About this speech." Cosette lifted a hand.

"Finally speaking up, eh?" Donovan's brows rose. "You weren't half as eager to answer our questions earlier."

She shrugged. "I don't like questions. I do have a statement though."

Really? I leaned forward in my chair and I wasn't the only one. Cosette had been helping us much more than expected, but she still wasn't very big on volunteering information.

"You're not to mention the word fey in this speech or any other contact with the humans."

That seemed extreme. I knew now that the fey had more magic than I'd thought, but they couldn't hide from the humans forever.

"Is that a threat?" Mr. Dawson's voice held a hint of a growl.

"Not mine." Cosette flattened her hands on the table. "I'm to tell you that the fey have no plans to announce themselves and if they're outed without their consent..." She wrinkled her nose. "Let's just not go there."

"What if they ask what you are?" I *could* lie to the reporters, but I wasn't sure what I'd say.

"I can go back to playing a witch if that's easier for you." Cosette glanced at Claudia, who hadn't said a word this whole meeting. I needed to talk to her again and check how she was getting through all this. "But my advice is that you speak for the Weres and *only* the Weres. Anything else is asking for trouble."

I nodded. "That seems reasonable." I barely felt right speaking at all, let alone trying to talk about witches or fey, or anyone else. Just to be sure, I turned to my cousin. "Is there anything you want me to say, Claudia?"

She jumped, grabbing her hands to her chest. "No... I..." Lucas squeezed her shoulder and they shared a look, him projecting confidence and love, before she continued. "I wouldn't feel comfortable speaking for the other covens, but Luciana was my coven leader..." Pain flashed across her features, but determination quickly replaced the hurt. "I trust you to speak for the few of us who are left. I know you'll make this about her without trying to paint the rest of us as villains. We can't have this ending in witch hunts."

My throat suddenly went dry. This was *a lot* of responsibility. But as I glanced around the table...

Cosette couldn't speak for us. She could barely speak for

herself. The members of the Seven I trusted most had all been caught on film, and I definitely didn't trust Lisabetta to talk about the witches in a positive light.

It had to be me. The realization made my heart pound, but it seemed too late to turn back. "Are we doing this now?" My voice only cracked a little.

"After you change." Dad gave a pointed look at my clothes.

I glanced down at my outfit—skinny jeans and an old Nine Inch Nails T-shirt. It was one of the first ones I'd screen printed. It had the downward spiral image on it. I figured after this morning, it was pretty apt.

"What's wrong with this?" I felt comfortable, and if I was going to do this, I should feel comfortable. Right?

"Teresa. A dress."

"Yes, sir." I gave him a little salute.

Donovan walked around the table to clasp my shoulder. "You're going to do great. I know you will."

Yup. Everyone had lost their minds today.

I turned to the other alphas. "It was nice meeting all of you."

"I'll go with her, if that's okay," Dastien said.

Mr. Dawson gave a small nod. "Probably best. Otherwise, I think she might run off."

"Pretty valid thought," I muttered, but all the Weres heard me and laughed.

On that note, I headed back to the dorm with Dastien. I dug out my one sundress, which had little yellow flowers on it, and slipped on a pair of sandals. Good enough.

I quickly put my hair up in a ponytail. I hadn't used any make-up since I'd gotten to St. Ailbe's, but I put on a little concealer, mascara, and lip gloss. If I was going to be on camera, I might as well look nice.

I exited the bathroom and held my arms out. "Well? How do I look?"

"Beautiful," Dastien said.

"Good answer. Otherwise, I'd have to hide under my bed for the rest of my life."

"Let's go. Get this done."

I nodded. "Yep. Rip this whole situation off. Like a Band-Aid. 'Cause it's gonna suck."

Dad was waiting for us in the dorm's common room. A few people were hanging out, watching the TV and snacking, but the talking stopped when I came in.

I really, really hated when that happened. And after today, I was pretty sure that would happen everywhere I went for a long time. "Please tell me there's time to practice this little speech?"

"Of course. Let's go back to the conference room."

"How's Mom taking all of this?" I asked as we headed outside.

He blew out a breath. "She's upset. She knew a lot of the people who died, even if she'd been out of contact with them for a long time. It still hurt her."

I hadn't even considered that. "I'm sorry."

"She'll be okay. Your brother wanted to come today though. I told him it was probably best if he stayed away."

"Why should he stay away?"

"I know that you can do this, that you're strong and can handle it. But this is going to be a circus, and I can't promise that some of these people won't act out. Your brother wouldn't handle that so well. He's spent his childhood protecting you, but he can't do that anymore. Not from this."

"I guess that's true. Sometimes I wish I could hide from all of this. Go home—" I looked back at Dastien, walking behind us, and then back at my dad. He worked hard to stay fit, but the worry lines were there. "But I can't. I'm different, and officially an adult."

"No. You'll always be my baby girl. You never get too old for that. And you're only a few weeks past eighteen. I'd hardly call that adult."

It was weird, him not knowing about last night. That I'd basically gotten married without him there. Without any of my family around.

Do you regret it?

Not for a second.

We can always have a more traditional human ceremony.

That would be nice, but it seems silly now.

We'll do it, but you have to tell Meredith.

Crap. I hadn't even thought of that. When I'd gotten ready for the ceremony last time, she'd helped. She'd been so excited. I should've told her what we were doing, but there hadn't been time. I hoped she wouldn't be too upset.

When we got to the conference room, Mr. Dawson, Donovan, Sebastian, and Lucas were having a hushed conversation in the corner. The rest of the alphas were gone, but Meredith, Chris, Adrian, Shane, Raphael, and Claudia were huddled together reading a newspaper.

"What's going on?"

Chris moved over so I could read the headline. *Eight Families Murdered By Monsters.*

Why had no one mentioned this?

Mr. Dawson separated from the group in the corner. "It just hit the news. There were a few gruesome murders around three in the morning last night. They weren't far from here—about thirty minutes away—in the outskirts of San Antonio." He paused, and his jaw ticked. "They're being blamed on werewolves."

That was stupid. Werewolves wouldn't hurt humans. Not unless they were defending themselves. "But they're not—"

"No." Donovan cut in. "These remains look like the policemen's."

The truth hit, and I sat down hard in one of the chairs. "Demons."

Luciana wouldn't... But obviously she had. I couldn't be totally surprised, but what did she stand to gain from that? Was she letting innocent people die just to make the Weres look worse?

"The crowd outside has grown. We've set up a podium and lectern just inside the gate. We'll let them in, you read the speech, and then there'll be time for questions. I'll be there with you, in case you're unsure how to answer. And if things get too heated, we'll cut it off."

This was getting better and better.

Dad handed me a small stack of notecards. I skimmed the words, and then looked up. "You can't be serious."

"It's okay," Mr. Dawson said. "Everyone has agreed on the content. It's time."

I blew out a breath. "If you say so..."

I spent the next hour going over the words. It wasn't a long speech, so I had it almost memorized by the time Dad called. In a daze, I walked to the gates with Dastien. The alphas and everyone else trailed behind us, but my thoughts were distant.

Whatever happened next, everything was about to change.

CHAPTER SEVENTEEN

AS SOON AS I stepped onto the podium, cameras started flashing. I could see through the flashes, but they still startled me. I nearly froze, but pushed myself to keep moving. I placed the now slightly crumpled piece of paper on the lectern. No less than ten microphones were attached to it, and I had to suppress the urge to tap on them while saying something like "Is this thing on?"

I laid down my notecards, spreading out the first few across the surface. Dad had said to focus on something above their heads, but all I saw were signs. Some were nice. Things like "We <3 Weres!" Others said some things that were not so nice about wolves and hellspawn.

A group of people stood behind me. Classmates. Cazadores. My friends. And Dastien.

You can do this, he said through the bond.

I took in a breath and prayed I didn't fuck up too badly. "Thank you for coming today." My voice wobbled and I cleared my throat. "I know the footage you saw was shocking." My hands shook, so I gripped the sides of the lectern. "You might also be shocked to know that werewolves have been around nearly as long as humans."

I couldn't believe I was here, telling the world these things. I forced myself to look up, over the crowd. "And, since they're a long-lived race, most of the people you see here—those all in black, and those behind me—have fought in many American wars. Including the one for our independence."

The silence among the crowd was eerie. Only the sound of camera shutters competed with my voice. "Werewolves have been protecting humans for centuries. Name a monster, and it most likely exists. Vampires. Demons." The card said pause, so I took a moment and then started again. The words were coming easier now.

"Our leaders have been planning to come forward, but we're extremely sorry that our presence had to come to light in these circumstances." I paused again, preparing for the hardest part. "Not everything that happened that night made it onto the video. The compound you saw is where the local coven of witches has made their home for the past fifty years. They lived peacefully within our community until their leader, Luciana Alvarez, turned to dark magic. Now Luciana has committed an unforgivable crime by murdering her coven and summoning demons into the world."

Some people shouted questions.

"I know this might sound crazy. Believe me, I didn't know that any of this existed until a few months ago. That's why I'm the one speaking to you today. I was a normal human girl until a few months ago when I became a werewolf. I've been where you are, and I know more than anyone what an adjustment this knowledge can be.

"But the pack is trustworthy. They've been protecting you without hope or desire for recognition or fortune. They would've stayed in the background, content to protect us from afar, but this time the evil is too great. If you saw the recent news from San Antonio, you know about the attacks. Those were not werewolf attacks. Those were demons.

"Luciana Alvarez is out there somewhere, and she's extremely dangerous. We're working with the police to bring her to justice, but we are coming forward to warn you and make sure that you have the facts. For your safety, please stay indoors after dark. If you see one of these monsters..." I held up the drawing Chris had sketched, "run. Do not engage. The officers who responded to the compound shot the demon many times, but bullets won't harm this type of monster. We've found that you'll smell demons before you see them. If you catch the rotten-egg smell of sulfur, take that as your warning to leave wherever you are and call the authorities."

I paused again. "It is our only wish to continue a peaceful existence, protecting you from monsters such as these. It is the pack's dearest hope that you will welcome us as part of your society, as we've already lived among you for a very long time."

I folded up the piece of paper, gathered up the cards, and turned to Mr. Dawson. He gave me a little nod. "I'll now answer some questions."

Everyone started yelling questions at once, and I had no idea who to call on. Dad came to stand next to me. "You first." He pointed to a reporter in the front.

"You said you didn't know any of this existed until a few months ago. What happened?"

Thank God Dad had prepared me for the likely questions. "I met my mate." The reporter waited for me to say more, but I wasn't going to volunteer anything more personal than that.

Dad pointed to someone else before the guy could think of a follow-up.

"How exactly did you become a werewolf?"

I'd been hoping for more questions about Luciana, but I

guessed that wasn't happening. "My mate changed me into one." We'd agreed that any mention of biting would open up a can of worms we didn't need right now, and I was technically telling the truth. Dastien *had* changed me.

After that, the questions came fast.

"Do you like being a werewolf?"

"Yes."

"Can you change forms?"

"Yes." From the way everyone waited after I said the word, I knew they wanted more from me than just yes, but I wasn't sure what else to say. They were going to be really disappointed if they were waiting for a demonstration.

"Can you think like a human when you're in wolf form, or do you truly become a wolf?"

"I can think."

"Would you ever attack a human?"

This was a tough one. I thought for a moment before speaking. "No. Not unless I was defending myself. We can all think and process information no matter what form we're in."

"Who was the girl with the sword?"

I wasn't touching that one. "She's a friend of the pack."

"But—"

"I can't speak for her. She enjoys her privacy." And any lie I gave could get me in just as much trouble as telling the truth.

"Do you have sex with wolves?"

What the hell kind of question was that? "No. I'm not into bestiality. Are you asking because you are?"

Dad cleared his throat. "My daughter is still in high school. Let's try and keep the questions appropriate to that age."

There was some tittering from the crowd.

"You said there were demons on the loose. Do you know how many? And what do we do to protect ourselves?"

Finally. Someone with a question I could deal with. "I don't know how many, and until Luciana is apprehended, it's safe to say she can keep calling them up. So, stay at home after dark. Keep your doors locked. And pray."

"That's not very reassuring."

"I wish I had something better to say, but I can only hope that she's found quickly."

"Why is Luciana doing these things? What's her motivation?"

I shrugged. Like I knew. The best I could come up with was her wanting more power, but she had plenty of that now. The latest attacks seemed like a plot to make the Weres look like villains, but beyond that, I kept wondering what her grand plan was. The destruction of all Weres? A world run by witches? Who knew at this point?

"Why does anyone do anything bad? Why do rapists rape? Why do murderers kill people? I don't know."

Dad gripped my shoulder and moved me gently out of the way. "That's all we have time for right now. Thank you."

The shouting drowned the rest of my thoughts as I stepped down from the podium. The reporters all pressed toward the barrier we'd set up. Only one person moved in the opposite direction. Raphael pushed through the crowd on his way back to campus.

I reached out to Claudia, and pulled her close so she'd hear me over the roar of the crowd. "Did I upset him?"

"I don't know. I wouldn't think so, but he's... He's not himself. He's been through a lot."

"Should I go after him? Apologize?" Although for what, I had no idea.

"No. Let him go. He'll be okay." The last sounded more like a question than a statement.

I understood. If it were my brother, I'd hope for the best, too. Still, as I watched the crowd part for him, I wondered if there was something more I could be doing for him. If there was something I *should* be doing for him. He'd been through so much already. But I couldn't think of anything that would be helpful.

Luciana had a lot to answer for. She'd destroyed her coven. Her family. Murdered so many people. It had to stop. And soon.

We had to find her before she killed anyone else.

CHAPTER EIGHTEEN

AFTER THE PRESS CONFERENCE, we grabbed food and headed to the labs. Now that we'd dealt with all the human drama, it was time to get to work. I had my messenger bag of stuff from Luciana's craft room to show Claudia, and she had stuff from Peru to show me. If she'd brought back whatever she used to cure Raphael, then it was probably something that could help us against Luciana and her demons.

Hope blossomed that we might *finally* have a way to take her down.

Claudia, Adrian, Shane, Raphael, Cosette, and Dastien gathered with me in the lab. I hadn't seen Beth since she found out about the coven, but I assumed the others were checking on her. The rest of the Weres were on guard duty. Dastien should've been with them, but he didn't want to be apart from me today, and I sure as hell wasn't going to argue. Although with Luciana on the loose and the ever-growing mob at our gates, they needed everyone they could get to keep the tension from boiling over.

Claudia placed her purse on the raised lab table. It clanged against the metal top. "All the objects I brought back from Peru are pure, white magic. They're potent, and I *think* they can be used to fight Luciana. The trick will be how we use them."

She pulled out the items one by one. The first was a bunch of tiny bundles of braided white hair. Next came a severed shriveled hand. A few days ago, that would've totally freaked me out. But after what had been done to *La Aquelarre*, one hand was no big deal. And it was loads better than the jar of eyeballs.

Then a ring with a seal on it came next. And last, a knife. Claudia arranged everything on the table before pulling out the last item. "This is the most interesting piece."

She held up a gray crystal. It looked like one of those cheap polished rocks they sold at rest stops. "Are you sure? I was thinking that hand was kind of the winner."

My cousin grinned. "I guess you're right, but the crystal killed a demon."

Now she had my attention. I took the crystal from her, but I didn't feel one lick of magic. "Are you sure it was the crystal? Not your own magic?"

"I'm sure. I think I used up all its magic when I stabbed the demon with it. It used to glow, like it was lit from the inside with a pure white light."

I laid down the crystal. "That would've been too easy."

Cosette touched the crystal and her eyes narrowed. "Can we get more of them?"

Claudia nodded and hope blossomed. "But it's a long trek. I'm not sure we could get someone there and back in time."

"How long could it really take?" I asked. "You got back to Raphael so fast. If we send someone the same way, it shouldn't be a problem."

She mumbled, mangling her words so much that even with my hearing, I couldn't understand what she said.

"What?"

She cleared her throat, but wouldn't meet anyone's gaze. Instead, she stared at the crystal. "I made a bargain with a fey to get me to Raphael."

Cosette jerked, knocking the crystal onto the floor. It skittered away, but everyone stood frozen. "I thought I expressly told you *not* to do that."

"I had no choice." Claudia rubbed her hands together. "My brother's life was on the line."

Energy vibrated off Cosette and I realized this was the first time I'd ever seen her angry. It made me worried for Claudia. By all accounts, fey could be tricky. Even saying thank-you could lead to bad things happening. Making a bargain could be deadly.

Cosette muttered fey curses as she picked up the crystal and then plunked it on the table. "What were the terms? Exactly as they were stated. And *who* did you make this bargain with?"

"I gave him a favor of his choosing—"

"No you didn't," Cosette's voice was so cold, the sound made me shiver. Claudia was definitely in trouble.

"There were terms..."

"What terms?" A wave of energy spiked from Cosette and she was definitely casting off a glow. "Do you even know what court this fey was from?"

"Cosette," I said. "Calm down."

Raphael cleared his throat. "I know that what my sister did might not have been the best thing, but I was dying. If you're worried about her, know that I'm willing to pay the price. Especially if it's something that could harm her."

"No!" Claudia hit her brother's shoulder. "It's my debt to pay."

"No. It's *mine*." Raphael crossed his arms as he stared down at his sister.

"Argue all you want." Cosette rubbed her temples, but at least she'd stopped glowing. "It doesn't work like that."

"It doesn't matter. I made the deal and I'm prepared to go through with it." Claudia pulled a chair to the table and sat. "We agreed that I wouldn't do anything bad or evil, or kill or hurt anyone. He also agreed that he wouldn't hurt or kill me or anyone I love. He can't steal my magic or bind me to anyone. If I have to go somewhere for the favor, Lucas comes with me. And whatever he asks can't override the agreement between the wolves and the fey."

"Mother of..." Cosette scrunched her eyes tight. "Give me your hand."

The deal sounded pretty airtight to me, but I kept my mouth shut. I wanted to see what Cosette would do.

Claudia offered her hand. Cosette took it gently and then closed her eyes, muttering something in her language. The seconds drew out as Cosette did... I wasn't really sure what she was doing, but when she finally let go, she pressed her forehead to the table. Her thick curls hid her face, but they didn't muffle her voice. "If this is a test, it's not funny."

We all exchanged glances. It looked like I wasn't the only one who couldn't tell whether this was seriously bad or if Cosette was just being dramatic.

Claudia broke the silence. "I made the deal and whatever I have to pay, it was worth it to save my brother." She shook her shoulders, as if she was physically pushing the tension away. "What matters now is how are we going to defeat Luciana?"

"I managed to salvage some books and things from Luciana's house before it was burned." I started unloading my messenger bag, piling the books and things on the table beside Claudia's relics. "In our defense, we had a bunch of dead bodies—including police officers. We couldn't just leave everything as it was."

"Right." The word was clipped. "That doesn't really help me as my whole life has been burned."

A wave of guilt had me hunching my shoulders. I should've been firmer about waiting. With the police footage leaking, destroying the compound hadn't even done any good. "You're welcome to stay here as long as you like."

"And the pack will help you relocate," Dastien chimed in. "Buy houses for each of you. We'll make sure you're not homeless and left in the lurch."

"That would be appreciated," Shane said. "I'm not sure where we belong now, but I'm not above taking some charity." He crossed his arms, showing off his tattooed biceps.

"We wouldn't do that to you," Adrian said. "The pack burned down your homes to hide our actions. It's standard that we'd put you up and help you."

If I hadn't been watching for it, I wouldn't have noticed the way his arm gently pressed against Shane's side. Adrian caught me looking, and I quickly turned my attention to Raphael. If Adrian wanted to have a secret, then that was his choice, but I hoped he'd confide in me when we finally had a quiet moment.

"How are you doing?" I asked Raphael.

"I'm okay. How are you?"

He was playing it tough, but I knew from experience what going up against Luciana was like. She'd taken something from me, too. "Doing better than before, but a brush with true evil leaves its mark." I paused. It probably wasn't the best time to bring this up, but if I didn't say something now, then I didn't know when I'd have the chance. "I upset you at the press conference."

He shook his head. "No."

Maybe I was being too sensitive, but I really felt like I'd said something to hurt him. "But you walked away..."

"You don't understand Luciana and why she's doing this."

"No." I shook my head slowly. "I don't. At first, I thought it was about the wolves, but now... I don't know why she's doing any of it. What's the point of attacking humans in San Antonio? It makes no sense." I blew out a breath. "Do you have any thoughts?"

"A few."

I motioned my arms wide. "Please. Anything could help."

He pulled over a stool, and sat down. "Sorry. I don't have all my energy back yet."

That sucked. I'd only recovered quickly from being drained because I was a Were.

"The thing you have to understand about Luciana is that she's not a strong witch—not on her own—and she never was. Yet, she was next in line for the coven because of her visions. She saw the future in her dreams, but it was always vague. Dream visions are never all that reliable. The waking ones get you closer to the truth." I briefly wondered if what I'd seen counted as a dream vision or a waking one, but Raphael kept talking before I could process. "Luciana kept seeing visions of war. She talked about them all the time. How she saw the wolves fighting us. She never saw the setting. She never knew the context. But she started gearing up for war."

I knew some of this already—about her weak visions—but hearing it now that I'd experienced the vaguer side of the future, it was as if the proverbial lightbulb had been lit.

"We weren't going to fight you," Dastien said.

"Now that I know you and I've been around the pack, I figured as much, but we didn't know before. Some of us thought she was being crazy and ignored her, but not everyone did. Those who believed her thought war was coming and started making preparations." Raphael leaned against the table for support. "Looking back, it seems obvious. For all I know, what she saw was the coven attacking the pack, not the other way around."

"Which has already happened." More than once.

"Exactly. The vision she was so afraid of could've easily been about the night that Daniel died." Raphael shuddered, and I wondered if he was remembering the attack. "But the vision consumed her. She became obsessed with it. Only it was a self-fulfilling prophecy. A few years ago, she changed. She did something and the light in her eyes was just gone. I don't know what it was—"

"I do," Claudia said. "She got some kind of charm or artifact from my ex-fiancé. His coven had something evil, and they were protecting it. Luciana only pretended to marry me off so she could get access to that object, although she never planned to really let me go."

"*That's* why?" Raphael sounded shocked.

"You didn't know this?" I asked. They were twins. I thought they shared everything.

"No. It's news to me." Raphael crossed his arms as he glared at his sister. The look on his face told me that he wasn't the least bit pleased by it either.

"I found out in Peru," Claudia said. "It's a long story. None of that matters right now. All I know is that he exchanged something for me, and whatever it was, it was bad. Really evil."

"That's messed up," I said.

"No kidding," Shane said. "How did your parents let that happen?"

She shrugged. "They were gone."

"Right." Shane winced. "I'm sorry. Stupid question."

"It's all right," Claudia said. "The point is, that was what changed Luciana. I won't—can't—defend her at this point, but after casting so much black magic... I just wonder how much of the original Luciana is left."

I didn't like where this was going. I'd seen visions of Luciana calling out to Satan and just by the look of her craft room, she'd been doing those kinds of spells for years. It wasn't a stretch to imagine that power consuming her. But she'd been in control in my nightmare vision, standing over that mouth of hell ...

Tapping on the table as I thought, I kept going back to Raphael's words. Now that the witches I trusted most were back on campus, it was time to get their opinions on what I'd seen. Dastien tensed beside me before I even opened my mouth.

"I've *seen* some things... Before we go any further, I think you should know what we might be up against. I'm starting to think this might be bigger than just her vendetta against the pack."

"What did you see?" Raphael asked.

I told them every detail I could remember, only leaving out the fey guy. I had a feeling that would set Cosette off again, and we needed to stay focused.

When I was finished, I sat on a stool. "So, we're in for quite a fight. Unless you think we can change it?"

"Yes... And no." Raphael was being completely annoying with his ambiguous answer.

"What do you mean?" I tried to keep the frustration out of my voice, but didn't do an awesome job of it.

"It means we'll probably end up in that church, but how we get there and the outcome could vary," Claudia said.

Dastien grasped my shoulder so hard it hurt. "See. I told you."

Raphael nodded. "The future is never set in stone. Destiny might put you in that spot, but it's up to you to choose what you do when you get there."

"Okay." I took a few breaths as that sank in. "Okay. So, we'll probably get to that point, but we can change things once we're there. So, we make that happen."

At least there was hope.

"We will definitely try to make sure that your vision ends a different way. But to do that, we need to be even more prepared, and we have to figure out where she's hiding out." Claudia sat up tall on her stool. "I tried to scry for Luciana, but I'm coming up with nothing. She must be somewhere that's heavily warded, so we'll have to find her some other way. In the meantime, we should start brewing potions to fight against her demons. From what I know, the veils between this world and the next are thinnest between three and four in the morning."

Wait. That actually lined up with what'd been happening. "That's when the demon killed those families last night. And when the demon crossed over in Luciana's house. But I thought it was because the cop crossed the circle."

Shane shrugged. "Could've been a happy coincidence. Or the demon could've been waiting there since the night before. I don't know what spells she used."

Right. None of us did. "Why that time in particular?"

"It's the witching hour. Not that I appreciate the name. But that's when ghosts, demons, and black magic are the strongest. So we need to be ready by that time tonight in case she's up to something tonight." Claudia motioned to the objects in front of her. "I'm not sure how to use all this, so there are no dumb ideas. And the books you brought back will certainly help. If any of them talk about summoning, then maybe we can use the spells to reverse engineer some counters."

I cracked my knuckles. "I'm so in for this. I'm tired of doing nothing. Let's take her down."

"Agreed," Raphael said.

We divvied up the books and artifacts. Dastien and Adrian started digging into the spell books while the *brujos* started pulling supplies and equipment from the storage closet.

We were done sitting around, waiting for Luciana to come to us.

For once, we were going after *her*.

And when the time came for us to meet in that church, I *would* be ready. I'd finally take Luciana down.

Because there was no way I was letting that vision play out. I had a future I wanted and, by God, I was going to fucking get it.

CHAPTER NINETEEN

IT TOOK SIX STEADY, brutal hours of mixing and baking and cross-checking spell books, but we ended up with ten variations of potions, each vial labeled with a number so we could weed out the ineffective ones. I'd suggested we modify my original potion using holy water and the saint's hand, but Claudia had multiplied it. She said holy oil would work much better than water. She disappeared for an hour and came back with this oil that smelled like heaven.

We took a break for dinner while the potions cooled in the lab, and decided the only way to test them was to try them out. Luciana had released demons last night, so chances were she might do the same tonight.

Mr. Dawson hadn't liked it, but he also hadn't been able to come up with a decent argument against it. If Luciana summoned any demons tonight, we were the best equipped to fight them. That was saying something about how unprepared we all were, but the fact remained the same. We couldn't idly stand by while humans were slaughtered again.

So, we dressed all in black and jumped into two of the huge black SUVs reserved for the Cazadores. We didn't have a destination in mind, but headed toward San Antonio and hoped that I'd at least get a feeling if I drove.

We ended up wandering aimlessly for hours. I tried to relax and keep my mind open, but nothing was coming.

I drove one car. Dastien sat in the passenger seat, and Chris, Shane, and Adrian were in back. Donovan drove the other car with Meredith, Cosette, Raphael, Claudia, and Lucas.

It was three in the morning. If something was going to happen, it was going to be soon.

"I'm starving," Chris said from the backseat. "We should definitely stop at Whataburger."

"How can you be hungry again?" Shane said. "You packed a lunch. How much can one Were eat?"

"More than you'd think," I said.

"Where does it all go?" he asked.

"If you figure it out, let me know." I took a turn down a residential street, weaving through the blocks. All the house lights were out, which was to be expected at this time of night. We hadn't come across many people. It seemed like the locals were taking my warning seriously.

I drove slowly, keeping an eye out for anything out of the ordinary. If something was going to happen, I wasn't getting any visions of it. At least not yet. The windows were rolled down so we could listen—and smell—for trouble. It was a little chilly, but nothing that a sweatshirt couldn't handle.

"Food," Chris moaned from the backseat.

I would've rolled my eyes at him, but I was starting to get hungry, too. "If we don't see anything in the next hour, we'll go to Whataburger."

"Do you see that?" Adrian pointed out the window.

I sped up, catching movement down the block, but laughed as we pulled closer. Two kids a little younger than me were making out on the lawn. A bike lay on its side on the pavement in front of them. The skunkish smell of pot drifted through the open window.

Teenagers... I said to Dastien.

You only just turned eighteen.

But I feel at least thirty. I feel like I get extra maturity points for all the shit I've gone through.

True.

The girl started to push at the guy with a whimper, and I almost got out of the car.

"Might want to head inside," Dastien called before I could do anything. "It's not safe out here."

They jumped and broke away from each other. The guy shot us a dirty look. "Fuck off."

Dastien flicked on the dome light, and they froze.

The girl grabbed the guy's arm. "She's that werewolf from the news."

"Just your friendly neighborhood werewolves." I motioned to the house. "Go home. Being outside at this hour isn't safe." And not just because of Luciana and her demons. Nothing good happened at three in the morning.

"Of course. Thanks." The girl seemed more than grateful.

The boy grabbed his bike and took off, and I waited as she scrambled up the lawn and went inside. She waved from the door.

This was good. I'd actually helped someone tonight, and that felt damned good. I waved and went back to coasting down the street. "Well, that was fun." Donovan had stopped behind us, but he followed as I turned down another street of sleepy houses.

Shane grunted. "Focus on your abilities. You have to harness them to find where the action will be tonight."

"What do you think I've been doing?"

"Nothing useful," Shane muttered.

I jerked the car to a stop and twisted to look at him. "Not cool. And you've got years of *brujo* practice on me. Where are all your brilliant suggestions?"

He stared at the ceiling for a second before meeting my gaze. "Sorry. It's not your fault. I'm just feeling antsy."

"I know it's been a really shit week, but let's try to hold it together." I hit the gas and tried to take my own advice. A note of sympathy passed through the bond and I glanced at Dastien. *You've been awfully quiet.*

I'm not sure how to help, Dastien said.

I tapped my fingers on the steering wheel. *Yeah, me neither.* If we were close to Luciana, I wasn't sensing anything. No magic. The night was quiet. *Maybe she's still lying low.*

No. She's got power to spare. She's not going to sit quietly by. Not anymore. He was quiet for a second, but I could feel his thoughts, like gears turning, clicking by as he saw them and dismissed the ones he deemed unworthy. *She's already started trying to make us look bad. I doubt anything's stopping her from doing more of that.*

If she's feeling vindictive... I chewed on my lip. Who was I kidding? It was Luciana. She was always feeling vindictive. *She'll try to get us where it'd hurt the most.*

But St. Ailbe's is too well protected. Everyone's already on alert.

Exactly. I was missing something. Something big. Last night, she'd let her demons tear through a few residential neighborhoods. Eight families were dead before the sun rose. She'd made the point that she could get the humans where they slept. They weren't safe in their own beds.

I thought of those families and hurt for them. I couldn't imagine the pain their loved ones were in. If something like that happened to my—

Fuck.

No. She wouldn't go after...

I swallowed as the realization sank in. No. She totally would.

Where the hell was I? We'd been wandering for hours. I slammed on my brake.

"What's going on?" Chris asked as Dastien's cell phone started ringing.

"You really think—" Dastien started but cut off when I shot him a look.

"Yeah." It was the most horrible thing I could think of, so why wouldn't Luciana try it?

My hands shook as I tried to work the navigation system. I needed to get to my parents' house. Now.

"Please proceed to the highlighted route," the robotic voice said, and I gunned it, taking the turn so fast I thought I might flip the SUV.

"The guards are still on my parents' house, right?"

"Of course. I'll find out who's on duty." Dastien punched the buttons on his cell. "Hey, Gill. Who's on the McCaides tonight?"

"Let me check." Rustling sounded through the phone like the guy was flipping through papers. "Shit. It was supposed to be Rory but he left with the others. I'm sorry. I don't know how this got overlooked."

I slammed the steering wheel. "You've got to be fucking kidding me."

"Send a team in *now*," Dastien growled. "We're on our way. We might have a situation." He ended the call. "They're okay. Don't worry. We don't know anything yet." Dastien tried Dad's cell, but he didn't answer. Neither did Mom. With each ring tone, my anxiety rocketed.

"Shit." My heart pounded, and I ran a stale red light. No one else was on the road in small-town Texas at this hour.

Donovan's headlights shone in my rearview mirror. If what I thought was going to happen was happening, then we all needed to get there. Five minutes ago.

"We'll get there in time," Dastien said.

"What about your brother?" Adrian asked. "He texted me to check on you after the press conference. He was thinking of coming down, but I don't know if he did."

That's right. Dad had told him not to come, but if Axel wanted to come home, he was home. He didn't always listen to our parents. Especially when it came to me. He was my first friend. For a long time, my only and best friend.

Dastien pushed his number, and my brother answered on the forth ring. "What the fuck, Tess? It's after three in the morning."

"Are you at home?"

"What?" He still sounded half asleep.

"Wake the fuck up. Are you at home?" I paused, but only for a split second. "Now. Answer me now." If he wasn't, then I was going to have Dastien keep calling my parents' phones until one of them answered or I got there.

"Uh." I could almost see him rubbing his eyes. We shared the inability to wake up quickly. We both needed a second to adjust, but we didn't have that now. "Yeah. Shit. Sorry. Yeah. I came home after class. I saw your press conference. I wanted to see you. Make sure you were—"

Thank God. "Go wake up Mom and Dad."

"No way in hell. Mom is a beast when she gets woken up."

True. But not tonight. "Wake them up. Then go downstairs and get the big canister of salt from the pantry. Bottom shelf on the right." I couldn't hear him moving. "This is life or death, Axel. I'm on my way, but you have to fucking move. It's three twenty-nine. I have a feeling when the clock hits three thirty, you're going to have some nasty visitors. You've got less than sixty seconds and no time to run." I put as much force into my voice I could. "Move fast."

"Shit. You're not fucking with me right now."

"*Jesus fucking Christ*, Axel! Does it sound like I'm fucking with you right now? This is not a joke. Move it!"

I heard the sheet rustling. "Mom! Dad!" He pounded on their door. "Wake up! Shit's about to go down."

The sound of his feet's hammering steps echoed through the phone. "Salt. Salt. Salt. Shit. I don't see the salt."

"Bottom shelf. On the right." That was where Mom always kept it.

"It's not there."

I took a breath. "Then she must've moved it." Where would she have put it? "Look on top of the fridge. Or beside the stove."

"Got it! What do I do? Shit, Tessa. I saw the news footage. Please don't tell me—"

We didn't have time. "Go into Mom and Dad's bedroom and pull their bed into the center of the room." The stairs squeaked as he ran back up.

"I'm putting you on speaker." The phone clattered. "We've got to move the bed."

"You're going to have them do a circle?" Shane asked over my family's talking.

I glanced at him by the rearview mirror. "Unless you have a better idea?" I hoped he had something more, but if not, this would do. For now.

"No. That's pretty solid. If they had some holy water or something—"

The sound of furniture squeaking along the hardwood floors filled the car.

"I have holy water," Mom said.

There was a huge bang, and Mom yelled, "What was that?"

The clock on the dash read 3:33. My stomach bottomed out.

"It came from downstairs. I think it's here," Axel said. "We moved the bed. What now?"

"Use the salt to draw a circle around it. Do *not* leave any gaps. Make one full circle and then go around again to make the line thicker. Mom and Dad, you get on the bed."

"How far away are you?" Axel asked.

"Five minutes," Dastien said. "Maybe less. She's driving as fast as she can."

My hands sweated as I gripped the steering wheel. I was already doing 80 in a 35 and I'd go faster if I thought I could handle the turns without killing us all.

"What's that smell?" Mom's voice confirmed my fears. "Oh my God. What's that smell?"

Shit. I was too late. "Axel. Are you done?"

"Not yet."

"Finish it. Now. Then get on the bed."

"Okay. Okay. Just need one more second. I've got one circle, but it's super thin. Going around—"

"There's no time. That smell is the demon. You better be drawing that circle from inside!"

Mom's whining scream sent chills down my spine.

"*Tsk. Tsk. Tsk.* No more."

The line went dead.

"Whose voice was that?" My voice sounded too airy, even to my ears.

"Stay calm. I'll call again," Dastien said.

This time, the call went straight to voice mail.

We hit a straightaway and I gave the car more gas. Whatever the speed limit was supposed to be now, I didn't care. My family was on the line. They didn't have magic. They had no weapons. And they couldn't heal like I could.

If something happened to them...

Dastien called Axel over and over again, and the sound of his voice mail message echoed in my ears.

It took forever to get there.

I screeched into the driveway, threw the car in Park, and jumped out. Donovan and his group weren't far behind us.

Dastien moved fast, tossing me my bag of vials as we ran into my house. The door hung off the top hinge and the screen was shredded.

Mom's prayers carried down the stairs and I took my first breath in what felt like hours...

Then I heard the hissing.

I climbed the stairs three at a time, only slowing before hitting my parents' room. Clutching a vial, I was ready to throw as I stepped to the doorway.

And froze.

Mom, Dad, and Axel huddled in the center of the bed, watching a figure slam itself into the salt circle. Mom was clutching an icon and rosary in one hand and throwing holy water from a small container at it with the other.

The demon ran at them again, and then bounced back, like it was hitting a wall.

If not for the sulfur burning my nose, I might not have noticed the figure was a demon.

It looked like me. My hair in a ponytail. Wearing the sundress with yellow flowers that I'd worn to the press conference. But the eyes...

Its eyes were two solid red orbs.

It hissed, and a wave of demonic energy rolled over me, making me dizzy. I gripped the doorframe. This one was *much* stronger than the last demon, and if I let it, it could suck the soul straight from my body.

Or my family's bodies.

I lifted my vial of brew number two as I entered the room.

Dastien was at my side and the others slipped into the room behind us.

"That thing doesn't look anything like the last one," Chris said.

"This one's a major demon," Cosette said. I didn't turn, but I hoped she had her sword ready back there.

"Mistress wants you dead." Its head tilted to the side as it studied each of us. Assessing us.

"Feeling's mutual." I said a prayer and threw the vial, but the demon didn't flinch as it shattered. "Shit. Twos are duds." Clinking sounded behind me as the *brujos* readjusted.

It swiped off the black sludge dirtying the sundress, and then shot me a look of pure rage that had me stumbling backward.

"We need more room to fight."

It slowly inched forward, as its red gaze darted among us.

I wasn't sure why it hadn't attacked yet, but that wasn't going to last. Once it was done assessing what we were and how to kill us, it was going to.

I backed out of the room, not wanting to turn around, but we needed to draw it outside. Not everyone could fit in my parents' bedroom. We were going to need everybody in this fight, and I wanted that thing as far away from my family as possible.

It started to move faster. "Run," I whispered.

The wolves heard and everyone else followed them. I quickly backed to the stairs—not wanting to turn my back to it—and then it leaped at me.

I jumped to the bottom of the stairs in one go. My hands touched the floor as I landed. The demon scrambled after me, knocking picture frames off the wall. It lunged, almost slashing my ankles, but Dastien grabbed me, tossing me out of the house.

A boom sounded as it tore through a wall. We only had a few seconds before it was on us again.

Cosette stood ready with her sword, and this time her skin was definitely glowing. "This one will be faster than the other. Get ready to try the new potions."

Adrian, Donovan, Meredith, and Chris had already shifted. Claudia waved her hands over them, drawing a few glowing knots. The saint's ruby ring glimmered on her finger. "I hope this will keep the demon blood from burning you."

Shane and a pale Raphael stood shoulder to shoulder. Shane held his first and middle fingers out, ready to flick some spell. A bead of sweat ran down Raphael's face, and before he stumbled back a step I had a moment to wonder if we should've left him on campus.

As I dug out another vial, Dastien's change ripped through our bond. Claudia drew another knot, and I felt her spell wrap around him.

Shaking off drywall dust, the demon appeared in the doorway.

"Stop!" I threw all my will in to the word. All I had to do was freeze it, and we could end this before anyone got hurt.

It stopped moving and I let out a breath as I turned toward Cosette. "It worked. Hurry and—"

Panic surged to me from Dastien, but that was the only warning I got.

A heavy weight fell on me, drowning me in choking sulfur. I hit the ground, and only just managed to get my hands up before the demon tore out my throat. Its claws flayed my side, and I screamed. The cuts burned like fire licking my skin.

Wolf-Dastien rammed it, and suddenly the creature's weight was gone. The wolves surrounded it, slashing out, but unlike the lesser demon, this one wasn't taking damage. Any hits the wolves landed just made it more pissed. I couldn't tell if

Claudia's spell was working because they couldn't make the thing bleed.

Raphael picked me up off the ground, and it felt like my side was being torn apart. The heat of the pain spread down my leg. We had to end this. Fast.

Claudia and Shane's hands moved rapidly. A burst of magic rippled through the air, but whatever it was supposed to do to the demon didn't work.

Cosette landed a few slashes, and *finally* a little blood oozed out. It coated her blade like dark sludge. The demon barked something and black flames erupted. Cosette shrieked, dropping the sword as it went up in a puff of ash and smoke. Her fingers were blackened, but she made a motion, conjuring a crossbow. "That one was my favorite."

My vision blurred at the pain in my side, but Dastien's strength rippled through the bond, giving me just enough power to steady myself.

He moved in front of me, protecting me as I grabbed everything I had in the bag. I'd lost potions three and seven when the demon hit me. I still had vials of five and nine.

"With the power of our Father, the Son, and the Holy Spirit, I banish you from this world, and send you back where you belong." I put all the force of my will into the words, believing them to be true. *Needing* them to be true.

When the glass shattered, the spell exploded. I hit the ground hard. The pain from my side stole my breath, but I knew I had to get up. I managed to get to my knees.

The demon's yellow dress had a blackened hole in the chest. Steam rose from it, but the damage wasn't enough to slow it down.

The wolves jumped back, but Cosette stayed on her feet, landing bolt after bolt in the demon's body. Her crossbow reloaded itself and her bolts hummed with magic that made the thing's skin sizzle and crack. It roared, lunging for her. She danced away, still shooting, but it moved too fast for her to get a kill shot.

"Keep distracting it!" I called. Trying to ignore the pain growing in my side, I hobbled to the other witches.

"Is that all?" Cosette laughed as she fired another bolt.

Shane, Claudia, Raphael, and I brought out every vial we had left. We surrounded the demon as Cosette darted around, keeping it blind. The wolves circled, driving it away from us with flashes of fang and claw.

Dastien stayed near me. He swatted the demon any time it got close to me, funneling power to me through our bond.

I met the gaze of the *brujos*. We'd talked about this in the lab. All of us would say the spell together.

"On zero," I said. "Three. Two. One."

We flung the vials and then said the words as we held out our hands. Magic flared between each of us to the others, creating a circle of light, and the vial exploded inside. The demon's shriek held a hint of my voice as it started to turn black. I winced until the sound choked off. Finally it was quiet as the demon turned to ash.

A fathomless hole crackled open, sucking the remains down into the fiery pits below.

I collapsed to the ground, breathing heavy. Blood soaked my shirt, and I wasn't sure how much longer I could stay conscious.

Hang on. Dastien yelled through the bond. I felt him running back toward the cars, as I stared up at the night sky.

I smelled lavender just before Mom's arms wrapped around me. I stifled a gasp at the movement as pain rippled through me. Sweat rolled down my back, and it wasn't just from exertion.

"You did wonderfully. Your *abuela* would be so proud."

I closed my eyes and rubbed my cheek against her arm. "I love you."

"I love you, too. So much." She let go. "My God. You're bleeding."

"I know." Everything looked blurry as she pulled away. "I'm going to need that holy water."

Dastien ran back from the car with a gym bag. He ripped the rest of my already shredded shirt off. "Shit. It took me twelve hours to heal the little spot on my back." I didn't bother looking. I could *feel* the cuts and whatever poison was in them working into my system. Seeing them would only make it worse.

My mom raced back. Her hands shook as she offered the bottle of holy water to Dastien.

He took it and looked at Raphael. "All of you will have to hold her down."

Strong hands on my arms, legs, and shoulders pressed me to the ground, but all I could see was Dastien. His eyes glowed bright amber. "Just breathe." And then he poured the contents of the bottle into my wounds.

My back arched off the ground as I screamed. The holy water felt like liquid fire, burning me from the inside out.

I screamed and tried to get away, but the hands held firm.

"It's still foaming. We need more."

"No," I moaned. "No more." I wasn't sure I could take it.

"I brought some. One second," Claudia said.

The sound of the zipper opening on Claudia's bag startled me. I closed my eyes, and then the hands pressed me down again. I wasn't sure how long the burning went on. It felt like eons, but was probably only minutes.

When it eased a little, I asked, "What now?"

"I'm done." Dastien brushed the softest kiss on my forehead. "I'm going to wrap it. It should heal okay now."

I nodded. He was gentle but it still hurt.

When he finished, I was exhausted, dirty, hungry, and thankful to be alive.

Mom's voice sounded at my side. "Come into the house. We'll get you something to eat." She started to get up but stopped. Her head bent over as she shuddered.

"Are you okay?" I asked.

Tears glistened in her eyes. "I've got both my kids here. Healthy and alive. I'll be okay."

"Okay." I tried to move, but any movement and it felt like I was splitting in two. Dastien leaned down, picking me up. Even that had me moaning with pain.

We passed Raphael, Shane, and Axel, who were already trying to fix the front door. The others had gone off to shift and put on clothes.

This was a victory. No one was hurt. Except me, and I'd live.

As Dastien carried me toward the door, I peeked over his shoulder at my parents' driveway. A dark spot marred the dirt. We'd only faced one major demon and it'd taken all of us to do it.

How in the hell were we supposed to fight more than one at a time and live?

Cosette stood off to the side, not glowing anymore, but playing with her blackened fingertips. I hoped it wasn't anything serious, but if she wasn't making a big deal of it, then I wouldn't either. She caught me looking and tilted her head at the charred spot. For once I was positive we were on the same page.

If being in that church was inevitable—destiny, like Raphael said—then we were going to need some bigger guns. Because this wasn't going to cut it.

Dastien set me on the kitchen counter then went in search of Oreos. Only eating my own bodyweight in cookies was going to help ease this kind of realization.

That and maybe two gallons of ice cream.

CHAPTER TWENTY

WE GOT BACK to campus as the sun rose. Exhaustion and a touch of pain made it hard to keep my eyes open, but hope coursed through me.

There was plenty to worry about, but as we walked back to the dorms—still coming down from our adrenaline high—we were united in friendship. Were. Witches. Fey. We'd fought a battle as one, and lived.

Sure. My side was still burning, but it'd heal. And if I thought about everything we still had to do, it seemed like an impossible feat. But looking back at how far I'd come—how far *we'd* come—it was impressive. Our potions needed some beefing up, sure, but before I left to stay at the compound, the were-wolves weren't the least bit friendly with each other. And the fey... But now we were fighting together. That felt like a victory. Maybe a small one, but it was enough for now.

Dastien and I followed Meredith and Donovan to the dorms. There was no way I was walking all the way back to Dastien's cabin—no matter how much I wanted the privacy. The term "dead on your feet" had been taken to a whole new level tonight. This morning. Whatever day it was.

Donovan showered first. When he was done, I took a quick one. Meredith was sitting on my bed when I was done. "You went through with it, didn't you?"

Dastien raised an eyebrow and motioned to the bathroom. *I'll give you a moment.*

I almost laughed. He didn't want to get in trouble for not telling Meredith. She always had a knack for seeing right through Dastien and me. "Yeah. We did."

She swatted my shoulder, and I winced. "Sorry! But I *knew* it. Something was up with you all day. You have to tell me everything."

"Sure. When I'm not so tired, and the guys aren't listening in."

"Girl time is needed. ASAP."

"Agreed." It seemed a little too good to be true that she wasn't upset with me over this. "You're not mad at me?"

"That you didn't tell me it was happening?" She shrugged. "A little, but I get it."

"Are you going to do the same?" I asked. "Before the battle?"

She glanced at the bathroom door.

What are you two talking about? Dastien asked.

Girl stuff.

He grunted. How much longer you need?

I dunno. A couple minutes? Maybe more. And no listening in!

He chuckled. I'll do my best.

"I don't know," Meredith said. "Donovan wants me to meet his pack. They have this whole elaborate ceremony in Ireland, but now... I don't know why we're waiting."

"This fight... I mean that thing nearly ripped me in two. If just one was hard, how are we going to fight more than that?" I blew out a breath. "I'm scared."

"Me, too." Meredith slouched down on the bed. "But we'll get her." The shower shut off, and she stood up. "I'm happy for you. You deserve a big slice of happy in all this crazy."

"Thanks. So do you."

She sighed. "I know. I'm just afraid what his pack will do if he comes back with some random chick. He was kind of a player back in the day and there are a bunch of she-wolves over there that are going to be pissed."

"When the time comes, if you want me to go with you to Ireland, I will. You've had my back and I will totally have yours."

"You've had mine, too." Meredith squeezed my hand. "I haven't forgotten what you did for me."

I shook my head. "That was no big deal." A little curse seemed like nothing compared to what we were dealing with these days.

"It *was* a big deal." She gave my hand a quick squeeze as the bathroom door clicked open. "'Night." She whistled at Dastien, who was still glistening from the shower and wrapped in a towel that was a little too small for him.

"Goodnight, Meredith." He gripped the knot of the towel as she slid past. Probably wise. His face was flushed when his gaze met mine. "We need to get you out of this dorm."

I laughed. "Or get you slightly bigger towels. Wouldn't want anyone sneaking a peek at my goods."

He grinned. "Your goods? I thought they were mine?"

"It might be your body, but it's mine, too." He jumped onto the bed, and suddenly I wasn't all that tired. "Just be careful. I'm wounded."

"I'll be really gentle." He lowered to brush a kiss on my lips, and grinned. "Very, very gentle."

I WOKE WITH A START, unsure what was going on.

"Who is it?" Dastien's voice rang out.

"It's Teresa's father. You have five seconds to get your ass dressed and out of my teenage daughter's bed," my dad's voice rang out on the other side of my door.

Oh shit, I said to Dastien as I pushed him out of bed. The movement ached along my side, but nothing like the pain from a few hours ago.

We'd put on clothes to sleep in—you never knew what was going to happen living in the dorm—but still, this was more than a little disconcerting. With my side still aching, it took me a second to pull a sweatshirt over my head. By then, Dad was pounding on the door again.

"Don't make me break it down, Teresa Elizabeth McCaide."

Shit. He three-named me. I checked that Dastien was fully dressed before opening the door. Dad was bracing to knock again.

He pushed past me. "What in the hell is going on here?"

I swallowed. "Dad..." I had no idea what to say. Not even the foggiest.

He knew this was coming, remember? We're not doing anything wrong. He faced Dad. "I know this must be difficult, but we talked about the bonding before, Mr. McCaide."

Dad crossed his arms. "Right." I was a little relieved to hear that from him, but the word was clipped. He was still angry.

But we'd been over this. I knew Dad wasn't happy—he'd made that known at my birthday party—but I'd hoped that he was over it by now.

"Tessa and I completed our bond two nights ago."

Dad's jaw ticked. "I thought that wasn't until the full moon."

Oh shit. Dad smelled like the sharp tang of anger. You think we should've waited until he wasn't so pissed to tell him?

Keeping it from him won't solve anything. "When Claudia returned fully bonded to Lucas, we learned it was possible without waiting until next month." I had to give it to Dastien, he was staying really calm, even while Dad was giving him the ninth-degree stare down. "I'm sorry we didn't tell you sooner, but with everything that's been going on, there's not been a lot of time. I hope you know that I love and respect your daughter more than anything or anyone in the world."

Dad ran his fingers through his hair, and it stood on end. "So basically my only daughter is married and I had no idea about it."

"Sorry." I winced. "We were thinking of having a wedding later."

His face told me exactly where I could stick that idea.

"Okay. I should've warned you. This isn't the best way to find out about us, but Dad—you knew this was going to happen after my birthday. It got delayed. That's all."

He rubbed a hand down his face. "I know. I just—when it didn't happen—I thought maybe it wouldn't. That you'd have more time being a kid. Go to college. All those kinds of things."

"I can still go to college. Once all this craziness is dealt with." Not that going to college was even on my radar at this moment. Anything beyond the fight with Luciana felt like a million years away.

"We'll talk about this later. I'm sure your mother and brother are going to want to know, too." He blew out a breath. "The FBI wants to talk to you."

Cops were one thing. I didn't like them—they made me totally nervous even when I hadn't done anything wrong... Except show up in a place with a few dozen dead bodies. But FBI? That was big time.

"Am I in trouble?"

"No. I think this is more curiosity than anything else."

"Why don't they talk to Mr. Dawson? Or Donovan? Or anyone else who's not a total newbie?"

"That's why they want to talk to you. Because you're new. They've already talked to Michael and a few others, but you're the one from the news, so they want you."

I tried to take a little bit of comfort in that, but nerves were still creeping in. "Okay."

"Get changed and dressed. I'll wait for you in the common room." He waited for a second, glancing from Dastien to me and back again.

Dastien laughed through the bond, but his face was a mask of seriousness.

You're not helping. I stepped past Dad and opened the door. "I'll be right down." He nodded and left without another word.

I closed the door and leaned against it. "Was it just me or was that super awkward?"

"It wasn't just you."

Laughing came from Meredith's room. "Yeah. Laugh it up, you two. Just you wait. I know your brothers' phone numbers. And your mother's. I can get them down here in no time for an awkward encounter of your own."

"My parents are happy about this. They're Weres. They were expecting me to pick a mate years ago."

She was right. They'd been super happy when Donovan claimed Meredith as his. "Damn it. Why am I always the newbie?"

"Because you *are* the newbie."

I strode to my closet. The hangers scratched the rail as I searched for something to wear.

What exactly should one wear when being questioned by the FBI?

Something that made me look as innocent as possible. I'd

worn all my dresses, so I picked a pair of dark jeans and a floral printed blouse. Anything I didn't have to pull over my head was a win. My side needed time to rest and not have me pulling on it.

I dressed as quickly as possible, sparing time for Dastien to redress my cuts with a fresh bandage.

"Do you want me to come with you?" Dastien asked me as I buckled my sandals.

I glanced at Dastien. "Is that an option?"

He gave me one of his trademark Gallic shrugs. "Might as well try. Worst they can do is not let me in the room."

I went back to the closet, dug out one of his button-downs, and tossed it his way. "Well, then you're coming with me."

Once he was ready, Dad escorted us to the conference room.

The two FBI agents sat at the opposite side of the table.

They rose together, and I knew they'd probably done this a lot. Except maybe not with werewolves.

"Tessa, these are Special Agents Ramirez and Morgan."

Ramirez had to be the short Hispanic agent. His navy blue suit hung a little baggy on him, but I could tell he had a reasonably fit body underneath. Not Were-fit, but fit enough. Morgan was a petite blonde. She seemed overly friendly with her megawatt smile, but something told me she wasn't all warm and bubbly.

At least I already knew which was the good cop and which was the bad.

"I'm sorry, but we only want to question Teresa," Special Agent Morgan said.

Yup. Not warm or bubbly.

I thought about arguing, but that seemed like a bad idea. Definitely not the first impression I wanted to make.

I'll be right outside, listening in, Dastien said as he brushed a kiss on my cheek. You need me, I'll be back. No matter what they want.

Thanks.

Dad nodded. "We'll be right outside. If you need me for any reason, I can come in as counsel."

"As we told you earlier, your daughter isn't in any trouble." Agent Morgan placed her folded hands on the table. "There's no reason to worry."

I tried to take that to heart as I settled down into one of the tall-backed leather chairs. I wheeled myself closer to the table and sat up straight. My side throbbed at the movement, but Dastien had been right. The wounds were already scabbed over. By tonight, they'd be red marks at most.

"We've talked to some of your fellow pack members." Ramirez said "pack members" like it was a question. "But we wanted to speak with someone who wasn't born into this world."

I nodded. I wasn't sure how much they knew, and unless they asked I figured silence was my best option.

"So, what do you think of the werewolves?" Agent Morgan asked.

That was an incredible vague and open-ended question. "They're fine. Some I really like. Some I don't. Just like anywhere else."

"And the witches?"

Where were they going with this? "The same. There are some here that I really like. Others, not so much."

"That's pretty honest," Ramirez said.

That wasn't a question, so I kept my mouth shut.

"Do you like being a wolf?" he asked.

I let out a sigh. "Right now, that's like asking if I like being short. It doesn't really matter because that's what I am, but I guess I know what you mean. It was hard at first, but I'm pretty okay with it. Running as a wolf is really freeing. And having enhanced abilities isn't a chore either."

"So you *can* change?" Morgan said.

"Of course." I didn't know that was in question.

"But you didn't the night you fought the demon?" Ramirez asked.

"I'm not the best fighter when I'm furry. I'm more of a help when I fight with magic."

"That's right. Mr. Dawson mentioned that you were special in that you come from a long line of witches."

I guessed I didn't mind that he'd told them, but it was a little odd that they'd been discussing me. "Yes. On my mother's side."

"So the wolves can't use magic?" Ramirez asked.

I thought about it for a second. True, they weren't as good as the witches, but they didn't totally suck at it either. They did their best with their metaphysics classes. "I wouldn't say that they can't do magic entirely. The pack is its own kind of magic. Not the same as what the witches have, but that doesn't mean it doesn't count."

"I see. And what kind of magic do you practice?" Morgan asked.

I raised an eyebrow. "I don't know. The good kind?" It seemed like an important distinction to make when Luciana was out there.

That got Morgan to smile. "Could a human use the magic that you use?"

Wow. Morgan had been quiet, but now she was blowing my mind with the tough questions. "Honestly, I don't know. I mean, I guess there's got to be a little bit of magic in us all, right?"

"And what about Ms. Alvarez? What are your connections to her?"

I tried to keep a look of disgust off my face. "I have none."

"Mr. Dawson has told us a little about the grudge that she has with the pack, but we'd love to hear it from your perspective. Why is she really killing people?"

God. If I only knew. "I was asked this at the press conference, and I don't know how much my answer can change. I mean, you must deal with this a lot. People do bad things all the time. Beats me why they do it." That was part of it. "But if I had to guess, it started out as her being afraid of the pack."

"So the pack started it?"

"No!" Shit. That's not what I'd meant. "No. Not at all. She's been acting out over the past few years. Some of my friends used to hang out with the coven members our age. But a few years ago, that all changed."

"How?"

I wasn't sure I should be answering this.

It's okay, Dastien said through the bond. Go ahead and tell them. Meredith won't mind. They need to understand how bad Luciana is.

Okay. But if she gets mad, I'm saying you told me to tell. "Luciana found out her son was hanging out with my friend Meredith. She cast a spell on Meredith that almost killed her. She's okay now. I broke the curse. But ever since then, the pack and coven have been estranged. When Dastien bit me, she took that as a personal affront and an act of war against the coven."

"Why would she do that?" Ramirez asked as he rested his forearms on the table.

I licked my lips. It was like with every new question, I was digging myself in deeper. At some point, I needed to just shut my mouth. "I was supposed to be the next coven leader."

"But you told us you had no ties to her?" Morgan asked.

"I don't. I never met her—or knew anything about being the next coven leader until recently." I paused as I thought about what I should say next. "This is all really complicated, but it boils down to her vendetta. And to be quite honest—I think it's driven her a little mad. Raising demons?" I blew out a breath. "She's crossed into extremely evil territory. Stopping her before she hurts more people is imperative."

"And how do you plan on doing that?" Ramirez asked.

"Honestly? I have no idea." Wanting to end this before I spilled any more pack secrets, I leaned forward. My side pinched with the movement, and I ignored it. "Can I ask you a question?"

Special Agent Morgan nodded. "Yes. Of course."

"What do you want from me?"

"You're very straightforward." Special Agent Ramirez leaned back in his chair.

I didn't think he did that because he was afraid of me, but I wondered... "It's been a really rough few days—as I'm sure you're aware. My father woke me up from only a few hours of sleep to come talk to you, and I just want to know what's going on. Am I in trouble?"

"No. Not at all. We've talked quite a bit to Mr. Dawson, and we understand what's going on with Ms. Alvarez."

Okay. Then, what was I doing here? "So, what do you want from me?"

"Basically, we'd like to have you as a point of contact."

A point of contact? "But I'm only eighteen. I'm sure Mr. Dawson or one of the other Alphas would love to be your point of contact."

"I've given my information to others, but I'd really like to form a relationship with you. You're eighteen. That's an adult in this country. You're part-witch. And, although Mr. Dawson mentioned that you only very recently had contact with any other witches, you managed to save some from Ms. Alvarez.

That tells me that I can trust you to do the right thing, even when it's hard."

I wasn't sure that was true, but I wasn't about to contradict him.

"You're also part-human from your father's side, which means you can understand what the general public is going through right now. Because you were bitten, you—of all the werewolves in this world—have a unique perspective on the supernatural world."

When he put it that way... "I guess that's all pretty accurate."

"Good. We wanted to interview you so we can get to know each other. As with any relationship, there needs to be a level of trust. We want you to trust us—to feel okay coming to us—when problems like those with Ms. Alvarez come up. In the interest of starting on good terms, we're going to pretend that your pack didn't break all kinds of laws while covering up a major crime, but next time, we won't. So, let's not have that happen again. If something comes up, we'd appreciate a call." He made it sound nice, but his voice had a distinct "or else" tone to it. He pulled out a business card and scribbled on the back. "That's my cell number. If something happens—especially when non-supernatural people are around—I want a call. No more burning houses to the ground."

I swallowed. They had a big point. We should have been in big trouble. Not that that had been my idea, but I wasn't about to stick it on Dad. Not to the FBI. "Got it. No more covering up crime scenes." Shit. Did I just admit to something bad? "Not that I was a part of anything like that."

Agent Morgan grinned. "We're aware."

My hands were sweating as she stared me down. "Can I ask you another question?"

"Sure."

"Which one of you is Mulder and which is Skully? Because you both seem very Mulderish with your blind belief in all of this stuff. It took me a while to come to terms with it, and I was a Were. I couldn't ignore it for long when people were shifting in front of me—when my own body wanted to shift. I had to adjust, and quickly."

Agent Morgan's smile broadened, and this time I thought it might be genuine. "Just as you said. No one gets to be skeptical when there's proof in front of you."

"Right." I guess that was true, but I'd had issues with it for weeks when I first got to St. Ailbe's. It took me a while to finally give in and let myself shift forms.

"And if we ever have any questions, we want you to be available to us," Morgan said.

I swallowed. That didn't sound too terrible, but I had a feeling it was going to be more complicated than that. "Okay." Wait a second. "Don't you need my number?"

Agent Ramirez grinned and it wasn't the nice one that Morgan had given me a second ago. The twinkle in his eye gave him an air of mischief. "We're the FBI, Miss McCaide."

That was totally creepy.

I took that as my cue to leave, and slid away from the table while the agents leaned in to talk to each other. Dad and Dastien approached me as I closed the door.

"Well," Dad said. "Is everything okay?"

"I think so."

"What did they want?" Dad asked.

I held up the business card. "Apparently, they wanted a contact. And they wanted to make sure I had their info in case something comes up. Some people—" I coughed to muffle FBI. "—frown on the whole let's-burn-everything-down-before-the-cops-get-here attitude."

Dad shrugged. "Seemed like a good idea at the time."

I snorted. "I still can't believe you showed up with gasoline. It's like I don't even know you."

"You know me as your dad. There's a whole other side."

I raised my eyebrows. "Really? Does Mom know about this side of you?"

"You'd be surprised what your mother knows."

Gross. "You're blowing my mind, Dad. I'm totally telling Axel."

"Well, there's no need for that."

I laughed. "There's definitely a need." Dastien had been awfully quiet. *Was everything okay out here?*

Yes. We sorted some stuff out, but it's okay now.

My cheeks heated and I started for the exit. "Now that all this excitement is over, I'm going back to bed. I only got—" I grabbed Dad's wrist and checked the time. "—three hours of sleep. I can't function on that."

"I thought you might want to go to the lab. Work on the potions."

I rubbed my eyes. "I probably should." He had a point. I was already awake. A couple cans of Diet Coke would probably fix me up. At least for a little while. "Okay. I just need to get out of this blouse—" I didn't want to spill something on it. It was the nicest one I owned. "—and then we'll head to the labs."

"I'm going to check on the agents," Dad said. "I'll come see you before I go." He pulled me in for a hug. I ignored the pain in my side and let myself hang on to him for a second before pulling away.

"See you later," I said.

"Yeah." He seemed sad as I walked out the door.

"Are you sure something didn't happen while I was in the room?" I asked.

"He realized his daughter was grown up." Dastien looked over his shoulder. "I think it must be a hard thing."

I glanced back and Dad was still there in the doorway, watching us. I waved, and he held up his hand in answer.

Funny. I didn't feel grown up. But Dastien was right. Things had changed. Starting the second he bit me.

I was never going to be able to go back home. I'd just realized that sooner than Dad.

CHAPTER TWENTY-ONE

I WAS PULLING on my favorite pair of comfy jeans when someone started knocking. I jerked, but my side barely twinged. At least my wounds were healing fast. The knock came again.

"What's with today?" I couldn't even change in peace.

Dastien laughed as he tugged a T-shirt over his head, and I stopped to stare at the ripple of muscle along his stomach.

Chérie. His voice rumbled through the bond.

The knocking started again. "Right. Right. The door," I muttered. "Who is it?"

"Claudia and Lucas."

I rushed to finish dressing. None of the witches had ever come into the dorms. I spared Dastien a second to make sure he was fully clothed before opening the door. "Hey. Everything okay?"

Claudia looked up and down the hall nervously. "Can we come in?"

I moved aside. "Yes. Of course." My bed wasn't made. I usually made it first thing, but the whole FBI thing had thrown me. "Sorry for the mess. It's been an interesting morning."

Claudia still wore the same clothes from last night—her

khaki skirt was wrinkled and her peasant shirt had a stain that smelled like coffee on the front of it. She held a thick, black tome out in front of her as she stepped across the threshold.

"Are you okay?"

"Yes. At least, I think I am. I just couldn't sleep. I close my eyes and—" She shuddered. "Anyway, I went through the books you brought back." She set the book on the floor. "I don't want it to touch where you sleep."

"Thank you." That was really thoughtful of her.

I sat next to her on the floor. Lucas stayed standing. He was in track pants and a T-shirt—which seemed to be the only thing he'd packed. At least as far as I knew.

Claudia opened the book. Its waxy black cover reeked like Luciana's room of torture, and I was suddenly grateful she hadn't put it on my bed. "See this?"

I tilted my head to try and make out the squiggly lines on the page. I got closer to the book, even though the scent of sulfur and blood was turning my stomach. "It looks like a map." I pointed to the blue outline. "That's definitely the US, but what are the lines? They're not states. And there's no river in that part of California." I leaned away from the book. There was something splattered on the page—something pink—and I wasn't sure if it was diluted blood or something else—and I really didn't want to find out. "What are they?"

"Ley lines," Dastien said from behind me. "I've seen maps like this before."

"They're lines of magnetic energy—or magical energy, depending who you talk to—that run through the world. You see these points where the lines meet?" She pointed to a few spots where a bunch of lines clustered together.

"Yeah."

"That's a vortex." Claudia sat back on her heels, and tugged on the hem of her skirt. "I saw this and it got me thinking.

Luciana has a lot of power now, but not as much as she'll need. Some people in the coven were so weak—it seems wasteful to drain them to get the few drops of magic they had..." Her voice wavered, and she closed her eyes, taking a slow breath. When she opened them, she seemed a little more together. "There are two small line intersections in Texas. Marfa and Enchanted Rock. But the church that you described... It sounds more like a church you'd find in the southwest." She moved her hand to the west. "In New Mexico, there are several adobe churches with stained glass windows. Some of them very old."

I wanted to stay away from all churches, but hiding wouldn't help anything. "You think she's going there?"

"Yes." Claudia pulled on her braid, like she did when she was nervous. "I think so. To the Santa Fe area specifically."

"How sure are you?"

Her gaze met mine. "Pretty sure."

Do you think we should go? I asked Dastien, hoping he'd say no. I didn't want to leave St. Ailbe's. Even with everything that was going on, it was my home. I felt the safest when I was here. And I didn't want to leave my parents. Especially after what had happened last night.

Her face has been plastered all over the news, so it makes sense that she'd leave town. We were expecting her to attack campus, but there has to be a reason she hasn't yet. I don't know what's changed for her, but if what Claudia says is right, then... His determination filled the bond. As he worked through his answer, I could feel him coming to a decision he was sure of. *Yes. We should go after her. We can't let her get away this time.*

If that was where she was, then yes, we should go after her, but we didn't *know* that. Why would she leave now? After all this time? I felt like I was missing a piece of the puzzle, and I didn't like that. Not one bit. *We don't have any proof that she went to New Mexico.*

What does your gut say?

I closed my eyes and tried to force a vision of the future, but I didn't see anything. I wanted to scream, but that wouldn't solve the problem. A part of me wished that I'd never met Luciana Alvarez. That I could still have visions like I used to. That I could touch something and see the past and—

Oh shit. I'm an idiot.

I'd been so focused on how my visions had evolved, that I'd forgotten how it all started. I hadn't even tried using them to see the past. Not for a while.

I reached for the book and hesitated with my fingers hovering just over the page. "I'm going to touch it and see whatever Luciana was doing with it last." I knew it. By saying it aloud, I reinforced my will. I placed my hand on the book and relaxed.

As I exhaled, the vision washed over me.

Luciana's craft room filled my vision. Flashes of blood. Death. A hint of sulfur.

But I wasn't seeing anything specific. Only flashes.

I focused, drawing power from Dastien, as I concentrated. This was the answer. I had to hang on.

Another flash. A splatter of candle wax. Some chanting.

And then the smell of sulfur grew. Luciana's face came into view as she placed the book on a stand. Her hair was pulled up into a braided halo on top of her head. Her long, flowy skirt brushed the floor, dragging through blood and goop that covered it, and I gagged. How could she wear anything that touched the floor in here?

She muttered something—maybe Latin—and then went to the book.

"You need more power, young one." A scratchy voice came from the center of the circle, but there was nothing there. "Go to

where the points of magic meet. Then you can raise me and my brethren."

"I'll have enough when the coven is drained."

"Not so. It takes more than the lives of one insignificant coven to open the gates."

She turned back to the book and her finger traced the lines, moving west of Texas.

I let go of the vision and wiped my hands on my jeans, wanting to get rid of the evil feel of her. Her oily aura was coating me, making me feel like I needed more than just a long hot shower to feel clean again. "Luciana's heading out."

This had started because of her vendetta against the wolves, but that couldn't be her end goal now. Not if she was leaving the state.

The demon last night had called Luciana "mistress," but this one was calling her "young one." Which meant I'd just seen her talking to something much bigger than a major demon. The possibilities of what it could be made my breath short.

Raphael had said she was losing herself, and Claudia confirmed it. After what I'd just seen, it seemed that both of them were right. Luciana wasn't just after the pack. Not anymore. "This portal thing will hurt more than us. We should talk to Mr. Dawson. Get the others. We need to go as soon as possible."

Dastien grabbed his phone from the bedside table. "I'll call him."

Lucas leaned quietly against the wall as we waited. He watched Claudia, and I wondered how they were doing. A lot had happened to Claudia in the past few weeks—including finding a mate—and I hadn't had much time to check on her in the last day. We'd been going nonstop.

I leaned close to Claudia. "How are you hanging in? Are you okay?"

"I know. I look like a mess." She fussed with her shirt. "But I'm officially out of clothes—I had to leave my new things in the middle of nowhere in Peru. And there's been no time for laundry. And..." She blushed. "It's a little embarrassing."

I had no idea she'd left her bags. Stupid. I really should've been taking better care of her. "That wasn't what I was talking about, but you shouldn't be embarrassed about that. I'm sorry that I didn't realize sooner. We'll get you some more clothes."

Claudia sighed. "We were planning on going to the mall, but there hasn't been time. Lucas needs some, too. We showed up in Costa Rica with what we had on us, and that was that."

"You should've said something. I'm sure I have clothes that will work for now. And I'm sure Dastien has stuff Lucas can wear until we get the rest sorted." Even if we left soon, we could hit a store to get them what they needed. "And how's Beth? I haven't seen her since you got back."

"She's not doing well." Claudia's voice cracked. "She won't leave her bed. Sh—she still had family there. Her sister and brother-in-law. And they had two kids."

"Shit. I didn't know. I'm so sorry. I would've..." I wasn't sure what I could've done differently. But something...

"You didn't know. Beth begged them to come with us, but they wouldn't leave. They didn't want to uproot the kids. I'm not sure what to do for her, except give her a little more time. She's not eating much, and..." Claudia's bottom lip wavered. "I just don't know what to do to make it better for her. For anyone." A tear slipped free, and she wiped it away. "It's all a huge mess."

God. "Huge mess" didn't even begin to cover it. "Did Shane have family there?" He'd seemed okay in spite of everything, but he could've easily been hiding it. I didn't know him well enough to get a solid read on him.

She blew out a breath. "His parents were in a car wreck a

couple of years ago. He's an only child. He had some cousins and an aunt and uncle, but they weren't very close."

"Hey," Dastien said. "Sorry to interrupt, but Mr. Dawson wants us in the conference room in five. I texted the others."

"Okay." Even if I'd already spent more time than I wanted to in there. "Did you hear the clothing situation?"

"Yup. We've actually got a storage room filled with supplies for guests—clothes, toothbrushes, toiletries... I'm sorry. I should've offered. I wasn't thinking."

Lucas stood upright. "Not to worry. I'm not fussy." That was the first time he'd spoken since he'd gotten here.

"We'll get you sorted after the meeting," Dastien said. "They might not be the best clothes ever, but they'll be enough to get you by until we have time for shopping."

I reached to take the book, but hesitated. I'd seen all I needed, and I'd spent more than enough of my life thinking about Luciana's craft room. "You mind taking that with us?"

Claudia picked up the book from the floor and held the disgusting thing at arm's length again. "No problem."

When we got to the conference room, the gang was already there. Adrian and Shane sat on the opposite side of the table. Raphael sat next to Shane. The three of them were laughing about something. It was good to see Raphael laugh. He was always so serious. Especially after everything.

Next to them, Cosette and Chris sat side by side, whispering, their heads tilted toward each other. When had they gotten so close? I leaned in, trying to listen just a little, but then I noticed Cosette's hand. She was wearing a glove.

On her sword hand. The one with the blackened fingertips.

She caught me looking and lifted her brows. That one motion shouldn't be so expressive, but I caught her loud and clear. Don't even *think* about asking. I was still going to—

because I wanted to make sure she wasn't hurt—but it could wait until there weren't as many people around.

Meredith and Donovan sat at the end of the table, talking with Mr. Dawson. They paused their conversation as Dastien shut the door behind us.

Claudia set the book on the table with a thud.

"What's going on," Mr. Dawson said. "Did you find something?"

"Claudia did," I said.

"Well, I found Luciana's book of ley lines, but Teresa had the vision."

"So you know what's going to happen?" Meredith asked.

I wished. "Not that kind of vision. I saw Luciana flipping through the book. We think she's heading to New Mexico. It would be awesome if we could find her before she does anything else terrible."

"A sneak attack," Chris said as he steepled his fingers. "I'm liking the sound of that."

"Me, too." Cosette's eyes flashed with bloodlust. "Let's see her fight for her life for a change."

"If this gets bad, you might need the pack with you," Mr. Dawson said. "We can't all up and leave now, though. There's too much going on."

"We'll have two Alphas—including myself—and some of these young wolves are pretty alpha, too. Not to mention a fey and a handful of witches," Lucas said. "It's a solid group. We can get there, scout things out, and then call you if we don't think we can handle the situation. New Mexico can't be a long flight from here."

Donovan shook his head. "Couple hours at most. I've got my plane here and—"

"You have a plane?" I asked before I could stop myself.

Meredith slapped his arm. "Yeah. You have a plane?"

The conference phone rang, and Mr. Dawson leaned to hit the button. "Yes?"

"You need to turn on the TV. The news..." Mrs. Kilburn—Mr. Dawson's secretary—said. "It's not good."

Someone clicked on the TV.

The anchor was narrating from off-camera, but I couldn't pay attention to what she was saying. My chest tightened as I watched the image.

There was a little girl on-screen. Toddler. Her hair was in tight ringlets and she wore a red and white gingham dress.

She was also tied to a chair. She cried and screamed while eight too-big-to-be-normal wolves circled, lashing out at her with their long claws. A Cazador wearing the usual all-black pants and shirt was asking her questions. There was no sound, but from the movement of his lips and the pause before the wolves moved into action, it was obvious what was going on.

A ringing sounded in my ears.

"Shit. That's Kaden asking the questions," Dastien said.

"Yes," Mr. Dawson half-growled the word. "A group of Cazadores found a demon. They were able to capture it, and proceeded to question it. They found it odd how easy it was to catch, having watched the previous footage, but they thought questioning it before killing it would be helpful in the hunt for Luciana." He gripped the chair in front of him so hard that it cracked. "I agreed at the time, but now I know. We were set up. The camera... It's placed a little too well."

It looked like the werewolves were torturing a child. A beautiful little girl.

We came off as complete monsters. The worst of the worst. Because if there was one thing everyone could agree on, it was that only a true monster would hurt the innocent.

Then the girl looked straight at the camera for an instant—a blink-and-you-miss-it moment. Her eyes were glowing bright red. If I hadn't been watching for it, waiting to see her eyes, I would've missed it, too.

This was bad. Beyond bad.

"As you can see, the wolves are not what they appeared." The image froze on a wolf ripping the dress with its claws. A male anchor filled the screen. His hair perfectly coiffed. "According to Teresa McCaide, werewolves are totally in control when in wolf form. Yet here they are, torturing a child. The public is calling for the police to bring the wolves to justice. The mayor of—"

I groaned as Mr. Dawson hit Mute. If I hadn't seen the demon that looked like me last night, I wouldn't have known they could look so human. I would've thought the Weres were torturing a child, too.

We had to get off campus. Before the cops came. Before the camera crews. Hell, before the mob with their pitchforks...

"If you're leaving, do it fast," Mr. Dawson said. "This is going to get ugly."

"Are you sure?" I asked. Leaving now felt even worse than before. The pack would have to be extremely lucky to avoid a riot.

"There are more wolves coming in to help," Donovan said. "They should be here tomorrow at the latest, but I agree. We should be gone in the next hour."

Donovan's words set us in motion. We hurried to get ready. Claudia and I grabbed our supplies from the lab, with a few extra ingredients in case one of us got hurt. We needed to be prepared.

Once that was done, I hustled to my room to pack a duffel. I grabbed my cell phone and charger from my nightstand. It seemed like only minutes had passed, but it was already time to go.

Whose car are we taking to the airport? I asked Dastien.

The Cazadores' SUVs are biggest. We'll need two. I'm heading that way.

The SUVs came loaded with supplies we might need, which was good because I was terrified we were forgetting something important. I made it to the parking lot and opened the back of the closest car. By the time I finished, the rest of the group was running down the walkway.

Yelling carried from the gates, much louder than before. People banged on the wrought iron, and anxiety gripped my heart. We weren't the bad guys here, but we sure as hell *looked* like the bad guys.

I honked the horn at the rest of our group. The faster we got out of here, the better.

Meredith, Donovan, Chris, Cosette, and Dastien threw their stuff in the back and climbed in. Lucas, Claudia, Raphael, Shane, and Adrian got into the other car.

"We ready? Seat belts buckled?"

A chorus of yeses and yeahs sounded, and I threw the car in reverse. As soon as the gates opened, people swarmed. It was a slow crawl out as people waved hateful signs at us and screamed their faces red. Talking about how evil we were. How we should die. Burn in hell. The noise was deafening.

I kept steady pressure on the gas. Their options were to move or get run over. I didn't really care which at this point. We had bigger things to worry about.

Demons to kill.

I thought about calling my FBI friends, but I was sure Mr. Dawson would be in touch. I hoped they'd take our side in all this madness.

A girl could hope.

CHAPTER TWENTY-TWO

I TEXTED my parents to tell them what was going on before we got on the plane. They were worried—hell, I was worried—but they trusted me to do what I thought was necessary. And this was definitely necessary. They swore they were moving to a hotel and would stay safe.

If I hadn't been so keyed up, I probably would've enjoyed the plane ride. It was a small jet, and it was *really* nice. The big leather chairs felt more like fancy recliners than airplane seats. A stewardess made sure we had everything we needed during the flight. It was a short trip over to New Mexico, but I spent most of the time talking strategy with Claudia. We weren't sure how long her spell could keep demon blood from burning the wolves, and that was a huge concern. It was okay last time, but all in all, the fight hadn't lasted very long. Ten minutes, max. The Weres needed to be able to fight for as long as it took.

But even as we debated whether the Weres should go furry or use weapons like Cosette, I was hopeful. For the first time in a long time, maybe even since I got to Texas, it was as if something was finally in my control. We'd spent so much time reacting—fighting when we had to, but waiting around for fights to start, that this felt like progress.

Donovan had two rental SUVs waiting for us when we landed, each with three rows of seats. I drove one car. Dastien, Chris, Meredith, Donovan, and Cosette were with me. Lucas followed behind with Claudia, Raphael, Adrian, and Shane.

We circled Santa Fe, trying to find a place to stay. Since I'd been on the news, and most of the others had been on the grainy cop-cam footage, we didn't want to stay anywhere too nice, but some of the Weres had high standards when it came to security. Someone had a reason we couldn't stay at every hotel and motel we'd passed so far. Too many people. Not enough people. Too accessible. Not accessible enough. Too many cameras...

After just the little bit of driving, it was obvious that a lot of the houses and buildings looked the same—dark tan adobe buildings. Maybe it would get old after a while, but for now it was charming. My favorite part was the busy plaza that the city was built around. It had perfectly even brick streets. Squat adobe buildings surrounded it, all the same shade of tan. People wandered from store to store. A group of Native Americans was selling art and jewelry on the sidewalk.

The sun was setting, and at some point the Weres were going to have to agree on a place to stay.

"There," Dastien pointed. "What about that one?"

"It's great. We're staying there," I said, cutting off any arguments. We were ten minutes from the central plaza. Just far enough that it wasn't super touristy. I pulled into the parking lot and stopped, checking out the place. "It looks a little too nice. Don't you think?"

He gave me one of his Gallic shrugs. "It looks decent to me."

I gave him my best you're-such-a-snob look. "Not everyone in the world has a castle to call home."

"I do," Donovan said.

What was with these werewolves? "Well, you're pretty damned old, right?"

"Aye."

"So, I guess that makes sense?"

Donovan muttered a comeback, but I ignored him. I was ready to stop moving for a little while.

"Raphael, you should get the rooms," Dastien said. "You weren't on the tape."

Raphael opened the door and hopped out. "Four rooms? Or more?"

"Four should do it," Donovan said.

After a minute, I undid my seat belt and glanced at the backseat through the rearview mirror. "Everyone doing okay?"

"Yeah," Meredith said.

Someone knocked on my window, and I nearly jumped out of my skin.

The woman had jet-black hair, and her eyes were dark as night. It wasn't her features that freaked me out, but the way she was looking at me. Her eyes narrowed like she was filled with hate. "I know why you're here."

She flicked her hand and a spell crashed into the car, lifting it on two tires for a second, before it crashed back down.

"Everyone okay?" Dastien yelled.

"Yeah," Meredith said from the backseat.

I stared at the woman. Witch. She was a fucking witch. But her magic felt different. It wasn't oily. Or greasy. It didn't have that tinge of evil that Luciana's had.

"She's not evil," I said.

Maybe not, but she's still attacking us. I'm getting out. You stay put.

What? No. We're both getting out of the car.

How the hell had she found us?

I moved to open the door, but the lady waggled her finger

225

and my window shattered. I huddled my head in my hands as glass rained down. Pin pricks of pain spread across my skin as the shards cut.

Dastien's anger and fear for me filled the bond. *Are you okay?*

Yeah, I said. Just a few cuts. I'll be okay.

"Shit. She locked us in," Chris said as he jiggled his door handle. "Careful. I'm going to break the window."

"Wait a second." The witch started mouthing another spell, but I had my own. "Unlock," I said, adding a little power from Dastien to amp up the words as I opened my door.

She hadn't been expecting that and was standing way too close. The door hit her, knocking her back so hard she tumbled across the pavement.

Careful! Dastien shouted. *Wait for me.*

The slam of feet hitting the ground filled the night as we rushed to surround her. The wolves were growling, tempers on edge. The *brujos* had their hands out, ready to deflect or cast a spell at any moment.

Dastien growled as he moved to my side. She lifted her hand to start another spell.

"I wouldn't do that if I were you." I held up my hands, letting my wolf surface enough to grow some impressive claws.

Dastien hadn't stopped his snarling and his eyes glowed amber.

The witch froze as she turned in a circle, finally noticing how grossly outnumbered she was.

Good. Now we could actually figure out what her problem was. "I know your magic isn't evil like Luciana's, so I'm going to give you the benefit of the doubt and assume this is some kind of misunderstanding. Is there something I can help you with?" I said in my best fuck-off tone. The glass cuts had already healed, leaving only little splatters of blood on my arms. I suppressed the urge to wipe them on my jeans.

"You attacked the Texas Coven."

Was she freaking kidding with this?

"Blessed be, sister." Claudia moved to stand between the pissed-off witch and me. "I'm Claudia de Santos of the Texas Coven, and this pack has done nothing but give us safe haven. Why are you attacking?"

The stumbled back and nearly bumped into Adrian. "Luciana came to us two days ago. Terrified. Asking for sanctuary. We saw what was left of the compound. These monsters—" she motioned toward me and Dastien "—killed everyone and burned it to the ground. We couldn't turn her away in her time of need." The woman lifted her chin high in the air, pretending she wasn't afraid of us, but her hands shook. The sickly sweet scent of fear permeated the air. "If you're siding with them, then you're a traitor to all covens."

Oh my God. I so didn't have the time or energy for this traitor BS. The woman needed a reality check, and fast.

"Andromeda spread the word among the covens." Cosette stepped forward. Her skin glowed in the night, and her hair looked like it was made of spun gold. She had to have dropped some kind of glamour or magic. "Luciana alone was responsible for the deaths in Texas."

"You're faerie." The witch's eyes widened at Cosette. "The one from the Denver coven...?"

"If you know who I am, then you know better than to come after my friends." Cosette loomed over the woman, still glowing. "Now, help me understand why you'd ignore the warning of my coven leader."

"There was no word from Andromeda." She shrank a little under Cosette's energy, but managed to shoot the rest of us a glare. "We've been on a retreat. We heard word from Luciana. She was waiting for us when we returned to our compound."

Cosette muttered something fey, but I didn't care who had and hadn't been warned. All I cared was whether this woman could point us to Luciana. And how we were going to keep her from reporting that she'd found us.

A flash of movement from the hotel entrance caught my eye. Raphael exited the hotel lobby and jogged toward us. The witch's back was to him, and he started motioning for a spell, but I shook my head.

The witch held out her hands to Claudia. "Why are you with them? How could you betray your coven?"

Raphael reached the circle and stepped between Adrian and Shane. "You shouldn't listen to Luciana," he said, and the witch spun to face him. "She drained the entire coven for the power to raise demons. She killed everyone. The only reason we're alive is because we broke our blood oath to her and—"

She scoffed. "No coven leader has demanded a blood oath in centuries."

"Luciana did," Claudia said. "She made every coven member pledge to her in blood."

"She couldn't..." A look of confusion crossed her face, and I knew we had an in. This woman knew where Luciana was. If we could get her to trust us, she could tell us.

"She did. She used the blood oath to murder our friends and families, sucking them dry of their magic. The wolves have only ever tried to help." Claudia sighed. "Please. Tell us where she is."

"I—I can't. Not until I talk to the rest of my coven."

No. "If you go back there and confront her, she'll kill all of you."

She stared straight ahead as she thought, not looking at anything. "I'll call them. They'll meet me at our sanctuary. We can come to an agreement there. Make contact with Andromeda. If everything is as you say, then—" She let out a slow shaky breath. Her eyes were glassy as she looked at me. "I'm sorry. If you had no part in this, then I apologize."

"That's okay. But please. Tell me—"

"No. I have to be sure. She came to us for protection. Before I break my word, and give her to the wolves that have been hunting her, I have to make sure I'm doing this for the right reason."

I hated this, but she seemed decent enough. She wanted to do the right thing, and that was all anyone could really ask for.

We should let her go. She'll come back with the information we need, and we'll have more witches in the fight.

Are you sure? What if she changes her mind? Or Luciana kills her?

She'll be back.

"Take my number," I said. "Call me when you decide."

"I don't need it. I'll just scry for you. If what you said is true, we'll help. But if it's not..."

Sirens wailed in the distance. "Do you hear that?" I said to no one in particular.

Hearing what I heard, the wolves all started moving toward the car, but when the witches didn't, I paused for a second to explain. "Cops are coming," I said to Claudia. "We can't stay here."

Claudia nodded. "Let's go."

"I'm sorry," the witch said. "My actions... If I'm wrong, I'll make it up to you."

I believed her. Maybe it was stupid, but I really did.

I believe her, too.

That made me feel better about my decision to let her go. "Better leave now. Or else we'll spend our night answering the cops' questions."

She spun and started running, but then stopped. "I'll be in touch. Either way," she said, looking back at me.

It was a little bit of a threat, but we weren't lying so it didn't bother me in the least. "We'll be waiting."

Everyone piled into the cars. I put the SUV in drive and exited the parking lot. *Do we actually have a lead?*

We do. Nicely done, chérie. I thought she was one of Luciana's, but you talked her down.

"You did good," Donovan said.

"Even though I let her go?" I was seriously hoping it wasn't going to turn into a problem.

"No," Meredith said. "You had to. If we forced her, she would've had that much more reason to believe Luciana's lies. At least letting her go might gain us some allies. We're going to need them."

I rolled my shoulders back, letting go of some of the tension.

This was good. Everything was moving along, and we had someone who could lead us straight to Luciana. We were right, and she'd realize that.

As we made our way through the streets of Santa Fe, the window being gone was actually a good thing. We listened for the sound of sirens, making sure to keep them in the distance as I drove through the night.

The cops gave up after a few minutes. The sirens stopped, and the tension in the car eased. Dastien turned on the radio, and the group finally agreed that any motel would do at this point.

It was late by the time we found a place, and I was bone-tired. I'd only had a few hours of sleep last night, and after so many in a row, I was well into the red zone of sleep deprivation. I parked the car, hoping no one tried to steal the SUV with the broken window.

While Claudia went to check us in, everyone piled out and

started grabbing bags. By the time she came back holding keycard envelopes, we were ready to head inside.

"How'd it go?" I asked.

"No one recognized me," Claudia said. "I paid cash for three nights. We've got two adjoining rooms on the second floor." We'd decided to keep the rooms to a minimum so we'd be in the same place if any other disasters happened.

"Perfect," Dastien said. "We've got the sleeping bags."

I didn't care what the room was like or what the sleeping situation was. As we walked up the stairs, my muscles ached and my skin itched—a sure sign that my wolf was closer to the surface than I'd like. If I didn't rest and eat soon, she'd take matters into her own hands.

Letting my wolf out now when cops, witches, and Lord only knew what else were hunting me was not an option.

Dastien wrapped his arm around my shoulders. *Just a little bit more. Then rest.*

I knew it wasn't far away, but I wanted all this drama with Luciana over. Now. I wanted to start my life with him. And I didn't want any more curveballs thrown at me.

But we still had the fight in the church to look forward to. I just hoped the New Mexico coven came through before that happened. If my vision could be avoided, that would be amazing.

For once, I wanted something to be easy, but there was no way a fight with Luciana was going to be anything other than horrible.

CHAPTER TWENTY-THREE

THE ROOM SMELLED like a mixture of piss, mildew, and pizza. The first two made it difficult to eat the pizza, but after a brutally hot shower, even with the overwhelming stench, I'd managed to eat two all by myself—which was a lot, even for a Were. As I ate, my wolf slowly settled down. At least that was one worry scratched off the list.

The potions brewing in the bathtub added to the general funk. We'd adjusted batches two and six, and were hoping they'd do more damage this time.

Batches one, three through five, and seven through ten had worked well enough on the major demon at my parents' house, so we made more using the same recipe.

Now we were on dinner break. Cosette had potion-stirring duty in the bathroom while the rest of us took turns looking up churches in the yellow pages. Who knew hotels still had phone books?

We narrowed the options down to five locations to check tomorrow. Scrying for Luciana was still a bust, and we didn't want to go anywhere blindly in the dark. Everyone had agreed that if we had to go up against another demon, we wanted to do it in daylight. And we hoped the witch would be in contact with us by morning.

"Ugh! What are we watching?" Meredith chucked a packet of Parmesan cheese at Adrian. "Change the channel."

We'd all crammed into one room, everyone sitting where they could find space on beds, chairs, and the floor. Dastien and I sat on a towel on the floor between the beds, mostly because I refused to sit on the carpet. It was a deep brown, with very short, bristly fibers, and it smelled. Bad. Plus there were mystery spots all over it. There was no way I wanted to risk getting a vision from it. This place would be a minefield if I wasn't careful.

Meredith complained about the TV again, and I sat up taller, so I could see around the crowd. I'd been so concerned about stuffing my face that I hadn't taken the time to check what they were watching. "Oh my God." I hit Dastien's shoulder. "What are they watching?"

"See," Meredith said. "Tessa doesn't want to watch it either."

I would've sworn that the TV was older than me. The snow-filled picture flickered in and out. I tried to make out the action but couldn't. "No. Seriously. Are they having sex or killing each other? I'm going cross-eyed trying to follow it." The noises and movements could've been either.

"I can't tell," Shane said. "That's why we stopped on this channel."

"And it was the only channel that wasn't talking about the pack. I think it's pay-per-view and we haven't paid, so we get a scrambled picture. But it's fun to try and figure out what's going on. I think they're having sex," Adrian said. "Shane thinks it's a horror movie."

Lucas grunted, and Donovan shared a look with him.

"What?"

Donovan shrugged. "Nothing. Just feeling a wee bit old at the moment."

"What? Eating pizza in a shitty motel too good for you, old man?" Meredith said.

"Not if you're here," he said with a flash of grin.

Chris and Adrian made gagging sounds.

"Oh God. Please don't make that noise. It makes me think about the smells in the room," Claudia said.

"Does anyone else think the carpet feels moist?" I asked.

"You've got to be kidding me!" Meredith jumped up to stand on the bed and swiped her hands over her butt. "I thought it was just me, but the blanket is damp, too." The springs in the mattress gave a squeaky cry, caving in under her feet. She fell into the dent, flailing her arms in the air.

Donovan caught her and pulled her out before she could fall. "Calm down, *a ghrá*," Donovan said. "You're going to break your neck with all this carrying on." His Irish accent thickened as he started laughing at her, too.

I don't know why that made me laugh so hard—I was probably more than a bit punch-drunk—but I couldn't stop. "You should see your face." My words were strangled through gasps.

Glass shattered in the bathroom, drowning out our laughter. Cosette cursed and then a soft, pearly light glowed from the door that was open a crack.

"You okay in there?" I called.

"Peachy."

Yeah. It was getting to be time to have a talk with her, whether or not people listened in. Cosette was still wearing her suspicious glove, and I'd rocked that style for enough years as vision protection to know that she wasn't trying to make a fashion statement with it. Something was up.

I polished off my last crust and was starting to get up when a flash of light exploded.

Dastien yanked me to his side and suddenly everyone was moving, taking defensive positions.

Cosette rocketed from the bathroom, fastest to react. "Show yourself."

The light slowly faded and, when my pupils adjusted, a guy stood in front of our locked door. Tall and lithe, he wore tight pants, tall boots, and a fancy tunic. His long white hair was clipped back and his cheekbones could've cut glass.

The fey guy from my vision. Which meant we were getting closer to the church.

I wasn't sure if I was glad he was here or terrified of what that meant. "It's you." The words were out before I could stop them.

Cosette spared me a withering glance and I winced. I was *so* going to pay for keeping that part of my vision secret. But she didn't have enough attention for me right now.

"No. Go home, Van." She drew out the soft A in his name until it sounded like fawn.

"I will." Van reached out to her, palm up. "And you'll be coming with me."

"Is that a command?" Cosette stilled, staring at his hand.

"A request. It's too da—"

"I know it's dangerous." Her shoulders relaxed as she let out a breath. "But I'm allowed to stay and clean up my mess. Go home before you get caught up in it."

"I won't leave you here to..." Van's voice trailed. Lightning fast, he grabbed her wrist and yanked off the glove. "You're injured."

Ugly black streaks spread up her hand. They were almost all the way to her wrist.

Shit. Why hadn't she said anything?

"Are yo—" I was going to ask what we could do to help, but

another flash of light nearly blinded me. Everyone lifted their hands to shade their eyes.

When I peeked through my fingers, my breath caught in my throat. Van glowed like the sun as he gripped Cosette's wrist. He radiated magic and my skin tingled—almost painfully—with it. His eyes burned bright silver.

Cosette's jaw was clenched, but she wasn't trying to pull away. Only, the longer he worked his magic, the more *she* started to glow. It was like pearly white light shone from under her skin.

I'd always known she was hiding herself from us. She'd proven that the first time she pulled her sword out of thin air. Now, she was casting off light, but I didn't feel a hint of magic from her. Was that just how she was supposed to look?

"Enough." Cosette jerked back her hand and finally the magic stopped.

"You can't stay here."

Van finally looked at the rest of us, and his lip curled a little at the sight of our room. I couldn't blame him, because I wasn't looking close enough to check, but I was pretty sure the brown stain on the wall was actual excrement. Still, it said a lot that he was standing in the middle of a group of worked-up Weres and *brujos* and couldn't care less about it. His silver eyes were all for Cosette.

She jammed her glove back on, covering the marks that hadn't budged. "I'm staying."

"Coco." Van sighed. "It was easy to track your magic. Others will be able to find you."

Coco? Who knew Cosette had a nickname? And who did she think was after her? This was getting juicier than Mom's favorite telenovela.

"I'm not likely to forget that, am I? Go *home*." Cosette pushed him toward the door.

"No." Van stood his ground. "I've found you and I'm staying. If you want me to leave, then leave with me."

Whoa. What was going on between them?

Whatever it was, I hoped Cosette would stay. We needed her, and if that meant Van had to stay, too, then we'd book them their own shitty motel room. We'd take as many fey fighters as we could get at this point.

"Anyone else wish they had popcorn for this show?" Meredith whispered.

"Me," I whispered back just loud enough so the wolves could hear. "This is blowing my mind."

Cosette turned to glare over her shoulder. *Whoops.* I guessed I hadn't been as quiet as I'd thought. She undid the chain on the door and nudged Van into the hall. "Let's finish this outside."

He walked out without looking at us, and Cosette pulled the door closed behind them. We all settled back down, except for Meredith, who stood to peek through the curtains. I was too exhausted to try to eavesdrop. I sank back against Dastien and let his energy wash over me, spreading calm.

"Who do you think he is?" Meredith whispered.

"I'm not sure." Claudia glanced at Lucas. He looked like he might know something about it. "But their auras were very similar. White and almost rainbow, although Cosette's is a bit brighter."

Lucas sighed. "It's not mine to tell her secrets. If you consider her a friend, you should be worrying more about that hand of hers."

I *was* worried about it. An injury from a demon had almost killed Raphael. Cosette was acting like she could handle it, but she also acted like she could handle everything. This was one thing I was pretty sure even she shouldn't be messing with. I hoped she'd let us look at it and see if we could find some spells to help her. "I don't know what's up with her, but I saw her friend in my vision."

"You *what*?" Cosette's voice from the doorway was like ice.

Right. She just *had* to come back at the right time...

There wasn't much I could say to defend myself. "I'm sorry. At first I was worried you'd leave if you knew. But then, with everything else that happened, there just wasn't a good time to bring it up again." I said the words, but they sounded like excuses, even to me. "We're going to need you in that church if we want to survive. I'm going to need you."

Cosette glared, and I deserved every ounce of her anger.

"I am sorry," I said again, hoping to reinforce the sentiment, but it didn't look like it was doing any good.

Her eyes narrowed at me. "I can't decide if I'm pissed or impressed."

"Impressed?" How was that possible?

"You got what you wanted, right? Very fey of you."

Is that a compliment? I asked Dastien. It didn't feel like one.

Probably not. His voice rumbled through the bond, a little amused.

"I'm the last person who can complain about keeping secrets." Cosette sighed as she tugged her bag out of the pile of gear in the corner.

Claudia stood. "You're leaving?"

I said a silent thank-you to her. I wanted to ask, but I'd already gotten enough of Cosette's wrath.

"For tonight." She let out a slow breath. "Van needs more convincing, but I'm going to stay and fight, so odds are he'll stay and fight with me."

I swallowed the "thank-you" that I wanted to give. "We really appreciate your help."

"Thank me by killing Luciana. That's the only way this is all worth it." She slung her bag over her shoulder. Her normal

AILEEN ERIN

humor came back as she took in the room with a smirk. "Also, I'll be sleeping in a feather bed that smells like jasmine. I think karma has done its work here."

"Lucky," Meredith murmured.

"We'll reinforce your wards before we go." Cosette eased the door closed, but her voice carried through, way more chipper than it needed to be "Don't let the bedbugs give you hepatitis."

Okay. Definitely not thanking her for that one.

"Well, that was awkward." Chris locked the door chain behind them, although it hadn't done much to keep Van out.

"Do you think they're romantic?" Claudia asked. "Or just friends?"

"It may be more complicated than that," Lucas said.

"How do you know?" I asked.

"We're in contact with our local fey in Peru. All I'll say is I've heard her name come up as a key player in the courts."

I paused to let that sink in, but at this point I was more shocked that she actually let someone call her Coco and live.

"We should call Michael again," Donovan said. "Give him an update and check on the situation at the school."

I nodded. We'd expressly avoided the news. The fight against Luciana was only hours away, and we needed to stay focused. Still, it was tempting. Donovan had been checking in with Mr. Dawson throughout the day. Word was things weren't pretty on campus. They'd managed to keep the police from storming the gates, but getting anyone to believe that the video girl was actually a demon wasn't a cakewalk.

A moan from the TV broke the silence.

"Jaysus," Donovan yelled. "Change the channel already." He got up, dialing Mr. Dawson as he crossed into the adjoining room.

The laughter started off soft, and then we were hooting at the TV.

"They're definitely having sex now," Adrian said, finally changing the channel.

"Just no more gagging noises. Please. I'm already worried how many showers it's going to take to get the ick of this place off me," Claudia said.

As they kept bantering and flipping through the channels, I leaned against Dastien, resting my head on his shoulder.

You okay? he asked.

Yeah. Tired, but okay. We have good friends.

He brushed my hair away from my forehead and placed a soft kiss there. *Yeah. We do.*

As I closed my eyes, I knew that we'd find Luciana tomorrow. One way or another, all of this would come to an end. And after, if I was lucky enough to live through it all, I was going to have years with my friends. With Dastien.

That was motivation enough for me to keep going. To not give up.

I had too much to live for to lose it all now.

CHAPTER TWENTY-FOUR

I'D HOPED to hear from the witch by the morning, but when that didn't happen we had to continue with our original plan. We all crammed into one SUV, and by the afternoon we'd realized what a mistake that was. There was nothing fun about a group of cranky supernaturals. Even though our rental had three rows of seats, that still left two people squished in the trunk. Cosette hadn't returned with Van. For now, that was okay because there was no way they could've fit, but I was starting to get worried.

It had taken forever to get moving this morning. Everyone wanted a shower, and with only two bathrooms that took for freaking ever. Then all the Weres needed food. By the time we hit the road to start looking at churches, it was already past noon. Although we figured that was an advantage if we were going to be up against demons.

Still, with no Cosette and no luck finding the right church, the mood in the car was tense.

"There's another option two miles away," I said.

Dastien was driving, and I was sitting shotgun at the moment, but we'd been rotating seats at each stop. Although, it wasn't a very diplomatic seat rotation. It was more of a mad scramble—people crawling over each other trying to get a good spot. Slowest got the trunk. And no one was playing fair. I had to warn Chris and Meredith more than once to be careful with the witches. But Raphael had been in the same window seat after the past three churches and he looked pretty smug about it, so I was thinking magic was involved.

"If she's at the last one on our list, I'm going to freak out," Meredith said as she leaned between the front seats. She blew a chunk of pink hair out of her face. "Are you getting any helpful feelings yet?"

"If I do, I'll let you know." I wished I had a better way to get us there, but I'd been so focused on the people in my vision, I hadn't been paying that much attention to the details. I knew the church we wanted was adobe and had stained glass windows, but beyond that, I had no clue. "Why don't you pick the next one?" I handed the map to her. We'd circled all the possibilities in red marker. Only three circles were left.

So at least this was almost over.

Still, every time we got to a church, our energy level amped up. When it was a bust, we all flagged. It was like a never-ending adrenaline roller coaster.

I just hoped we found Luciana before dark.

Meredith picked the next church and we were off. It took about ten minutes driving north of the city. We followed a few winding dirt roads until we ended up at a weed-choked parking lot. The church was rundown and slowly being swallowed up by desert vegetation.

The adobe was right, but I didn't see any windows. It had small bell tower and ornately carved wooden doors. One had an image of Our Lady of Guadalupe and other was the Sacred Heart of Jesus. Whoever made them was an amazing artist. They'd made the wood come to life.

But as I took in the building, I knew something was off. "It's not the one from my vision, but..." There was a funny feel in the air. Almost a compulsion to run away. It reminded me of the wards on the compound, although it wasn't nearly as strong. "Does anyone else feel that?"

"Yes." Claudia rubbed her arms. "It's warded."

At least I wasn't imagining it.

"I don't want to go in there. Not even a little bit," Shane said.

"It's just a little magic," Raphael said. "Maybe the local coven uses this spot. If you guys want to stay here, I'll check it out." He hopped out of the car before anyone could stop him.

I shared a look with Dastien. *Should we follow him?*

Better not let him go alone, Dastien said. Claudia was already on his heels anyway.

Guess we're going, too, then. I grabbed my messenger bag of potions and followed after them. I still didn't feel right about this, but we had to at least check it out.

Raphael was almost to the door when the clouds shifted. For a second, the sun flashed and a blinding beam of light reflected off something on the front stoop.

I squinted at the spot. Faint and barely visible, a silver line arced out from under the doorway, embedded in the floor-boards. I would never have noticed it if not for the change in light.

But why would there be a silver arc in the floor?

My chest tightened. He couldn't touch it.

"Wait!" I raced to Raphael, yanking him back just before his foot stepped over the line. "Wait."

"What?" Raphael pulled free from my grip. "We have to check inside."

"It's a trap. Look at the silver line. If that's part of a circle and we cross it, who knows what could happen."

"Where?" Claudia asked.

"Just tilt your head." I pointed to the spot.

"You're right." Claudia's eyes widened and she gripped Raphael's shoulder.

The Weres had caught up to us, but still stood back.

"What does that mean?" Meredith asked. "Is this the right church or not?"

"This isn't where she opens the gate to hell, but there's something else here." I stared at the door. Doing a spell to make it open wouldn't have been that hard, but I was worried any magic would set off the wards. "We need to go in. There's something about this place..." The wind shifted, and I lost my train of thought for a second. "Do you smell that?"

"Sulfur?" Claudia asked.

"That." Chris leaned in a little closer and then shook his head. "And death. There are bodies in there."

"I knew those wards felt familiar. They're Luciana's." Claudia tugged on the end of her braid.

"Do you think she's still here?" Meredith asked.

"No," Claudia said. "I don't think she'd stick around after killing again."

Shit. Now we really needed to go inside. But crossing the wards would signal Luciana we were here, and if we broke the circle, we could release a demon or anything else she might've left to surprise us. A total double whammy of a trap, but I wouldn't expect anything less from Luciana at this point.

"Any suggestions how to do this?"

Light flashed and a few of us jumped as Cosette and Van appeared. They held hands, but Cosette pulled away as soon as the light was gone. Van didn't exactly scowl, but he didn't look happy about it either.

"Good morning, friends." Cosette smiled, too coy for her own good. She wore skinny jeans and a flowy white top that hung off her shoulder. Her hair shone in clean, glossy curls. I wrinkled my nose at her. She actually smelled like jasmine. How unfair was that?

"Where the hell did you come from?" Chris asked.

"I second that," Meredith said.

She shrugged. "My magic's restricted. Van's isn't."

Not exactly an explanation, but it was as good as we were getting out of her. She nudged Van, who took a step forward. "I didn't mean to interrupt you all so rudely last night. You may call me Van. I'll be your ally as long as Cosette is."

Cosette rolled her eyes. "By that he means he looks forward to fighting with us."

"That's great," Chris said, his voice rasping a little, "but I'm still stuck on where the hell did you come from?"

"We were nearby, watching." Cosette gave a vague wave. "We didn't feel the need to ride on your roof rack."

No one could blame her for that. She'd showed when we needed her and that was all that mattered.

I turned back to the wooden doors. The carved handles were works of art on their own. I hated that Luciana had turned such a pretty place—a sanctuary—into something evil, but the scent of demon and death, combined with the slimy feel of her wards, couldn't be ignored.

"Can you guys just beam us in, or whatever it is you do?" I asked Van.

"That wouldn't be wise." He narrowed his silver eyes at the door. "However we cross the line, it will release what's being bound. Better to go through the door and fight it face-to-face."

That made sense. It sucked, but it made sense. "So, what now? We just can't leave a demon in there waiting for someone to stumble in and set it free. And if Luciana has killed again..." It didn't feel right leaving bodies here. The last thing we needed her to do was use them to make more demon-zombies like Daniel.

"I'll check the perimeter," Donovan said. "Might be there's a window we can peek through and see what we're really up against." He tromped through the scrub, disappearing from view.

Van went the other way, apparently wanting to check things out on his own, and the rest of us stepped back from the wards.

I moved closer to Cosette. "You okay?"

She shrugged. "Things could be worse."

That wasn't an answer, but at least she didn't seem hurt or pissed. I had more questions about to bubble free.

Dastien moved to my side before I could open my mouth. *I don't think it's any of your business.*

I suppose, but it's my fault I didn't warn her about the guy. I can't help but feel bad.

Donovan stumbled from the other side of the chapel, ending the chance I had to ask her anything.

A stray branch caught Donovan's cheek. "Damn it all," he said as he wiped off the blood. "There's nothing back there but woods. The walls are solid. Not a window or door besides this one."

"We *can* break through the ward," Cosette said. "But Luciana could be waiting for us to do just that."

"Maybe we should just go," I started. "I mean, is it worth—"

A soft scream echoed from inside the church.

We all froze.

"Please tell me there's no one alive in there." Because if that was a human, then we had to go in. Screw the wards. Screw the circle and whatever was inside it.

"Help me!" The woman's voice rasped. "Please." She was so hoarse, my throat burned in sympathy. "It's going to kill me."

Before I could do anything, before I could even think about

how to go about this without setting off any traps, Raphael was moving. Any one of the Weres could've stopped him, but none of us really wanted to. There was someone in there who needed our help. We couldn't ignore that. No matter what we might face inside.

He ran up the stairs, threw open the doors, and froze. "Oh shit."

I started after him but a wave of energy blasted me back.

Air whipped against my face as I flew through the air.

Dastien screamed my name, his fear ripping through our bond.

I landed with a thud, but something soft was between the ground and me. The scent of pine told me who it was. Dastien had softened my landing.

Thanks. You okay? I asked.

Yeah. I've taken worse hits.

The others?

We weren't close enough to get hit by the blast. I barely had time to catch you.

Next time maybe catch me before I hit the ground. I groaned as I rolled off him. Even with him there, it still hurt to hit that hard.

His soft laugh ran through our bond. Why don't we just try to not have a next time? Okay?

"Teeereeeessa." The way Claudia drew out my name lifted all the hairs on my arms.

I slowly turned to the doors.

Raphael was scrambling down the stairs. Beyond him, a figure moved back and forth, just out of the reach of the sun.

A major demon.

This one looked like a teenage girl dressed in skinny jeans and a black T-shirt, but the way it moved its head wasn't natural. And the red eyes were unmistakable. My side had healed, but I'd gotten lucky the last time. I couldn't get that close again.

"It won't come outside while the sun's high," Raphael said. "I don't understand how it's even here."

"She must've summoned it last night," Shane said. "It's been trapped there all day."

"This one's more powerful than the last." Cosette yanked off her glove and tossed it. A shining new sword appeared in her hands.

"They're dead..." Claudia's soft voice drew my attention to the church beyond. The pews were set at a diagonal, leaving a wide center aisle. Lumps filled that space. Some bigger. Some smaller. A foot stuck into the aisle near the back.

Bodies. She'd drained the New Mexico coven. That was why I hadn't heard from the witch again.

The demon whirled, heading into the darkness of the sanctuary.

"Help!" The call sounded again.

It wasn't too late to help at least one of them. "Stop!" I threw my magic at the demon, putting all my will behind the word, but it barely froze for a second. We needed more firepower. "Everyone got your vials?"

Raphael ran back to the car, but the rest of us were ready. I grabbed a few vials from my bag and left the flap open for easy access. The other *brujos* came to stand beside me, potions in hand.

Raphael came back with a metal bat.

"You sure about that?" I asked.

"Yeah. You guys have it handled on the potion front." He gripped the bat with both hands. "I want to try this way."

"Van." Cosette nodded toward Raphael. "Soup that up for him."

Without missing a beat, Van touched the bat, mouthing a spell. When he lifted his hand, the metal glowed.

"That'll work," I said. The Weres had all agreed on a formation and shifted. Lucas, Donovan, and Dastien were closest to the door, while the others fanned out behind. We'd talked potion strategies, but I said it aloud one more time. "I'll take the lead, and you throw behind me. Cosette and Van will jump in when there's an opening." Everyone nodded.

Another scream, this one of pure pain and terror.

I licked my dry lips. "Let's do this."

"With the power of Jesus Christ, I banish you." The words activated the potions, and I tossed them through the open doorway. An explosion echoed inside the sanctuary, and I rushed inside with the wolves at my side.

The demon lay on the ground, arms splayed wide. I almost celebrated.

Then it levitated two feet off the ground and flipped onto its feet. It hissed and lunged for me at full steam.

Oh hell no.

I threw three vials as I backed up, but that didn't stop it. I would've turned and run, but the wolves jumped in front of me. Dastien dodged and Lucas almost got a mouthful of it.

Adrian flew at it, but the demon slashed out with its nails. Adrian yelped, tumbling into a pew.

Shit.

Shane got to his side first, chucking vial after vial, but the demon saw Adrian's blood and kept heading for him.

"Hey!" I tossed a vial and invoked it. It exploded on the demon's back, sinking a small crater into its skin. *That* got its attention.

As the demon started for me, I spotted Cosette and Van slinking into place behind it. We'd talked out this scenario on the plane. We just needed a little time for the fey to get in place.

Then Claudia, Shane, and I would throw our potions, and Cosette—and now Van, too—would go for the head. The wolves would keep it distracted and herd it where we wanted.

"You will not defeat the mistress." Its voice was a hair-raising, high-pitched rasp.

I stopped moving.

It talked. Holy shit. Was it talking to me? About Luciana?

"If you tell us where she is, we'll defeat her," I said, trying to bait the little monster. "Don't you want to be free of her control?"

It hissed, and goose bumps ran up my arms. "The mistress is not Luciana. Not anymore." It laughed the same laugh I'd heard from Raphael not so long ago. Not a similar laugh. The *exact* same laugh.

I spotted Raphael on my right, twisting the bat in his hands. His jaw was clenched tight and little lines formed around his mouth.

A woman coughed from the front of the room. It sounded wet, like she was bleeding. Hurt.

We needed to end this, and soon. But if we got some information before we killed this thing, even better. "I bet your mistress is too scared to face us. She ran all the way here, but we'll find her."

It laughed again as it levitated off the ground. It hadn't even turned to listen to me. Instead, it stared straight at Raphael "I remember you," it said. "Your soul was tasty. Kept a few bits of it for myself."

Raphael roared and swung the bat, aiming for the demon's head. Light flashed as it connected and the demon flew across the room, slamming into a pew. Wood splintered around it.

I strode to it, holding a vial ready. No more beating around the bush for this girl. Not if it was going to torment my cousin. "If your master is so powerful, then where is she?"

"Not telling."

I threw the vial. It screeched in pain as its skin melted, steam rising as the potion bubbled. The smell it gave off—like burning plastic—reeked.

"Where is she?"

"Not—"

I threw another vial. Then another. Claudia and Shane started lobbing potions, too. Its skin made a sickening crackling noise as the potions hit, but it was still breathing. Still alive.

The demon gave off an ear-splitting cry as it flew into the air.

I dodged, throwing myself on the floor.

Shane yelled, and my blood went cold.

We needed to end this now.

I kitted up, and threw three more vials before reaching into my bag. Claudia met my gaze, her hand raised with her own vials. "Cosette!"

Claudia and I threw our vials in unison.

"My pleasure." Cosette hooked arms with Van and he launched her into the air. She flew, sword raised and glittering. The blade came down, decapitating it in one glowing strike.

The earth cracked open with a roar and a flash, sucking the demon back to hell.

Eerie silence echoed through the church for all of five seconds.

Then a gun cocked.

"SFPD. Drop your weapons. Now." No less than ten cops swarmed into the sanctuary, guns out. Some of them wore Kevlar vests, others had shotguns instead of handguns, but all of them looked like they weren't fucking around.

Wolf-Dastien nudged me with his head, and I closed my eyes. This was so not happening.

"On the ground. All of you. Any wolf that makes a move toward us gets a silver bullet right through the eye."

A gunshot we could heal. But I wasn't so sure about silver bullets, let alone a silver bullet to the head. I lifted my arms in the air and got to my knees.

"Everyone. On the ground."

I spared a glance for the others.

Shit. My cousins and I were the only ones cooperating. A bead of sweat rolled down the nearest cop's cheek. All of them reeked of the sickly sweet scent of fear. One wrong move and they'd all snap.

Help me out, Dastien. We have to cooperate. "You guys have to get down," I said just loud enough for the Weres to hear.

"No," Donovan growled the word. He must have just shifted back. I peeked at him, off to my right. Even standing there, naked as the day God made him, he looked fierce. Waves of alpha energy rolled off him, and my throat tightened.

This could go bad. Very quickly.

"Yes. You will."

"They have a gun pointed at my mate. I'll not be surrendering."

The other wolves growled.

"You should listen to your friend. Down on your knees," one shotgun-carrying cop said as he took one step forward.

"You all will shift back and be nice to these police officers." I raised my voice loud enough for everyone to hear. "We have to make a choice. We could force our way out of here, but is that the right thing to do?"

"Maybe Donovan has a point," Adrian said. "If we don't leave, we'll be tied up with the police, just like Luciana wanted."

Dastien's anger rolled through our bond. Even my own mate thought I was being dumb, but I couldn't give in. A mistake here could destroy the trust between humans and werewolves forever.

I swallowed down my nerves. "I'll call the FBI, and they'll help clear this up. We need to show the humans we can work with them or they'll see us as nothing more than animals. If we don't go with them now, peacefully, we'll ruin any chance of them trusting us. Monsters like Luciana will come and go, but the rest of our lives with the humans—we can't throw that away."

I cleared my throat. "Officers. The wolves are going to shift now, and they'll need the clothes from our car. I'm sure you're already searching it, so if you'd please bring the bags here for them, we'll happily go with you. We have two injured humans. One badly hurt. I don't know if she's still alive. And Shane? You okay?"

"Hurts." His voice was strained. He just had to hold on. A few minutes more.

None of the cops moved.

"Please. We're going to need an ambulance."

"We already called one."

I let go of a little bit of tension. I was going to have to get the EMTs to use holy water on them, but maybe... "We haven't done anything wrong here. This is the work of Luciana Alvarez. It's exactly the same as what happened in Cedar Ridge, Texas. If you get us the clothes, we can sort this all out."

"She needs to drop her weapon."

I looked at Cosette. She bit her lip as she eyed the door. "Would you rather I just made this all go away?"

Tempting. *Really* tempting. But I shook my head. "We tried that last time and look where it got us. We have to cooperate."

"Fine. But I'm not kneeling in demon ashes." Her sword winked out and she brushed her hands on her jeans.

"What the fuck was that?" a cop yelled.

Ugh. Way to diffuse the situation. I waved my hands, drawing the cops' attention back to me. "Please, don't be afraid. The wolves are going to shift now."

One by one, the guys took their human forms until only Meredith was left. She huddled against Donovan's legs and I didn't blame her.

"Now, we need our clothes. Please."

A cop disappeared and came back a minute later with one of the Cazadores' duffels of clothes. He tossed it toward us.

The guys held out their hands and slowly reached for clothes. Everyone was moving very slowly. Carefully. Making sure there were no mistakes. It was necessary, but we didn't have this much time. Adrian and Shane—not to mention the woman—needed help now.

My arms ached, but I wasn't about to lower them.

"What about that one?" One of the cops motioned at Meredith with his guns.

Donovan growled.

"Calm down," I whispered. "That's my friend Meredith. She's a minor and would like some privacy to change."

She approached the bag, grabbing the sweats in her mouth, and then slowly walked behind a pew. A few moments later, she stood, fully clothed.

"Thank you," she said.

This isn't going to go well, chérie.

Yeah, but we're screwed either way. At least now we can be seen as cooperative.

"Everyone outside. Move it. Now."

Ordering wolves around was bad. Ordering an alpha was pretty damned stupid. And ordering Alphas like Donovan and Lucas while pointing guns at them and their mates...

Their power rose, brushing against my hair.

Help me. I called to Dastien. We can't hurt the cops.

"Move!" The cop yelled, shoving a gun in Claudia's face.

Lucas' power rose, and Dastien finally started to realize what I'd known all along. *Take what you need.*

"We're going with the cops." I put everything Dastien and I had behind the words—commanding them to start moving. Lucas and Donovan turned their power toward me. I had to grit my teeth against the massive force of alpha energy, but I wasn't backing down. "We have to do this or we'll just prove we're the monsters they fear."

Meredith's lips were pressed tight as she stared down her mate. From the look on her face, she was giving him a solid dressing-down.

"She's right. Let's go," Meredith said. She raised her hands as she moved slowly toward the cops with me.

The cops moved quickly, cuffing Meredith and me before moving on to the rest. I kept my eyes on the Weres. If anyone was going to act out, I had to stop it. We couldn't afford to open a rift between the supernaturals and humans. Not if we had any chance at peacefully coexisting.

I expected the most trouble from Van, but he'd disappeared without ever being seen by the cops. That was probably for the best. As it was, Cosette had done some Jedi mind trick on them, holding her wrists together so they seemed to think she was already cuffed.

I knew we could get out of this, but that was what worried me. All it took was one slip—one lost temper—and humans would get hurt. Then we'd have to run. And if we ran now, we'd be running for the rest of our lives. Anger burned inside me.

There was no way the cops would've known to come to a random church in the desert. The demon was just to keep us busy. Luciana must've called the cops as soon as we crossed the wards. If we went with them quietly, no one would be able to stop her.

So either way, Luciana won.

I took in the scene. All the dead bodies. Their skin gray and shriveled. I didn't need to see their eyes to know what they looked like. Shane lay on the floor. Blood seeped through the leg of Adrian's pants. We were a mess.

And now Luciana had more than enough power to do what she wanted. She'd wiped out two covens and gotten us out of her way. If they threw us in jail for the night there'd be more than enough time for Luciana—mistress or whatever the hell she was now—to open her portal.

Sirens rose in the distance as the ambulance approached. First, we had to make sure Shane and Adrian were okay. Then we'd deal with Luciana.

I hoped for the last time.

CHAPTER TWENTY-FIVE

THE SCENT OF STALE, cheap coffee wafted through the station. The process of getting booked took forever. Like multiple hours. Especially since only a couple of us had any form of ID.

Good thing Van hadn't stuck around. Who knew what the officers would've made of him?

Cosette was bad enough on her own. The cops had been giving her a hell of a time, which I didn't really blame them for, given the whole pulling swords out of thin air thing. Then she'd charmed one of the police dogs somehow. Now, she sat in the corner with a German shepherd curled up at her feet, and it growled at anyone who came close, including its handler.

Knowing Cosette, it could've been worse. I was just glad she was making a show of cooperating instead of trying to magic this away like she so obviously wanted to. It was way too late to undo the situation.

Our big problem was that the cops wanted answers. None of us had anything to say that they were willing to believe. It left us at a stalemate, but at some point they were either going to have to trust we were the good guys or decide we were the monsters.

The cop who seemed to be in charge—Wilson—had left us in a room with one officer—Yeats. She was a heavy-set woman with hair in an unflattering pixie cut. She watched us as we sat quietly in our chairs like good little citizens.

The room's white walls and gray-speckled linoleum floor were clean enough, but the smells of blood, sweat, and vomit were ingrained underneath the scent of cleaning products. A table took up space in the middle of the room, but none of us were using it.

A blinking red light flashed on the camera in the corner. Someone, somewhere was watching us. I wondered what they were thinking. Which side would the coin were we going to land on? Friends? Or not?

As we sat in silence, waiting for what felt like forever for something to happen—one way or the other—the only sound in the room came from the large clock on the wall as the hands ticked. It was driving me mad, constantly reminding me that time was slipping away.

At least Adrian and Shane weren't dealing with any of this. They were at the hospital. Under guard, but still, they weren't being interrogated. Shane hadn't looked good. I'd heard Adrian convincing the EMT to treat him with holy water before we were hauled off, but I was still worried. Adrian seemed much better off than Shane, and I didn't think it was just our speedy healing time. Maybe the reason Dastien and I hadn't been affected by our demon-inflicted wounds like Raphael had been was because we were Weres. What if witches were easier to possess?

I had a feeling Shane was going to need more healing than just holy water. Something more like what Claudia did to

Raphael. Only we were stuck at the police station, and we hadn't heard a word about them in hours.

Cosette sighed as she scratched her police dog behind its ears. "Anyone else ready to walk out of here? Because I am. At any moment."

"No." It was the first time Donovan had spoken since we'd gotten to the station. "I wasn't thinking straight. The sight of a gun pointed at Meredith set me off—"

"Same here," Lucas said. "Don't beat yourself up about it."

"Aye. But it was shortsighted. Teresa here was the only one who kept her head, apart from the witches. If we'd done what we'd wanted, the humans never would've trusted us. We'd be hunted. Our children would be hunted." He stared at the wall in front of us. "No. This was the only way."

"I kept my head," Cosette muttered before turning to me. "If we're not breaking out, can I at least summon my Kindle? This is dead boring."

"No summoning." I was too wound up to get bored, but it was still taking too long. I had to do something to move the process along.

"Can I have my phone call, please?" I asked Officer Yeats. "It's my right. And we haven't been charged with anything. I should get a call."

A wrinkle appeared between her eyebrows as she considered my question. "I'm not sure werewolves have rights."

It didn't sound like she was trying to be rude, but instead was trying to reason out whether I should be able to make a call. That was the only reason I was able to maintain my cool. Thanks to Dad's coaching over the years, I already knew how to argue my case.

"I was born in Los Angeles eighteen years ago. My parents are human. I have a valid US birth certificate, and you saw my valid driver's license when you booked me. By not allowing me my phone call, you're violating my rights as a US citizen."

She sighed. "Fine."

Thank you, Dad, for making sure I know my rights. I smiled at her. "Is there any way you can get my wallet? There's a business card inside. I just need the number."

She crossed her arms as she stared me down. Then she let out a huff and turned on her heel. When she came back, she had my sparkly silver wallet in her hand.

Maybe she wasn't so bad after all. "Thank you."

She handed me a portable phone, and I started dialing. Seconds later, the phone was ringing. *Answer. Please answer.* If this was really my one call, I didn't want to waste it on a voice mail. I wasn't sure I'd get another call if no one picked up.

"Special Agent Ramirez here."

A sigh of relief escaped me before I could stop it. "Hi. It's Teresa McCaide."

"Teresa." He drew out my name, his voice a degree—or ten —colder than our last meeting. "I've been expecting your call."

"Well, I'm calling." I cleared my throat. "I'm at the fine police offices of Santa Fe."

"What a coincidence. I just got off a plane in Santa Fe. I thought we discussed you calling me *before* the fact?"

I winced at his annoyed tone. "We didn't know what we'd find here. Now that we did find something, I'm calling."

"Next time, you call me first."

"I'm sorry. Next time, I promise I'll call first." Maybe. If I could.

"Good thing I've already been apprised of the situation and why you're being held or else I'd be really annoyed."

I never thought I'd ever be in a position where the FBI would be pissed at me. Yet here I was. Special Agent Ramirez was definitely ticked off. "The thing is... I need to get out of here. Luciana is going to do something very bad, and if we're not there to stop her... Well, it's going to be worse than what she did last time. Much, much worse. A little help would be very much appreciated. If there's anything you can do to speed this along?"

Officer Yeats cleared her throat and tapped her watch.

I nodded. Time was almost up.

"You're going to have to sit tight. I'll see what I can do once I'm there, but they're officially holding you for questioning. They could keep you there for up to twenty-four hours. Unless they get a judge to sign off for more time."

No. That wasn't going to happen. Even twenty-four hours was way too freaking long. We needed to get out of here like yesterday.

"But I'm sure I can do something about it once I get there, provided you fill me in on what's going on."

"Absolutely." I looked at the clock on the wall. "How far away are you?"

"I'll be there in less than an hour."

That put him here after midnight. Much too late.

The line went dead before I could argue with him. I handed the phone back to Officer Yeats. "Thanks."

He seemed pissed, Dastien said through the bond.

I know, right? It feels like no matter how hard I try, I'm messing it up. My knee bounced as I thought.

Hey. You're doing a good job.

But even you disagreed with me about going with the cops, and—

And I was wrong.

I tried to take solace in that, but as I sat there, listening to seconds tick by on the clock, it was hard not to question my decisions.

We had to get out of here. Soon.

I was sitting with my eyes closed, waiting for the Special Agent Ramirez to make his appearance, when magic brushed along my skin. It felt dirtier than the interrogation room and motel room put together. My chest tightened as I slowly sat up.

"Claudia?"

"I feel it, too," she whispered.

Luciana's magic. It had a certain flavor of disgusting that I'd become familiar with.

I glanced at the clock. Ramirez should be here any minute, but it wasn't going to be soon enough. Not anymore.

It was starting, and the humans were so not equipped to handle anything like this. The Weres in the room were tense, barely hanging on to their human forms, and the twins had turned a shade of green.

I started pacing the room. It was another fifteen minutes before I heard faint gunshots in the distance.

"Do you hear that?" Meredith asked.

I nodded.

"What do you think Luciana's doing?"

"I don't know, but magic's crackling along my skin." I cracked my knuckles. "We might have to break out of here."

"Midnight seems too early for this much black magic," Raphael said. "It would be much stronger after three. Why would she jump the gun?"

"Maybe timing doesn't matter as much if you have two covens' worth of magic." Now she had enough power to open her portal and then some. My anxiety level went through the roof. My skin itched to change, but I kept pacing. Hoping that the movement would help maintain my form.

This was it. Luciana's endgame was starting. Everything I feared could come true...

We were trying to be good little werewolves, but if Ramirez didn't show soon, we were going to have to make a run for it.

If a hell portal opened and no one stopped it, none of us would have to worry about the long term anyway.

CHAPTER TWENTY-SIX

FOOTSTEPS THUNDERED DOWN THE HALLWAY, stopping at our door. Special Agents Ramirez and Morgan stepped into the room.

Morgan scanned the room before fixing her gaze on me. "What's going on out there?"

Dastien rose from his chair, but I grabbed him before he could move. *Stay calm.* "I can't say that I know what you're talking about."

"Officers were called to a church. The neighbors reported weird chanting and something that smelled like a broken sewer line." Ramirez looked pale.

"Demons."

Special Agent Morgan nodded. "These little raccoon-size monsters are spewing out of the church, and the police are doing everything they can to stop them—but apparently bullets only slow them down a little. Shotgun shells work okay, but they're having some serious trouble containing the problem."

"Raccoon-size?" That was new kind of demon to me. Even the minor ones were much bigger than that. But the fact that shotguns were working on them was seriously good news.

"You have to let us help you," Donovan said. "Luciana Alvarez is very dangerous. She's not going to stop with these little demons. The minor and major demons that we've seen... Even if you slow them, they can't be killed by human weapons. They have to be decapitated or burned to ash with potions or magic."

"Jesus," Officer Yeats said. "It's not like we go around carrying swords these days."

"I have a sword," Cosette said. She conjured it for a second to make her point clear.

"And we have potions," I added. "And wolves with fangs and claws who are much stronger and faster than humans. Please. Let us out, and we'll take care of these monsters." The fact that there were so many had my hands shaking, but I shoved them into my pockets.

A call came through Officer Yeats' radio. I couldn't understand anything that was being said—it was all static and yelling and some sort of code.

"Wilson's out there," Officer Yeats said. "He's the one in charge. I don't have the authority to let you go. I don't—"

"You can release them into my custody," Ramirez said with a smile. He touched Officer Yeats' shoulder. "I'll take care of the rest. You'll get the paperwork you need, and I promise you won't get into any trouble."

I held my breath as she considered. After a long second, Officer Yeats gave a sharp nod. "I'll get your things."

She came back with my messenger bag, as well as Shane, Raphael, and Claudia's stuff—including Raphael's bat. I slung my bag over my shoulder and started toward the exit.

Agent Morgan jangled some car keys. "I grabbed these from Yeats. She said it's the second on the right." She turned to us. "I didn't realize there were going to be so many of you."

We piled into a van with an SFPD emblem on the side.

"Do you know where you're going?" I asked.

"I think I can get us there." She flicked on the sirens and peeled out of the parking lot.

I slammed into Dastien as she took a corner. "Jeeze," I yelled over the siren. "Do all agents drive like this or is it just you?"

"All agents," Ramirez said. "It's practically a job requirement."

Gunfire rang out through still the night, and we quieted down. The streets were clear. Not a soul in sight. And I hoped there wouldn't be.

As Morgan turned a corner, the church came into view. The light from the helicopter overhead made it as good as daytime wherever it shone. The cops were firing, some in riot gear. Others just in Kevlar vests. Some hid behind their cars, but the rest were moving toward the demons, firing their shotguns and reloading as quickly as possible. With each blast, little bits of demons went flying.

But the demons weren't like the ones we'd seen before. They were the size of large raccoons. Their fangs dripped black goo that scorched the ground it touched. They swarmed out of the church like giant ants. I could see maybe a hundred of them, but more were coming out of the doorway every second.

The maybe thirty cops surrounding the church were barely keeping the swarm at bay. Their shotguns were pretty effective at killing the demon-raccoon things, but I wasn't sure if that'd last long if minor demons—let alone major ones—started coming out.

We had to hurry. If Luciana hadn't summoned any bigger demons yet, then maybe there was still time to stop her. In my vision, there'd been minor and major demons in the church. So, the portal wasn't open yet. At least not all the way.

We skidded to a stop just outside of the ring of cop cars.

I slid down from the van—unable to tear my gaze from the

front of the church as a demon leaped at a cop—gaining at least four feet of air—landing on the cop's face. He cried out as blood spewed. The cop hit the ground, and another cop charged beside him—firing two shotgun blasts at the demon, point blank, as it came at him. Another three officers covered him while he dragged the injured cop to safety.

"Who's in charge here?" Morgan called, drawing up to her full height as she approached the densest pack of officers with Ramirez by her side.

I shuddered. We needed to get into the church or we might all be dead soon.

Dastien gripped my hand. *You okay?*

I pressed my forehead against his sternum and breathed in his scent. *I'm terrified of going in there.*

We can do this. We've been preparing for it. We're ready.

Maybe. But if this was my last moment with him, I wanted to savor it.

"Officer Wilson and Chief Lauler have agreed that being supernatural creatures, you might have some insight into this problem of theirs." Agent Ramirez motioned us forward.

Thank God. "Luciana is going to be behind the altar. I'm going in—straight for her," I said. "As soon as she dies, her spells should die, too, and all the demons will get sent back." I hoped without me having to jump into any portals.

My stomach knotted, and I felt like I was going to throw up.

Breathe, chérie. I'm not going to let that happen.

We might not have a lot of options.

Then we make options.

"If not?" Deputy Wilson asked.

"Then we kill them one by one," Donovan said.

I turned to the chief. "The only human inside there right now is Luciana, right?"

"None of my guys have gotten through the bottleneck at the door. What's going on in there is anyone's guess."

I cracked my knuckles. "Fine."

I turned back to my friends. This could be my last moment with them, but I didn't want to think like that. I couldn't think like that. Not now. "Y'all ready?"

There were some nods. Some yeahs and yeses.

I would've done a huddle with a "Go Team!" but that felt cheesy. So, instead I said, "Let's go get this bitch. And then let's go home. I'm tired. And would love to not sleep in a fucking motel again."

"Me, too," Claudia said. "That place was gross."

"Y'all are bunch of whiners," Chris said.

We laughed, and I stepped up to Dastien. I wrapped my arms around his waist as I looked up at him. *If we get through this, I want to go on a honeymoon.*

His dimples deepened. *Where to?*

I don't know. A tropical beach with white sand and clear waters.

Sounds perfect. He brushed a kiss on my forehead.

Do you think we'll get through this? With everything I'd seen, we were still here. I wasn't sure how much we could change or if it'd be enough.

Absolutely. There's no other option.

I leaned back from him, stealing some of his confidence through the bond. "Okay."

"Okay."

I nodded. "I'm ready." I said the words even though I wasn't sure they were true. Not even a little bit. I knew how badly this could go.

I knew that I could die. Dastien could die. Everything I knew could be over.

But that didn't change anything.

We had to fight.

The only thing I *did* know was that Luciana wasn't getting out of this alive. No matter what. I was ending this.

Now. Tonight.

With determination burning through my veins, my gaze darted to each of my friends before settling on Dastien again. "Let's do this."

Dastien, Meredith, Donovan, Chris, Lucas, and Adrian were already shifting. Some of the cops cursed, stepping back as they took in the sight.

You shifted, I said to Dastien. *You weren't shifted in my vision.*

He stuck his wolfy tongue out and tilted his head. Right. We're changing that vision. It's going to be different. Might as well start now.

"You coming, Van?" Cosette gestured and a sword appeared.

"Of course." He was suddenly at her side, already gripping two swords.

"Show off." She rolled her eyes and conjured a second sword, not to be shown up.

Claudia drew spell knots, warding each of us against the demon blood.

I grabbed two vials. "Everyone have enough?"

Raphael pulled the last vials from Shane's backpack and shoved them into his pockets. He gave his bat a little test swing. "Ready."

"What about you, Claudia? Vials?"

She grinned, and it was about as mischievous of a grin as I'd ever seen from her. "I'm ready." Lucas bumped her hand. "And I've got my wolf."

"Good." *Love you,* I said to Dastien.

But there were no promises in life. No guarantees. I had to

live every day like it was my last, and do my best to make my life count. So, that was what I was doing.

And if we survived tonight, that's what I'd continue to do. "Let's do this."

A call went up among the cops. Some yelled out to not shoot the wolves. Others yelled about not shooting the witches.

I held up the two vials. "With the power of Jesus Christ, I banish you from this earth." I threw the vials, and started running before the explosion hit.

CHAPTER TWENTY-SEVEN

LITTLE PIECES of demon bodies rained down on me, turning quickly to ash, as I hit the pavement in front of the church. Claudia's spell held—their acid-like blood rolled off me without even the slightest burn. There might be a lot of these raccoon suckers, but they were much easier to kill than the bigger demons.

Claudia tossed another two vials, and the heat from exploding potions licked along my face. I reached into my bag and grabbed two more. We'd made a bunch more at the motel, but we didn't have a limitless supply. We needed to get in there and get this done before Luciana fully opened that portal.

We were maybe ten feet from the front door of the church. Not much farther to go.

"In the name of God, the Father, I send you back to hell." I threw the vial, and more demons turned to ash. Dastien jumped on one, ripping its head off with a well-placed bite.

"One more blast and we'll be inside," I yelled.

Claudia stepped up beside me. "One. Two. Three." We said the words, tossing the vials in unison, and then charged the door.

Inside looked just like my vision. The portal wasn't open yet, but there were at least twenty minor demons and half as many major standing in the circle Luciana had drawn in front of the altar. Pews were turned on their sides—some ripped apart. Red flares lit the inside, giving everything a hazy, red glow. The helicopter's spotlight shone in through the broken stained glass window.

My throat tightened. *Dastien?* I felt him beside me, but I didn't dare look away from what was in front of me. He sent me strength through our bond, and I could breathe a little easier.

I stepped farther into the church, focusing on the altar in the front. There was movement there.

Luciana.

She shouted something in a language I didn't understand, and the demons started moving toward us.

A major demon caught my attention as its red gaze stared. Its scaly gray skin glistened pink with the flares. It was taller than the rest, with muscles that looked like it could rip me apart. "Teresssssssa," it hissed.

I didn't hesitate to reach inside my bag. "In the name of Jesus Christ, I send you back to hell." Three vials hit it at once, but it kept coming.

"You're mine, Teresssssa," it said as its leathery skin smoked, burning from the spell.

"Not likely," Cosette said as she swung her sword, severing its head. "Did they send a demonic memo around with your name?" she asked as the demon turned to ash and was sucked back where it belonged.

"That was creepy as fuck." I reached into my bag, and my fingers brushed the bottom. Only three more potions, and then I was going to have to rely on my spells—which I sucked at—or go wolf—which wasn't my best fighting form.

The pews were all over the place. I stepped over one, and a

small demon—no bigger than a child—clawed at my foot. "Try that again, fucker!"

I shifted my free hand, going half-hand, half-paw—thick, razor-sharp claws extended. I slashed its arm, and the limb fell to the ground with a satisfying thud. Black sludge spewed from the dangling limb and the demon leaped at me, baring a full mouth of pointed teeth.

I twisted my body and slashed, and the demon burned as it died, turning to ash.

Not a move I normally would've tried, but it worked. Confidence boosted my energy level.

I needed to get to the altar. I jumped on one of the overturned pews and could still see Luciana moving behind the altar. I took a quick glance around the room.

Chris was fighting a demon with Raphael, whose bat swung, slamming a minor demon in the head.

Cosette and Van were caught up fighting two major demons. They were holding their own, but those demons were fast. And two more were coming up behind them. "Behind you, Cosette!" I shouted. She heard me and whirled, just in time.

The wolves were fighting, claws slashing wherever they could find a target. I spotted Claudia, and started for her. "Do you have more vials?"

"Take Shane's," Raphael yelled from behind me. I spun around as he tossed me the backpack. "I'm doing well with the bat."

I caught it and knelt, dumping the vials into my messenger bag—much easier access.

I lifted my head just in time to see a demon's nails coming right for my face.

Dastien leaped into it, knocking the demon to the ground just before it made contact. I activated a vial, throwing it at the demon. Dastien slashed its neck as the vial hit, and the demon turned to ash.

Hands shaking, I went back to dealing with the vials.

That had been way too fucking close. Dastien came up beside me.

I'm heading for the altar, I said. Watch your back. Don't let my vision happen.

He yipped.

I took off running, leaping over demons and dodging around them. I reached into my bag, pulling out two more vials. "In the name of Jesus Christ, I banish you." The vials activated.

I was almost to the altar, only two feet away. I raced to it, but a flash of light blinded me as Luciana finished her spell.

I flew through the air as her slimy magic hit me and my back slammed against a pew. I lay there, shaking off the hit, and a demonic howl echoed through the night. Followed by another.

I sat up enough to see the portal open—a bottomless pit. The jagged circle yawned deep into the ground. Its edges were tipped in red, making it look like glowing charcoal. I couldn't see down it from here, but the scent of sulfur was so strong it was almost unbearable. It made my eyes water. There was a rumbling from deep within the pit. The little demons that we'd fought outside were still coming out of it, but something else was working its way up.

I had to close it before whatever that was made it to the top.

Dastien was still in wolf form. I closed my eyes for a second and saw the fight through his eyes. He was dealing with two minor demons. Pain from a long scratch along his back beat against him, but he was ignoring it.

This was it. This was my vision.

Now I had to change it.

Watch your back. One's going to come at you from behind. Don't get distracted. I'm going after Luciana.

I hopped onto a pew. The wolves were slashing at the demons, working together with Claudia and Raphael. Claudia fired off a few spells, tossing them in different directions to help the wolves. Raphael's bat glowed as it slammed into a minor demon's head, turning it to ash.

Cosette and Van were killing it. Literally. Dead demons piled around them. More were climbing over the bodies of the fallen, but as they fought—back-to-back—they looked invincible. Their shining blades slashed violently, but somehow gracefully, through the air.

I hoped everyone would stay safe as I focused on my goal. On my enemy. I trusted them to keep the demons under control and out of my way while I worked my way to Luciana.

She stood next to the pit, hands held high above her head in summoning. Her skin had taken on a green tinge, far beyond any olive undertones. Her long frizzy hair was around her face instead of her usual braided halo and her flowing skirt was shredded along the bottom. I couldn't make out her words, but the magic started to build. It brushed against me like sickening oil on my skin, and my stomach turned.

I started forward, jumping from one pew to the next. They were broken and on their sides, but I managed to balance.

I quickly activated a few vials, feeling them heat with magic as I held them. "Luciana."

She lowered her arms and tilted her head toward me. The pit stopped rumbling, so that was a start, but the sight of her made me wobble on my perch.

Her eyes were solid red orbs. Her two front teeth had lengthened into fangs.

My arms lowered as I gasped in shock. What the hell had she become?

She laughed, and it was the deep, rasping laugh of a demon.

It was true. She might have started out as a witch who

wanted power, but she was fully demon now.

I threw the vials just as Luciana started moving her fingers.

Her spell hit me, knocking me to the floor. Three rat-size demons scuttled toward me, and I couldn't stop myself from screeching. I kicked them away before they could bite.

I kitted up, and she was there. Standing in front of me. Spit dripped from her fangs. "You're mine now, Teressssa."

That voice. It wasn't her. My eyes widened as my breathing sped. I had to move.

She weaved her fingers in a fast spell, and I flew across the floor. My head crunched against a pew, and blood dribbled down my forehead.

I sat up, and the world wobbled. I tried to shake off the dizziness, but I didn't have time. Luciana was already running for me.

I had one more vial. I quickly muttered the words and threw.

Her shoulder jerked, but she was still coming for me. The vial hadn't done anything to her. It didn't even burn her skin.

I reached into the bag again, and my fingers brushed the canvas.

I had no more spells. No weapons.

Dastien howled and I felt his fear for me, but there was nothing he could do. Nothing any of them could do. They were busy fighting for their lives, too.

Fear made my blood run cold as Luciana cackled and lunged at my leg. I tried to roll away, but her nails dug through my tender muscle.

I screamed.

"Your magic will be mine."

"No!" I was stronger than this. I kicked at her face, but she only jerked back an inch.

Holy shit. The demon in her was too strong.

I sat up in one quick motion and jerked her nails out of my leg. My whole calf went numb, but I threw her off. She hit a pew a few feet from me and lay still for a second.

She craned her neck at an impossible angle. I looked into her eyes and in the blood red orbs, I saw myself burning in a pool of flames. I blinked and her eyes were plain red again.

My mouth went dry. The demon was trying to scare me—and doing a damned good job of it.

I got up, hobbling as I dragged my injured leg. What the hell was I going to do? I was out of potions—but they were useless anyway. I'd kicked her hard enough to break her neck, and she just fucking shook it off like it was nothing.

I heard her laugh, and the hair on the back of my neck stood on end.

The pew behind me slammed into my legs, and Luciana cackled again.

I glanced back. She was maybe ten feet, staying just far enough behind me to taunt me.

I moved faster. I needed cover. I had to figure something out before she got tired of chasing me and ended this.

"You're a wolf!" Cosette's voice cried out. "Be a wolf and end it before we all get killed."

She was right.

But I was also a witch. I needed to be both if I was going to win this.

I leaped over a pew to gain some distance from her. My leg protested, foot slamming into the wood as I fell to the ground.

Luciana climbed on top of it. "Nowhere to run now."

I made a quick knot in the air, moving my fingers fast. Willing it to work. When the knot completed, the magic slammed into place. She hit the knot and bounced back a few steps.

Thank God my magic held long enough for me to let the

wolf out. But only in my hands.

My fingers lengthened, and I picked myself up off the ground just as she swung at me

I twisted and her fist went right past my face. She kicked and I blocked. Luciana might not have known how to fight, but the demon sure as hell did.

I let instinct take hold. All Dastien's years of knowledge poured through me, and I used them as I waited for her to give me a window.

Her shoulder dropped, and I swiped. "Die!" I poured all my will into the word. My nails ripped across her neck, parting her skin as if it were butter. As her blood—black and red—slid over my hands, coating my skin, I was glad Claudia's magic was still holding.

I waited for Luciana to fall to the ground—to turn to ash—but she was still moving. Slower now.

"Die!" I yelled again, throwing more power behind the word. This time she staggered as I swiped my claws across her stomach.

I didn't waste time. "Die!" I let the power fly as I hit her again. She froze and started to fall.

I caught her before she hit the ground and gagged at the feel of her demonic energy in my arms. Her heartbeat was slowing as blood poured out of her, and I dragged her to the pit.

I stared down it, and hoped this was enough to put a stop to the chaos around me.

Dastien was still fighting demons. He was hurt, but not down.

The sounds of demons screeching and hissing, as we whittled down their numbers told me the tide was turning, but it wasn't over.

I had to close the portal.

The little demons had stopped pouring out, but inside the

pit a giant demon was clawing its way to the top. It looked like it was made of molten lava, scarring the rock with fire as it climbed. It spotted me and roared, moving faster.

I didn't want to have to jump, but I had to throw Luciana in. Her magic had to be stopped.

As the demon inside Luciana died, her eyes turned back to her normal brown. Her skin wasn't quite so green. Confusion crossed her face as she glanced around the church.

"I'm sorry for what I'm about to do." My voice sounded much stronger than I felt.

Her life was slipping away. It'd been only moments, and I wasn't sure she could understand me, but Luciana's face relaxed like she was giving me the okay.

"Lord, save us from what she's done. Help us stop the death." I pushed her body into the pit. "Send these monsters back to hell."

Luciana's body tumbled as it fell. The demon roared as she passed it.

I waited, watching it fall, hoping that the portal would start to close, but nothing happened.

Oh shit. The portal wasn't closing. The demon was moving fast.

A howl echoed through the church. Not a demon.

Dastien!

I felt his pain through the bond. Claws scored his back as demons surrounded him.

Closing the portal would kill off the demons that pinned my friends down everywhere I looked.

I had to close it. Now.

In my vision, it was me jumping with Luciana that had stopped everything. Sacrificing myself would work. But as I stood there, gazing into hell...

I didn't want to die. Not now. Not yet.

I had to try to close it with magic first. If I couldn't, then I'd jump before Dastien or anyone else had to die.

I raised my hands in the air, mimicking Luciana. "Close." I focused on the pit and pushed all the magic I had at it.

It stayed open.

Dastien's whimper of pain hit me as another demon got its claws in him. I didn't need to see him to know what was going on. The bond was wide open.

But if I could see, then I could draw power, too.

I pulled from our bond, taking as much power as I could get. "Close!" I drew the word out, screaming until my voice broke. My skin tingled from the magic.

I pulled again—more this time. From the pack. I felt all the ties that held us together, and yanked on their magic as I screamed the word.

It still wasn't enough.

Shit. A tear rolled down my cheek. I stepped to the edge and took a breath.

Looking down, I nearly threw up. I couldn't believe I was doing this. I felt empty. Broken. I didn't want to die, but the lava demon was almost to the top and I wasn't sure any of us would be able to stop that one if it got free.

Three other wolves howled. I glanced around the room one last time. Claudia's shirt was torn, her hair coming free from her braid. Lucas was beside her, fighting, as Claudia moved her hands in a spell.

Raphael stood with Chris, fighting to keep their own between two minor demons and a major one across the room.

Meredith and Donovan were guarding the door—stopping any demons from escaping.

Cosette and Van were fighting their way to Dastien, but most of the last demons were swarming them.

Dastien was surrounded by five demons. A little rat-size one was on his bloody back, biting into his neck. The fey couldn't get there in time.

I didn't have a choice.

This was it.

I'm sorry. I tried. But I have to stop this. I love you. Please be strong for me.

His rage and denial beat against me, but I closed my eyes and took a breath.

I had to be strong. I could do this.

Just before I jumped, a furry head butted against my legs, knocking me away from the pit.

Donovan was next to me, and I gripped his fur. "I have to jump. It's the only way."

Before I could take the last step forward, his command rolled over me.

The power of the Seven slammed into me, and only my grip on Donovan's fur kept me from toppling into the pit.

Within a second, I was pulling power from him. From every wolf alive.

Through him, I could feel the Cazadores approaching. They were too late to fight, but they'd be here to help clean up.

I could feel the people who'd left the pack. Imogene. Shannon.

Shannon sent an apology back and opened up completely, giving me everything she had. Stopping Luciana was bigger than our petty differences.

Power poured through me—from every Were alive—until I thought it was too much. I was burning up, but I held it inside.

And then I felt Lucas. He had a lot of power, but through him—I could feel my cousin. Claudia's ability seeped into me, amplifying all the magic I held. Multiplying it.

It was too much. I couldn't hold it in anymore.

"Close now!" I screamed the words, letting out all the built-up power in one huge blast.

An explosion hit and I was blown back, slamming into one of the fallen pews.

The light was so bright, I couldn't see. I squeezed my eyes shut.

The demons cried out as one, and then there was nothing but silence.

No more hissing. No more scuttling of nails. I could hear my own gasping breaths as I waited for something to happen.

Soft wisps brushed my face, and I opened my eyes.

It was raining ashes.

My heart raced as the last of the magic faded from my system, making every part of me—my skin, my teeth, my nails —tingle.

I sat up, and the pit was gone. The floor was there—blackened in a ragged circle—but the portal to hell had disappeared. The demons were gone. Dead. All of them.

A series of wolf howls broke the silence, and I started laughing.

I was so exhausted—my head was pounding, every muscle in my body ached, and that wasn't the worst of it. My leg was both throbbing and on fire. I wasn't sure I could put any weight on it. But every pain was worth it. The demons were back where they belonged. Luciana was dead. The portal was closed.

And Dastien and I were alive.

It was okay. I fell back against the ground, crying tears of relief.

Chérie. Dastien's hand brushed against my forehead.

I grabbed him before he could pull away. *You're okay?*

For once, I didn't care that he was naked in a room of people. "I need to see your back." He turned so I could see, but he looked mostly okay. There were little red marks on his back, but no bloody gouges. "What... How..."

He grinned, and my heart warmed. "I was hurt badly, but when you killed them, the wounds started healing. It was like the supernatural hurt disappeared, and I could heal like a Were should."

My wounds hadn't gone anywhere but I didn't care. If that was the price I paid to stay out of hell, then I'd pay it. Gladly.

I jumped into his arms, and he laughed as he fell backward to the floor. *I'm okay. I promise,* he said as he ran his hand down my back.

Cosette cleared her throat, and I shoved Dastien away. "Shift! There are people around!"

He chuckled and then shifted. I knelt down beside him, and ran my hands through his fur.

That was how Agent Morgan found us. "You look okay, but it's torn to shit in here."

"We're okay," I said, even though I could barely believe it. "I think I might need some stitches and a gallon of holy water for my leg, but we're okay."

"That was some fight. Those things—they just disappeared." Strands of her hair had torn free of her ponytail, and her dress shirt was half untucked. "You all did a great job. I don't know how you pulled it off, but when we're cleaned up a bit, you'll have to share the secret to fighting those things."

Horror filled me. I wasn't going to be working with the police, let alone the FBI. With Luciana gone, there wouldn't be any more demons showing up. I was hoping this would be my last battle for a while. "Have you talked to Donovan Murry? He's super good at this stuff, and he's a very powerful alpha. I can introduce you."

She grinned. "Don't sell yourself short. I heard what you did this afternoon. The wolves were going to fight the police. You stopped it. Kept a clear head and saw the bigger picture." She reached an arm around me, helping me limp my way to the exit while wolf-Dastien kept pace beside us. "I have a feeling this is going to be the start of a very healthy relationship."

She was out of her mind. Once she realized there were other Weres—who were much better at all this stuff—then I'd be off the hook. I hoped.

As we made our way toward the exit, I spotted Cosette and Van leaning together and talking. Cosette was waving her hands, arguing with him again.

I hoped this didn't mean she was leaving. I was just starting to get used to having her around.

Raphael and Claudia were talking as they reclined against the back wall of the church. She absently ran a hand through Lucas' fur. Chris, Meredith, and Donovan were lying on the floor together in wolf form, catching their breath.

I sighed. "Well, I guess we better go face the music outside. Any of you wolves want to shift so I don't have to talk to the cops alone again?"

None of those jerks changed.

"Fine. I guess it's on me then." But you better stick by my side, even if you stay wolf.

Dastien laughed at me through the bond. You're the one who told me to shift back.

Well, it's better than being naked in front of everyone, right?

As we stepped outside, the light of the helicopter shone down on me, and I raised my arm to block it.

For a moment, just the sound of the chopper filled the night, but then the cops started cheering. Whistling. And I took a breath.

This. This was good.

I let the last bit of guilt for what I'd done in that church slip free. I was sure I hadn't seen the last of it, but for now—I let go.

We'd survived and I was beyond ready to go home.

CHAPTER TWENTY-EIGHT

ABOUT TEN MINUTES after I exited the church, the Cazadores showed up, with Mr. Dawson and some of the alphas in tow. They took over the scene, helping with cleanup and making sure all the injured officers were properly taken care of. Some of the cops didn't like the idea of pouring holy water on their injuries, but after what they'd seen—it didn't take too much work to convince them.

In all the chaos, Cosette disappeared with Van, but I was sure she'd be back before long. I owed her big time, and from the looks of things, she might need my help.

We all split up to take care of ourselves. Dastien checked both of us into a new hotel so he could look after my leg, while the others went to see Shane and Adrian at the hospital. Adrian was doing fine, but Shane...

I'd wanted to go help, but I was fully burnt out. Closing the portal had used up every ounce of energy, and after getting my leg treated, there was no way I could do anything but pass out.

So I did. For a glorious twelve hours.

When I woke up, Dastien ordered room service. I hadn't looked at our room too closely last night, but Special Agent

Morgan had recommended a hotel right off the historic plaza, and in the light of day, it was luxurious. Light-years apart from that disgusting motel. The bright white, fluffy duvet and soft mattress made me feel like I was sleeping on a cloud. I never wanted to get out of bed, but when the food came, Dastien handed me a fluffy robe—which was like being wrapped in heaven.

I tore through the best eggs Benedict with avocado and roasted tomatoes, a mountain of pancakes with a side of bacon, and Nutella-stuffed French toast. My stomach was full in the most amazing way. I stumbled over to the bed, face-planting into the soft, pillowy covers.

"I could do that again."

The bed dipped as Dastien sat beside me. "Do what again?"

"Another round of breakfast." I lifted my head up. "What do you say? Again from the top?"

Dastien laughed. "How about you let me check your leg and then we'll talk?"

After the initial washing with holy water—which hurt like a bitch—he'd wrapped my leg in gauze. Now it was in full-on itching mode, which told me it was probably healing just fine on its own.

"Do I have to?"

"Yes. The itching is driving you crazy."

"I haven't said a word about it." I'd been super proud of that lack of bitching about it, when all I wanted to do was grab my fork and go to town on my leg.

"It's almost all you're thinking about right now. I want to make sure it's not infected."

I guess it could've been worse—I could've become possessed from it. But still, I didn't understand how I could get an infection. "I thought that couldn't happen to Weres. We don't get sick."

"It's not likely, but with a supernatural hurt..." He slapped my butt. "Come on."

I grumbled as I rolled over and slid up the bed. Dastien was in a robe, too, but it fit his larger frame much better than mine did. As it opened, revealing just a bit of his chest, I tilted my head to stare.

"I'm being objectified again." He gave me a little wink before carefully unwinding the bandages.

"You like it."

"From you, sure." He hissed as he looked at my leg. "We might need more holy water. It's healing slower than your side. And the edges are all red. It doesn't smell right."

"Does it smell like sulfur?"

"No," he drew out the word. "But it smells off."

Pouring more holy water on it sounded like a whole bunch of no fun. "Have you heard from Claudia?"

He squeezed my foot. "You'd know if I had. I think if something was going wrong, we would've heard by now."

I hoped so.

"Quit worrying. You've done enough of that the past few weeks to last us at least the next decade."

"Clearly you don't know me very well. I can always come up with something to worry about."

Dastien chuckled. "I know you better than you know yourself, which is why I'm not going to let you invent new worries." He stood up. "Your leg—"

Three soft knocks sounded on the door.

"Please tell me you read my mind and went ahead and ordered another round of room service."

Chris' rasping laugh came from behind the closed door. "Come on. Let us in."

Dastien strode to the door. "Any of you have more holy water?"

Claudia pushed past everyone. "Why? Is something wrong with her wounds?" She was freshly showered. Her wet hair was pulled back in a loose braid. "What's going on?"

I tightened my robe as Lucas, Chris, and Adrian came into the room. "It itches. Like, a lot," I said to Claudia. "But I think it's going to be fine."

She leaned in to it, touching it gently. "It's red around the edges."

"How's Shane?" I said, hoping to change the subject.

"Recovering. He needed a little spell intervention, but now he's healing just fine. Raphael's with him. We'll stay here a few days while he recovers."

I nodded. "Makes sense."

"I think I'm going to stay, too," Adrian said from the doorway.

I smiled at him. "Sure." I hoped Shane appreciated how awesome Adrian was. "So, when are the rest of us heading home? Where are Meredith and Donovan?"

"They're arranging the travel," Chris said. "We should be ready in the next couple hours."

I let out a relieved breath. "Good."

"Did you happen to see the paper?" Adrian asked.

I glanced at Dastien. *Did we get one?*

No. They asked, but I didn't think we needed one.

"*Why?*"

"This was in front of my hotel room door this morning." Adrian pulled a folded newspaper from his back pocket and threw it on the bed. I grabbed it, opening the page as Dastien sat beside me.

An image of Dastien and me plastered the cover. We were exiting the church with Agent Morgan, him at my side in wolf form. We looked like we'd been through hell. Blood ran down my leg, but I was smiling.

Seeing myself on the front page of an actual printed newspaper was totally surreal. I swallowed. "Uh. Is this for real? We're really on the front page?"

"Of every newspaper in the country—hell, probably in every country, too. It's all over the news."

This is crazy.

Well, at least it seems like they trust us now, Dastien said.

That was something.

"Okay." I rubbed my hands together. "Well, we better get dressed if we're leaving soon."

"Oh no you don't." Claudia wagged a finger at me. "That leg looks infected. You don't need more holy water—I don't feel any evil in it—but you definitely need antibiotics."

I plopped back on the pillows. "I'm a werewolf. I don't get infections anymore."

"Apparently you do if it's a cut from a psychotic, demon-possessed witch," Chris said. "We can call Dr. Gonzales. I'm sure one shot and you'll be fine."

"Shot? You have to be kidding me." I groaned.

"You can take on Luciana and a church full of demons, but one shot has you shaking in your robe?" Claudia said.

Dastien started laughing.

You're not helping. "I just don't like them. Okay? And for the record, I was scared last night. More than scared. I was terrified."

"I think we all were," Lucas said. "I've seen a lot of battles in my life, but that was truly terrifying. You did well."

"Thanks," I said. "That means a lot coming from you."

He nodded. "I'm only stating the truth."

I stared at the ceiling for a second, before giving in. "Fine. Call Dr. Needle-Happy and let's get this over with. As nice as this bed is, I'd like to be home tonight."

"Agreed," Dastien said. "The sooner we're back home, the sooner we can put all of this behind us."

A quick call to Dr. Gonzales, and we were off to see the doctor that had helped Adrian. The shot wasn't that bad, plus I got to check in on Shane, who was recovering well. Better than I'd hoped.

Two hours later, we were heading to the airport with Meredith, Donovan, and Chris. The others would come in a few days. Although, I wondered how long Claudia would really stay or if they'd head to Peru. Selfishly I wanted her to stay, but I knew she'd have to do what she felt was right. And Lucas had a pack to look after.

Everyone was exhausted on the quick flight home. Donovan offered to drive when we landed, and I was more than happy to let him.

As we got closer to St. Ailbe's, cars lined the two-lane farm road. I leaned around the passenger seat, trying to get a better view of the crowd ahead.

"If they're telling us to burn in hell again, I'm going to lose it," I said.

"*Non. Chérie. Listen.*"

I lowered the window a little. "Is it just me, or do they seem happy?"

"They're definitely happy to see us," Meredith said.

Instead of blocking our way, the people actually moved, allowing us through the gates. A lady patted the window as we rolled by. "I love you," she said. "Turn me into one of you."

"Girl doesn't know what she's asking," I said.

Dastien poked my side, making me laugh. "Hey. It didn't turn out so bad."

Two girls, a few years younger than me, waved a sign that read, "We <3 Werewolves!" in glitter puff paint. They shook it in front of the car, screaming their heads off like we were the hottest boy band.

"I guess when you stop a murdering witch, people like you. Who knew?" I laughed. "But these people are crazy."

It took us nearly twenty minutes to make it through the gates. I would've abandoned the car, but even if the mob was for us this time, I was a little afraid of them.

As we exited the car, I saw my parents and Axel. *You called them?*

He nodded. I knew you'd sleep better if you saw them.

Even with our bond, he always managed to surprise me with his thoughtfulness. It was one of the many reasons I loved him. *Thanks.*

Of course.

"Mom! Dad!"

Mom let out a little squeal and closed the distance between us. "I'm so proud of you. I don't know how you did it, but you're amazing."

Axel pulled me from Mom. "Kind of badass."

I shoved him.

"You did good, kiddo." Dad brushed a kiss on my forehead. "Let's go get some food. I hear the cafeteria is pretty good."

"Yeah. It's pretty decent." I turned to my friends. "You guys coming?"

Meredith scoffed. "Me and food? Yes."

Dastien came up behind me and wrapped his arms around my waist. I leaned back into him.

So, when are we leaving? he asked.

We're going somewhere? For a second, I was worried. I didn't want to have to deal with another catastrophe. Not yet.

I thought you wanted to go on a honeymoon.

I spun in his arms. Hell yes. When can we leave?

I'll talk to Michael, but we could sneak away in a few days. I just want to make sure your leg is fine before we go.

It's fine now.

You're limping.

Eh. It's not a big limp. I wrinkled my nose at him. It honestly didn't hurt anymore. And ever since I'd gotten the antibiotic shot, I was feeling much better. Not that I'd ever admit that to Dr. Gonzales.

I want two weeks. At least. Maybe three. He wasn't countering me. Hell, I could go for longer. I was just waiting for him to say no. *Or a month. A month sounds good, right?*

Dastien gave me a big grin, dimples and all. *You won't hear any complaints from me.*

I nearly rolled my eyes. The boy was letting himself get steamrolled, and he was definitely enjoying it. *And we go wherever I want?*

He raised an eyebrow. *Within reason.*

We'll see. I had plans. Places I wanted to go. Things I wanted to see. Hell, maybe we could finally see Paul van Dyk play. Or Above and Beyond. That would be amazing.

Luciana was gone, and we'd survived. From here on out, I was going to try not to worry about my visions. Obsessing over what might happen had led Luciana down her path to evil and I wanted nothing to do with that slippery slope.

Instead, I was going to live every day to the fullest.

I'd looked death in the face, and it had changed me. It made me want to embrace everything that life had to offer.

I was going to spend time with my friends, and maybe help Chris find a girl. Because, seriously, the boy deserved someone amazing. I wanted to continue getting to know my cousins and learn more about my magic. And if Meredith wanted me to go with her to Ireland, I'd be on a plane with her in a heartbeat.

Because family and friends were what mattered, and I wanted to appreciate them.

Starting with Dastien. After all the crap we'd been through, we deserved a vacation.

Maybe somewhere tropical. Or maybe to his castle in France.

Count me in, Dastien said. For all of that.

I pulled him down for a kiss. *You better be.*

Je t'aime, chérie, he said through the bond as he brushed a soft kiss against my lips.

Getting to this moment had been long and hard, but now that I was here—it made me appreciate what I had even more.

Staring up at my mate—surrounded by my friends and family—for the first time in my life, I felt really and truly lucky to be me.

I wouldn't trade a thing.

Want more from Meredith and Donovan?

Check out **Shattered Pack**,

Book Six of the Alpha Girls Series.

Meredith Molloney never thought she'd find a mate, let alone someone like Donovan Murry—one of the most powerful Alpha werewolves alive. Now that she's no longer cursed and the evil Luciana Alvarez has been taken care of, she thinks life will finally settle down. Boy, she has never been so wrong.

In the middle of the night, Donovan gets a call telling him that his pack has gone to pieces. The news that his second in command has been found brutally murdered has Donovan packing his bags for Ireland, but the last thing Meredith wants to do is go with him. Cosette just warned her that the Irish pack isn't so happy about Donovan's choice in mates.

But Meredith's never let a few angry wolves stop her, and she's not about to start now. She's faced down much worse the past few months. But when she gets there, she finds that it's not just an angry pack that stands in the way between her and her Full Moon Ceremony with Donovan.

Meredith is thrust into a deadly game of pack politics, one a fey beast has happily joined. When the magic and dust settle, she knows she'll either have everything that she wants or lose it all.

Tessa and Dastien are back in ***Being Alpha***,

Book Seven in the Alpha Girls series!

For the first time since Tessa met Dastien, life is quiet. The evil witch, Luciana, is six glorious feet under, St. Ailbe's is closed due to human trespassers, and people are finally getting used to the fact that supernaturals exist in the world. It seems like the perfect time for a honeymoon.

After traveling to Dastien's house in Provence, clubbing in Paris, and attending Meredith and Donovan's Full Moon Ceremony in Ireland, Tessa and Dastien head to the Caribbean. Their trip is turning out to be the honeymoon that fantasies are made of-sunset cruises, long walks on the beach, and every romantic cliché you can imagine. Tessa couldn't be happier. Except that Tessa's visions are on the fritz. She hopes that means that nothing is brewing. That everything is quiet because all is well. But Tessa's never been one to assume anything.

When she's magically attacked and nearly dies, Tessa knows she can't ignore the signs anymore. Something huge is going on. As much as she doesn't want to call an end to their six-week honeymoon, it's time to head back to Texas.

Whoever messed with Tessa is in for a rude awakening. Because if there's one thing fighting rogue witches and werewolves has taught her, it's how to be Alpha.

Now available from *USA Today* Bestselling Author, Aileen Erin
Off Planet, Book One of the Aunare Chronicles.

In an all-too-plausible future where corporate conglomerates have left the world's governments in shambles, anyone with means has left the polluted Earth for the promise of a better life on a SpaceTech owned colony among the stars.

Maité Martinez is the daughter of an Earther Latina and a powerful Aunare man, an alien race that SpaceTech sees as a threat to their dominion. When tensions turn violent, Maité finds herself trapped on Earth and forced into hiding.

For over ten years, Maité has stayed hidden, but every minute Maité stays on Earth is one closer to getting caught.

She's lived on the streets. Gone hungry. And found a way to fight through it all. But one night, while waitressing in a greasy diner, a customer gets handsy with her. She reacts without thinking.

Covered in blood, Maité runs, but it's not long before SpaceTech finds her...

Arrested and forced into dangerous work detail on a volcano planet, Maité waits for SpaceTech to make their move against the Aunare. She knows that if she can't somehow find a way to stop them, there will be an interstellar war big enough to end all life in the universe.

INK MONSTER
NEWSLETTER

STAY UP-TO-DATE WITH
EVERYTHING AILEEN IS
WORKING ON --
INCLUDING SPECIAL SALES,
BEHIND-THE-SCENES CONTENT,
AND MONTHLY GIVEAWAYS!

SUBSCRIBERS ARE
AUTOMATICALLY
ENTERED INTO
MONTHLY
GIVEAWAYS FOR
SIGNED COPIES AND
MORE!

Subscribe at: https://www.aileenerin.com/subscribe

ACKNOWLEDGMENTS

Thank you again, to all my readers! To all of you who have reached out to me, thank you! I love hearing from each and every one of them.

To my amazing editor, Lola Dodge: Thanks for always kicking my ass and pushing me to make it better. You're the best!

To the lovely ladies at INscribe: Thank you for everything you do! You're an amazing team, and we're so lucky to have you on our side.

To Kristi Latcham and Cathleen Stern: Thank you for powering through proofing! I suck at finding typos. Y'all are awesome!

To my family and friends: Thanks for understanding when I go full-hermit! I'm now out and about, and ready for some fun. ;)

And last, but never, ever least, to Jeremy: Your constant and unwavering support—even when I'm second-guessing every-thing—is such a blessing. I'm so thankful that you're in my life. I couldn't imagine up a better husband, best friend, and partner. You're the bee's knees. <3

Aileen Erin is half-Irish, half-Mexican, and 100% nerd—from Star Wars (prequels don't count) to Star Trek (TNG FTW), she geeks out on Tolkien's linguistics, and has a severe fascination with the supernatural. Aileen has a BS in Radio-TV-Film from the University of Texas at Austin, and an MFA in Writing Popular Fiction from Seton Hill University. She lives with her husband and daughter in Texas, and spends her days doing her favorite things: reading books, creating worlds, and kicking ass.

For more information and updates about Aileen and her books, go to: www.aileenerin.com

Or check her out on:

 facebook.com/aelatcham
 twitter.com/aileen_erin
instagram.com/aileenerin
bookbub.com/authors/aileen-erin